Readers love
SJD Peterson

Something's Brewing at Joe's

"It had gripped and held onto me with its hot and sizzling chemistry, its humorous and sexy bantering, and, its kept-me-on-the-edge-of-my-seat suspense. I love, love, loved it!"

—Gay Book Reviews

Override

"The strength of *Override* is definitely the strong and steady connection between Seth and Donavan and their growing romance."

—Sinfully: Gay Romance Book Reviews

"I loved this story. Little angst, no anger issues, no overblown drama, just two men finding a way to meet in the middle and merge their worlds."

—Alpha Book Club

Limitless

"I recommend this to everyone who's intrigued with BDSM, the Dom/ sub relationship, the concept of pain mixed with pleasure, and flawed, realistic men who more than deserve a happy ending."

—Long and Short Reviews

By SJD Petereson

Published by DREAMSPINNER PRESS
www.dreamspinnerpress.com

Remember When

SJD PETERSON

DREAMSPINNER
PRESS

Published by
DREAMSPINNER PRESS

5032 Capital Circle SW, Suite 2, PMB# 279, Tallahassee, FL 32305-7886 USA
www.dreamspinnerpress.com

Remember When
© 2017 SJD Peterson.

Cover Art
© 2017 Garrett Leigh.
http://blackjazzpress.com/
Cover content is for illustrative purposes only and any person depicted on the cover is a model.

ISBN: 978-1-63533-678-8
Digital ISBN: 978-1-63533-679-5
Library of Congress Control Number: 2016921401
Published August 2017
v. 1.0

Printed in the United States of America
∞
This paper meets the requirements of
ANSI/NISO Z39.48-1992 (Permanence of Paper).

To all those who believe in fate and dreams come true.

Prologue

"WE SHOULDN'T be doing this," Nelson Maitland whispered.

His best friend, Lucas Rollins—or Luke, as Nelson called him—lifted his head from where he had it buried in Nelson's crotch and peeked out from beneath the covers. "Why not? It feels good, don't it?"

Oh yeah, it felt good, fabulous. His entire body tingled, and he was an idiot for even considering they stop. Nevertheless, as good as it felt, Nelson couldn't seem to stop worrying about getting caught. "What if your mom comes in?"

"She won't." Luke recovered his head and licked the tip of Nelson's penis again.

Nelson released the death grip he had on his pillow and shoved the covers off Luke's head. "Wait. How do you know she won't? What about your dad? Your little brother?"

Luke huffed a breath and crawled up the bed. He lowered himself between Nelson's legs, their naked bodies touching in all the right places. *Naked! Oh geez, what if we are caught! How are we going to explain being naked!* His heart started pounding so fast he thought for sure it would leap out of his chest.

"We're not going to get caught. Now will you shut up? You talk too much."

Nelson started to protest, but Luke pressed their lips together. It was clumsy and sloppy, especially after Luke pushed his tongue halfway down Nelson's throat. But suddenly he didn't care about anything except the way Luke was moving his body and their privates were rubbing together, and Nelson forgot all about Luke's parents and kid brother.

It wasn't until they were lying next to each other breathing hard and sticky that Nelson's worry started gnawing at his gut again, but it was no longer Luke's parents who created his unease.

"Luke?"

"Yeah," Luke whispered in the now-dark room.

"Do you think Pastor Collins ever lies?"

"I don't think he's allowed to 'cause he's a pastor."

Nelson looked up, watching the shadows from the trees outside the window dance across the ceiling. He worried his bottom lip as he considered Luke's answer. He supposed Luke was right. Pastor Collins was supposed to teach them about sin. It was against the rules of the Bible for pastors to sin, and that included lying. Luke's belly flipped sickeningly. There had to be another explanation. "Do you think maybe he doesn't know everything about the Bible or sometimes preaches from a different book?"

"I don't know. Why the sudden interest in the Bible?"

"I was just thinking of something he said in church the other day. You know about sinners. Do you think we made God mad?"

"For what?"

"For what we just did," Nelson explained. He was unable to put a name to it. Sure, he knew all about the birds and the bees, but they were boys. Nothing he'd heard or read said anything about two boys being together. All his friends were chasing after the girls, and here he…. Well, maybe Pastor Collins was right. Maybe what they were doing was unnatural.

"I don't think so. We were just playing around, Nelson." Luke yawned and rolled over, pulling the covers up. "Now will you go to sleep?"

"I know, but—"

"Pastor Collins was talking about sodomites, Nelson. We ain't them. Besides, it's not like anyone will ever find out. We're going to be best friends and roommates forever, right?"

"Oh yeah," Nelson responded, feeling better. They'd promised each other they were going to join the rodeo and see the world.

"Now stop worrying and go to sleep."

"Night, Brobdingnagian."

"Night, Runt."

He and Luke didn't have to worry about what Pastor Collins said because they weren't going to lie together as a man would with a woman. There would be no women or marriage in their lives. Nelson smiled as he drifted off to sleep. It was going to be him and Luke against the world forever.

AN AUDIBLE "oomph" escaped Nelson as he hit the ground with a hundred-and-fifty-pound Luke on his back. The football Nelson had been clutching to his body popped free, but he couldn't even attempt to go after it. He opened and closed his mouth a couple of times, but nothing came out. He didn't even care about the game anymore as panic started to surge through him when nothing went in either. He couldn't breathe! He was going to die. His short thirteen years of life flashed by, ending in a headline that read: *Scrawny Kid Crushed By Best Friend*.

Nelson tried to force air into his lungs but again unsuccessfully. His arms, pinned beneath him, put added pressure on his chest, constricting it further. He needed to move but couldn't. His muscles refused to respond, and his panic turned into full-on hysteria.

Luke rolled off Nelson, grabbed the back of Nelson's shirt, and yanked him up to his feet. "What's wrong with you?"

Nelson clutched at his chest, tears rolling down his face as he continued to try to breathe.

Luke took Nelson's shoulders in his meaty hands and shook him. "Stop it, Nelson, you're scaring me."

You're not the only one. Another attempt, a weird sound, and suddenly his lungs reinflated, and he began gasping. The rest of the guys surrounded them, all staring at him and asking him what was wrong. Nelson could now breathe, but tears were still streaming down his face. The fear that lack of oxygen would kill him passed. But now he was pretty sure the embarrassment would.

"Just got the wind knocked out of me," Nelson wheezed. He wiped at his damp cheeks, then glared at his best friend. "Jesus, Luke, you weigh a ton."

Luke grinned and tussled Nelson's mousy brown hair. "Not my fault you're a runt."

Nelson slapped Luke's hand away. "I'm not a runt, you Brobdingnagian," Nelson countered. He tried for a harsh tone, but it came out as a squeak that, of course, caused everyone to laugh.

"Alright, Mickey Mouse, I think that's enough football for you today," Luke announced and slung his arm over Nelson's shoulders.

None of the other guys argued with Luke, and they began to disperse. Luke had been blessed early by the puberty gods, and he had a good fifty pounds on most of the boys at Sipel Middle School. Nobody wanted to go up against him. Luckily for Nelson, he and Luke had been neighbors and best friends since they were five. Luke could easily rule the kids within the neighborhood and at school by pushing his immense size around. But Luke was a kind-hearted giant. Still, their friendship assured no one ever picked on Nelson.

Nelson ran his hand over his chest. "Man, you really knocked the hell out of me. I thought we were supposed to be on the same team."

"Sorry about that, little man. I tripped over someone. Hell of a run you had going there. You'd have gotten a touchdown for sure if I wasn't so clumsy."

Now how was he supposed to stay mad at Luke when he was complimenting and apologizing? He couldn't. Crap, who was he kidding? He never could stay angry at Luke for long. All Luke had to do was look at Nelson with those big blue eyes and turn on that dimpled smile, and Nelson would forgive him for stealing the stars and moon. Nelson brushed the grass from his pants and shirt, then shrugged. "It's okay. Scared me for a minute when I couldn't breathe, but I'm good now."

"Oh man, I know. Freaked me out too."

"Hey, Luke! You forgot your ball," one of the guys called out.

Luke released his hold on Nelson and started to run. "I'm going long."

Nelson watched in awe as Luke's long legs tore up the field as he sprinted across the grass. The ball reached him but was well above his head. At the last second, Luke jumped, stretched his well-toned arms, and grazed the ball with his fingers, tipping it. Luke spun, grappling to get his hold on it, and then fell on his back, the pigskin landing on his chest. He wrapped his arms around it and clutched it to his chest.

Everyone, including Nelson, clapped and cheered when Luke stood up, a satisfied grin stretching across his face as he held the ball over his head. He tucked it under his arm and took a bow.

Nelson shook his head. Man, the guy could do anything. He was tall, athletic, handsome, and smart. Nelson was one lucky fellow to have someone like Luke as his closest friend. Only Nelson worried they were growing apart. Sure, they still stayed over at each other's house on the weekends and any other night that wasn't a school night, but much to Nelson's disappointment, nothing had happened in bed except sleep the past year. However, Nelson thought about their secret a lot, especially when he was lying in the darkness of his room, and Luke made an appearance in his dreams most nights.

Nelson was too scared to take the initiative, and Luke didn't seem to be interested in their secret games anymore. Nelson tried his best to let it go. But it was getting harder and harder to ignore. He didn't understand what was wrong with him. Luke had told him it was normal, lots of guys experimented when they were kids, and it didn't mean they were gay.

Luke was never wrong.

There was always a first time because he was beginning to believe Luke was wrong about the gay thing. Instead of chasing the girls like the other guys did, Nelson couldn't stop thinking about his best friend. He shouldn't want to hold Luke's hand, run his fingers through his wheat-blond hair while looking into his big blue eyes. He shouldn't want to press their lips together, run his hands over his muscular chest, but God help him, he did. Perhaps he was still a kid, and once he matured, he'd finally outgrow the forbidden desires plaguing him. He hoped so, anyway.

Luke jogged back to Nelson. "Did you see that?"

"Nice catch."

Luke shook his head. "Pure dumb luck, that ball falling on my chest like that."

Nelson started to respond, but then Luke pushed the ball into Nelson's gut and slung his arm back over Nelson's shoulder. His throat went dry, and a tingling sensation raced down his spine, settling into his groin. Even Luke's innocent touches were enough to make his dick start to fill. He spun away, flipped the ball up, and caught it.

"Nah, that was pure athletic talent," Nelson finally got out past his constricted throat.

"Aww, thanks, little man, but seriously, I didn't think I was going to get that one. I think luck had a lot to do with it."

"If you say so." Nelson walked backward, needing to keep some space between them, and tossed Luke the ball. "Mom's making meatloaf tonight. What about yours?"

He and Luke always checked the cooking schedules of their moms, compared notes, and then decided which house to eat at. It was rare they didn't both choose the same meal.

Luke threw the ball to Nelson, then wrinkled his nose. "Meatloaf? Yuck! We will be eating at my house tonight. Dad's bringing home pizza."

"Oh, Mrs. Maitland, I love your meatloaf. I love everything you cook," Nelson said in his best impersonation of Luke. He tossed the ball back to Luke, and before taking off running, he added, "I'm so telling. It's your fault I have to eat that crap."

"You wouldn't dare!"

Nelson didn't respond. He sprinted across the field as fast as his legs would go. He didn't dare look back and waste precious seconds, knowing Luke was right behind him. He'd catch up soon enough with his longer stride. Nelson was getting better. He nearly made it to his driveway. He slowed down to make the turn around the rosebushes, and Luke sprung. He wrapped his arms around Nelson and lifted him off his feet.

"You tell your mom, and I'm gonna beat your scrawny little butt."

Nelson reached back and tickled Luke's sides and wriggled free when Luke started laughing and squirming. Nelson ran up the driveway. "Going to take a shower and let Mom know I'll be eating at your place, and then I'll be over."

"Okay, see you later. Oh, hey, you should grab a bag and just stay over tonight."

"K," Nelson tossed over his shoulder and headed for the house.

HIS BELLY full of five slices of pizza and half a liter of pop, Nelson stretched out on the old couch in Luke's basement. He folded his arms behind his head and relaxed while Luke went through the video cabinet.

"What are you in the mood for tonight? Comedy, action, or horror?"

"My gut is too full to laugh. How about scary?" Nelson suggested.

"That makes no sense at all."

"Sure it does. Laughing makes my belly hurt; horror makes my chest hurt."

"I stand corrected." Luke rummaged around in the cabinet and then turned, holding two tapes. "Zombies or Freddie?"

The last thing Nelson wanted was to watch someone munching. Dang it, he loved zombie movies. He shouldn't have eaten so much. "Let's hang out with Freddie tonight." They could do an *undead* marathon after church.

"*Nightmare* it is," Luke said and loaded the VCR. He hit the play button, grabbed a bag of chips from the bar and sat on the floor, and leaned back against the couch.

"How can you still be hungry? You ate twice as much as me, and I feel like I'm going to burst."

"I'm a growing boy," Luke mumbled around a mouthful of chips. "Now shut up and cut that light. The movie is starting."

Nelson turned off the lamp and then stretched back out on the couch. They'd already seen the show at least a dozen times, so it wasn't long before Nelson was dozing off in between screams. He'd open his eyes again and be able to catch back up with the movie quickly. He'd just started to slip back off to sleep when Luke tapped his shoulder.

"This floor is hurting my butt, scooch up."

Before Nelson had a chance to respond, Luke climbed over him, shoved him forward, and lay down behind him. They'd been staying at each other's houses since kindergarten, and it wasn't unusual for them to lie on the couch together. Nor was it out of the ordinary for them to wake in the morning in Luke's full-size bed wrapped up in a tangle of arms and legs. The last few months, however, Nelson found Luke's closeness uncomfortable, or more like weird. With Luke's warmth pressed against Nelson's back and his strong arm draped across him, the tingling started trickling down Luke's spine. And if that wasn't bad enough, he was painfully aware of Luke's dick pressed against his butt.

For some reason Nelson still didn't understand, Luke had stopped touching Nelson like they used to. Luke explained they were becoming men, and the things they did as children had to stop. Nelson had tried to put it out of his head, to stop wanting to touch and kiss Luke's naked flesh, but it was impossible. Over the last year, his desire for Luke had only increased. While Luke and the rest of the guys were having first dates, first girlfriends, Nelson wanted nothing more than a boyfriend. More specifically he wanted Luke as his boyfriend.

What is wrong with me?

He didn't understand why he couldn't be more like Luke and the rest of the guys. Why he couldn't put those childhood experiences behind him and grow up as Luke had. He was thirteen, for Chrissakes, a man. He wasn't supposed to be thinking about Luke like this, and he sure shouldn't be popping a boner. *Oh God, what if Luke feels it?* His hand was close, and if he moved it an inch downward, he would—

Nelson jumped to his feet.

"Where ya going?"

"Too much pop. Be right back," he lied and rushed up the stairs.

Behind the locked door of the bathroom, Nelson held on to the counter and hung his head, breathing harshly. Why was this happening to him? A better a question was why couldn't he make it stop? He was going to lose his best friend if Luke found out, Nelson was sure of it. How could he not lose Luke? He was a freak.

Shame engulfed Nelson. His eyes filled with tears, spilled over, and rolled down his cheeks. He knew the difference between right and wrong. He went to church, wasn't a bully, tried his best in school. He'd lied about breaking his mom's lamp, sometimes told fibs about having his homework done. He was far from perfect, but he couldn't think of a single thing he'd done bad enough to deserve what was happening to him now. He didn't want to be different from the rest of the gang. Dammit, he wanted to go out on double dates with the other guys, wanted to add to the conversation about girlfriends, and he didn't want to lie anymore.

A sob escaped him, and he turned on the taps to drown out the sound. "Please, God, make it go away. I promise I won't lie anymore, and I'll tell Mom about the lamp. Please just make it go away," he whispered.

Nelson grabbed a washcloth, ran it under the cool water, and then laid it against his face until the tears stopped and he was able to swallow down his sobs. He lowered the cloth and stared at his reflection, his eyes puffy and red-rimmed. "Now you look like a freak too."

A soft rap on the door was followed by Luke's low voice. "You okay in there?"

"Ummm… no. Too much pizza and pop made me blow chunks." Nelson squeezed his eyes shut and laid his head back. Less than five minutes, and he'd already broken his promise to God, but he couldn't tell Luke the truth. Ever.

"There is some Pepto-Bismol in the medicine cabinet."

"Okay, thanks. I'll be right down." Nelson waited until he was sure Luke had moved away from the door before he opened his eyes. He couldn't even stand to look at himself in the mirror. He flushed the toilet to give credence to his lie and then shut off the taps. Maybe he did deserve this punishment. He was a sinner, and the lies were getting easier and easier to tell as the guilt got harder and harder to swallow.

FOR TWO weeks he continued the deceit. Stomach ailments, headaches, poison ivy, homework, and a multitude of other reasons why he couldn't hang out with Luke. Nelson would have sworn the worst punishment that could be bestowed upon him was the unnatural desires he'd had for his best friend every time Luke touched him. He was wrong.

Nelson stood at the back door, his legs shaking so hard he didn't know how they were keeping him up. "You're kidding me, right?"

"I wish I was," Luke responded sadly. He then turned and sat down on the top stair and hung his head.

Nelson pushed the screen door open, reeling from the shock. He barely made it the three steps before his knees gave out, and he fell on his ass next to Luke. "When…?" Nelson's voice cracked, and he had to swallow hard before he could continue. "When are you leaving?"

"Dad's leaving Monday, and Mom and I will join him in two weeks," Luke replied without lifting his head. He was silent for a long time before he whispered, "They're putting the house up for sale."

Nelson didn't know how to respond. Wasn't sure he could with the lump that lodged in his throat. Christ, he could scarcely breathe, and it was taking every bit of willpower he had not to fall to the ground in a fetal position and cry like a baby.

California? That was on the other side of the country. It might as well be on the other end of the world because Nelson knew he was losing his best friend, and they'd never see each other again. What was he going to do without Luke? Who would he hang out with, eat dinner with, watch zombie marathons with?

He heard Luke sniffle, and it was all it took for Nelson to give in to his own grief. He wrapped his arms around himself and rocked as the tears fell. The sobbing intensified when Luke pulled him into a hug and cried just as hard. Nelson poured out his anguish as only a child could. Powerless to change the course they were barreling toward. Too young to fully understand why. Only knowing an adult's decision was destroying his world. He suddenly hated Mr. Rollins. Would never forgive him for taking Luke away.

They clung to each other well after the tears stopped flowing. Nelson's anger at the injustice growing until it burned off the rest of his grief and left him with nothing but red-hot rage. He jumped to his feet, fists clenched as he stomped down the stairs. "He can't do this," he screamed. "He can't make you move."

Luke caught up quickly and grabbed Nelson's arm, stopping him. "He doesn't want to move. His company is doing this."

"Then he can get another job!"

Luke sighed heavily and gave him a watery grin. "I've argued every reason I could think of. We have to move. I don't want to. It sucks, it's unfair, and I hate it! But there is nothing we can do about it."

The anger seeped from Nelson like a deflated balloon. "Then what's going to happen to us?"

"We're still going to be best friends. We'll talk on the phone every day, and you can stay with me on every holiday and summer vacation. And when we turn eighteen, we can hit the rodeo circuit together."

"Hey! Maybe I can talk my dad into moving too. I bet there are lots of jobs in California for police officers."

"Yeah, I bet there are. It's a big state, and the best part is, we won't ever have to shovel snow again. We can spend Christmas on the beach." Luke wiped at his eyes, a genuinely happy smile lighting up his face.

"And we can send pictures of us surfing to the rest of the guys who are going to be stuck under a hundred pounds of winter clothes."

"And we'll be tanned and buff and have the hottest girlfriends," Luke said with a wink.

Nelson liked the idea of them being tanned and buff and living on the beach but wasn't so keen on the girlfriend part. He wasn't going to dwell on that one negative, but the rest of it sounded amazing. "We're going to have the best life ever," Nelson hooted.

"Yup," Luke agreed. "Race you to the ball field? I can't wait to tell the other guys."

"Right behind you," Nelson called, having already taken off on a dead run, leaving Luke to catch up.

It was the last time he and Luke laughed together. Two weeks later Nelson stood in the center of his street waving goodbye to Luke. Their plans and dreams were crushed when Nelson's dad refused to move. His only consolation was his parents agreed to let him visit Luke in the future.

Nelson had no clue how impossible it would be to keep his promises.

Chapter One

Reunion
Ten years later, 1998

THE AIRPORT was a bustle of activity, people racing by to catch their flights, kids screaming, and the whole scene a clusterfuck of mass confusion. Nelson scanned the monitor for his flight, relieved when he found it and the words *On Time* displayed next to it.

He hated flying, and unexpected business trips with an hour to pack really pissed him off. Nevertheless, with only six months at TFA Technologies, he was the rookie. He hadn't earned his stripes yet, and as such got the shitty last-minute jobs.

Glancing at his watch, he discovered he had an hour before his flight boarded and went in search of an airport lounge. A shot of Woodford should calm his frayed nerves. Because the lounge was packed with commuters, Nelson took the only seat available at the bar. He ordered his drink on the rocks and then pulled out his Palm Pilot and brought up his itinerary. With the rush order to get his ass to Seattle, he hadn't even had a chance to take a minute and discover where he was going beyond the city and who he'd be meeting once he arrived. The only info his boss gave him was a software system had crashed and to get on a plane, and he'd get further instructions later. So here he was. Good thing he hadn't given in to his new urge to get a puppy. It would have been a selfish act borne out of loneliness and not right for the animal. Last-minute flights across the country were a prime example why he didn't need anyone or anything dependent on him. Still, it would be a lot less lonely around his place with someone there who cared if he came home.

Since moving to Minneapolis, he hadn't made any friends to speak of. Working twelve-hour shifts and spending his evenings reading over policy and procedures, blah, blah, blah, he had no time to hit the gym three days a week, plus eat and sleep. It wasn't that he was ungrateful for the opportunity. He was happy the job afforded him to be on his own for the first time—dorm rooms so did not count as being on one's own, especially with a slob for a roommate and eating on Mom and Dad's dime.

Hopefully this trip would prove to his boss how competent he was, and he'd finally get his first raise. He'd settle for hourly with overtime rather than a salary increase, but that wasn't going to happen.

The bartender sat Nelson's drink down in front of him. Nelson thanked him, paid his bill, and took a sip of the flavorful bourbon. He didn't make enough money yet to indulge in the finer things. However, since this was TFA's tab, he was going top shelf.

"Nelson! Nelson Maitland?"

Nelson turned to find a tall, quite broad, and muscular man standing behind him with a wide, dimpled grin. Nelson blinked at him in confusion. How in the hell did this guy know Nelson's name? It took several ticks of the clock before it dawned on him who he was looking at. He blinked again to make sure he wasn't seeing things, but the man was still standing there.

Nelson jumped to his feet. "Holy shit! Lucas Rollins, is that you?"

"In the flesh. Got a hug for an old friend?"

Nelson wrapped his arms around Luke and patted his back. "Jesus, it's good to see you." He stepped back and looked up—Luke was a good four inches taller than Nelson—and met Luke's gaze. "How long has it been?"

"Ten years, dude." Luke shook his head. "How time flies. Man, it is good seeing you. How have you been? You live here in Minneapolis? How's your mom and dad?"

Luke threw questions at him rapid-fire without giving Nelson time to respond. When he started to chuckle, Luke stopped talking and laughed with him. "Sorry, I was rambling. It's just… Damn, I can't believe it's you."

"I know, right? Who would have thought, after all these years, we'd run into each other here? You still in Cali?"

"Yeah. Hey, if you have time, I've got a table over there," Luke said with a nod toward the back of the lounge. "Why don't you join me, and we can catch up."

"Sure." Nelson grabbed his drink and followed Luke through the crowd.

Wow was right. *Holy shit, ten years*. He spent the first year after Luke left checking the mail every day, completely miserable and blaming himself for Luke having to move away. At thirteen he thought his life was over, couldn't understand why the world was still spinning when his had stopped. However, as they said, life went on. Eventually he pulled his act together, made new friends, and grew up. A part of him never stopped hoping to see Luke again. One never truly got over their first love, or their first crush, so it was incredible to see him again. It was just.... *Wow!* The sentiment could also describe Luke. The guy was well over six feet tall, and holy fuck, was he thick with bulging muscles. Hints of the cute face Nelson had remembered so fondly were there—the sweet dimples and upturned nose—only now brown stubble covered the jaw, his square features more prominent, masculine. Luke's wheat-blond hair was now streaked with nearly white stripes, and his skin was a dark-olive tone that spoke of many hours in the Southern California sun. Luke looked the stereotypical SoCal inhabitant. *He must be living in Malibu because Luke definitely deserves to be around the beautiful people.*

"Okay, let's try this again," Luke said once they sat at a small table. "You live here in Minneapolis, or just passing through?"

"I moved here six months ago. How about you? You still living in Cali?"

"Yeah, I'm in Malibu."

"Figures." Nelson couldn't help it. He started to snicker. His skills of observation were obviously quite stellar.

Luke frowned. "What is that supposed to mean?"

"Nothing, ignore me. I get a little weird when I have to fly. So what brings you to the Midwest?"

"Just came from New York City on business. I got to make a quick stop in Seattle before heading back home."

"Seattle? No shit. That's where I'm heading."

"Flight 4023?" Luke asked with a hopeful expression on his face.

"No," Nelson responded with real disappointment. It would have been great to spend the next few hours catching up. "Hey, how long are you going to be there? Maybe we can meet up for dinner or something?"

"Just a couple of days. It would be great to catch up and talk about old times. Let me give you my business card." Luke pulled out his wallet from the inside pocket of his coat and slid a card across the small round table.

Nelson accepted the card, shocked when a jolt raced up his arm when their fingers brushed against each other. He hid his reaction to the power of such a simple touch by keeping his head down and examined the card.

Rollins Financial Services

Lucas Rollins
Vice President

"Vice president, huh? I'm impressed." Nelson retrieved his business card and handed it to Luke. "Hate to disappoint, but I'm but a lowly intern computer geek."

Luke accepted the card, studied it for a second, then slid it into his pocket. He smiled at Nelson. "You could never disappoint me. Well, unless you were, like, a serial killer or mugged little old ladies."

Nelson's cheeks heated with the compliment. He hid his embarrassment behind his glass and took a healthy swig. "Neither of those are on my bucket list."

"Didn't think so. Anyway, my job really isn't that impressive. I've been the vice president since Dad started the company when I was seventeen. It's a fancy title he gave me so I would be his gofer. It's not that consequential when I tell you I got the title when there were only two employees. Me and Dad." Luke chuckled and then took a swallow of his beer.

Luke's lips pressed against the mouth of his bottle drew Nelson's gaze. Phew, if Nelson didn't get the same all-over tingling sensation Luke had produced in him when they were kids. He shifted in his chair and spread his legs, needing a little room for his growing erection. Damn thing had a mind of its own. Nelson grabbed his glass, forcing his gaze away from Luke's throat or any other part of him, and downed the rest of his bourbon.

Needing to get his mind out of the gutter, Nelson asked, "Other than work, what have you been up to? Got a wife and family to go with the grown-up title?"

"Oh hell no. No little woman at home. Don't you remember when we were younger we vowed to never get married? I kept my promise, did you?"

Nelson held up his fingers in a Boy Scout salute. "On my honor, I promise to never marry."

They both laughed at the old memory.

"I had a steady girlfriend for a while," Luke said and shrugged. "She started talking marriage recently, and I fled. Scared the hell out of me, I tell ya."

Girlfriend. Nelson swallowed down his disappointment. It would have been too much to hope that Luke swung his way. "I can imagine."

"You got you a girl?" Luke asked over the rim of his glass.

"Nope." *No boyfriend either.* "I've been so busy with school and working, I haven't had time to date."

Luke frowned. "Hey, you got to make time for fun. Without it you'll get old before your time."

"Yes, but without working all the time, I go hungry and homeless," Nelson countered.

"Gotta find balance, dude. Yin and yang, ya know?"

Luke had always been laid-back and very much balanced. It was a big part of why he'd been so popular in their old neighborhood. He worked hard, played hard, and had a big heart. It was good to see it appeared his old friend hadn't changed in that respect. Nelson, on the other hand, worried about everything. Always had.

"Flight 4023 now boarding at gate C," a female voice announced over the loudspeaker.

"Shit, I gotta go," Luke grumbled. "Usually I'm complaining about delayed flights, and now that I want it to be late, no such luck." He downed the rest of his beer and went to his feet. "Anyway, come give me a hug."

Nelson shook his head but stood just the same.

Luke wrapped Nelson into a bear hug. "It's good seeing you, Runt."

"You too, Brobdingnagian."

Luke laughed. "I haven't been called that in years."

Nelson looked up at him. "It's even more appropriate these days."

"I tried to get you to eat your Wheaties, but would you listen? Noooooo."

"I didn't like those," Nelson pointed out and wrinkled his nose. "Besides, I'm pretty sure it's more about good genes rather than cereal choices."

"We shall never know now." Luke winked. He picked up his briefcase and flashed a brilliant smile that hit Nelson right in the center of his chest. "Call me when you get to your hotel, and we'll hook up for dinner."

Nelson held up Luke's business card and flicked it with his finger. "Looking forward to it."

Luke waved over his shoulder before he disappeared around the corner.

For a trip that had started out in panic and irritation, it sure as hell was looking up. For the first time in his life, he couldn't wait to get on a plane. Dislike of flying be damned. He was going to spend time with Luke on the other side of the journey.

He downed the rest of his bourbon and whistled as he casually strolled to his gate. His steps were light, and if he walked with a bit more sway, it was because the sheer fucking happiness was too big to contain.

WATER DRIPPING down his body, Nelson stood in front of the bathroom sink, brushing his teeth and running a comb through his hair at the same time. Fuck, he should have called Luke after he showered. What were the chances Luke was staying at the same hotel? Ten years he hadn't seen him, and not only did he run into him in a random city, they were heading to the same destination. Man, maybe there was something to all that talk about fate and destiny. Unfortunately he didn't have time to ponder it.

"Dammit, why in the hell did I agree to meet him down in the lobby in fifteen minutes? I need more time."

He rinsed and spit. Tried in vain to do something with his wet mop, then raced out of the bathroom to dress. *So much for having a little time to primp.*

Nelson froze, jeans in hand. "Primping?"

Had he lost his goddamn mind? Luke was a friend he hadn't seen in ten years, not a potential date. He shook his head at his stupidity. Just two old friends having dinner to catch up on old times. It didn't matter that Luke was still the hottest guy Nelson had ever laid eyes on. Maybe Luke had become a jerk. Perhaps they no longer had anything in common. Hell, just because they rubbed off on each other a couple times, shared a few blowjobs, it didn't make Luke gay. A lot of adolescents experimented. It didn't mean anything. Besides, Luke talked about a steady girlfriend. "So put your dick and your hope away," Nelson warned himself.

The jeans weren't the easiest to get into with wet skin, but he managed. Somehow he was able to dress, fix his brown mousy curls—sort of—spray on a little cologne, and was downstairs in the allotted time. He was presentable, but sure he looked frazzled. Of course, when he spotted Luke leaning against a pillar, Luke appeared calm and relaxed and, man oh man, did he look presentable. He was wearing tight jeans and a baby-blue dress shirt the same color as his eyes that accentuated his deep tan. He wore his hair styled back, the longish strands tucked behind his ears, and from this distance, it looked dry, unlike Nelson's wet mop.

"Just dinner with an old friend," he mumbled. He ran his fingers through his hair one more time and took a deep breath.

His hands were shaking so badly he shoved them into the pockets of his jeans to hide his nervousness. With as much confidence as he could muster, he strolled over to Luke.

Luke smiled when he spotted Nelson. "Hey."

"Hey." *Oh, that was original.*

"The receptionist said they have excellent food in the Torch Light, but if you'd rather get bar food, we can hang out in the lounge."

"Might be hard to talk in the bar," Nelson pointed out.

"True. Torch Light it is. We can always head to the bar later."

Nelson walked along with Luke, doing a little mental math. He had to meet his client at seven in the morning and still had to go over the notes his boss had sent him. He was young. As long as he got back to his room by, say… two… three at the latest, he'd be good.

The restaurant was high-end. White linen tablecloths, fine china, cut-crystal wineglasses. *The whole nine yards of way too fancy for me to be here.* The other patrons wore slacks, dinner coats, and dresses. Nelson was way underdressed, as was apparent from the disapproving looks he was getting. However, since Luke was dressed casually as well, it did make Nelson feel marginally better. He pointed out the dress code as soon as they were sitting and the host had walked away.

Luke waved a dismissive hand. "Like I care. My money spends just as easily as theirs."

Nelson shook out his napkin and laid it in his lap. "I'd have thought, you being from Malibu and all, you'd adhere to etiquette. You know, wear nothing but the finest everywhere you went."

"This is my finest. Best pair of blue jeans, that is," he chuckled. Luke then tilted his head. "Does it really bother you? We can go somewhere else if you prefer."

"Nah, I'm good. Hell, I don't even own the finest pair of anything."

"My kind of guy," Luke said. He flashed that stunning dimpled smile before hiding it behind his menu.

Nelson hid the goofy grin Luke's comment sparked behind his own menu. *My kind of guy. I wish.* With a silent sigh, he studied the choices, nearly choking when he caught sight of the prices. No way in hell would his boss cover this tab. For dinner with a client, improbable but not impossible, but with an old friend? That would be a big fat hell no. Oh well, he liked bologna. Good thing too since that's what he'd be eating for the next week after covering this meal.

Everything sounded fancy as hell, just like the décor. Nelson had no idea what to order. He'd only been to one haughty restaurant in his life, but he hadn't cared about the cost since he was fifteen at the time and with his grandparents. He'd just have whatever Luke was having. He set his menu aside and took a sip of his water.

When the waiter came over, Nelson nearly choked again when Luke ordered the filet mignon and a bottle of red wine.

Nelson sighed internally. *Make that bologna for a month.* "I'll have the same minus the wine. Water is fine for me."

"You don't like wine?" Luke asked.

"Never acquired a taste for it. Actually, I've never tried it," he admitted.

"I hadn't either until I spent some time in Napa Valley. It grows on you."

"Like a fungus?"

Luke threw his head back and laughed. The sound was deeper than Nelson remembered, but it still had the same effect on him, and he laughed along with him. Some of Nelson's favorite childhood memories were of Luke's laughter and his charming smile.

"Damn, Nelson, it's so good to see you. I can't believe it's been ten years." Luke pursed his lips. "How in the hell is that possible?"

Nelson didn't know how to answer that. He remembered the first year after Luke left as some of his darkest days. Each one seemed to last an eternity, as did the ache in his chest. Eventually he set aside his childish dreams, and each day thereafter became a little easier until he was finally able to move on and begin to live again. Looking back, ten years did seem to have flown by. Now sitting across from Luke, a pang of sadness struck Nelson. Apparently, the sense of loss never completely left him. He was beyond ecstatic to see Luke again, but he also couldn't help but feel cheated for all the years he'd missed.

"Life has a way of doing that. People get busy," Nelson finally responded.

"Don't I know it? I live out of a goddamn suitcase. I've been to some great cities but rarely have time to stop and thoroughly enjoy them."

Nelson played with his napkin, folding and unfolding it, and nodded. "That sucks and, unfortunately, I may be heading down the same path. My boss gives me about a ten-minute notice before I have to pack, then rush to the airport."

"Damn, that's harsh. I thought I had it bad. My boss tries to, at least, give me a week's notice. It doesn't always happen that way, but he tries."

"That's because your boss is your dad, and your mom would probably spank him if he was mean to you," Nelson teased.

"There may be some truth to that," Luke snickered.

"How are your parents and brother, by the way?" Nelson asked.

"They're great. Dad is working from home a couple days a week and leaving the traveling to me, which makes Mom a lot happier. Colton is still the irritating little shit he's always been, but he's a good kid. What about your parents?"

"Same as ever. Mom's still working at the school, Dad with the force, although he's been promoted to lieutenant. Hell, even the house hasn't changed in ten years. My room looks the same as it did when we were kids. How sad is that?"

"Same shit-brown walls and deer horns."

"They are antlers, thank you very much," Nelson corrected. "You never did appreciate my Wyatt Earp obsession."

"And you never appreciated color. Anyway, I think it's cool you still live there. I wish I could have grown up there. I miss the old stomping grounds and the gang almost as much as I've missed you."

Nelson's gut fluttered pleasantly with Luke's admission. Luckily he didn't have to try to respond, as the server chose that moment to bring their drinks and a basket of fresh bread.

They spent dinner in the past, chatting about the kids in the old neighborhood, the ones still there, what they were up to, and those who had moved away. Luke also spoke of his high school years in Cali. The conversation was light, casual, and surprisingly, the years slipped away. Nelson found it as easy to talk to Luke now as it used to be. Funny enough, they didn't talk much about themselves, nor the present. It seemed appropriate to start at the beginning. A chance to relive and reconnect.

At the end of memory lane, Luke dropped his fork onto his empty plate and pushed it aside. He wiped his mouth, sat back in his chair, and stared at Nelson while he ate the last of his dinner.

Nelson put his finger to his mouth. "What? I got something in my teeth?"

"A computer geek, huh?"

"Yup."

Luke pursed his lips and squinted. "Nope, I just don't see it. I mean, you were always the smarter one, but computers, huh?"

Nelson washed down the last bite of his steak, then set the plate aside before answering. "Actually, my major was in business management, but luckily I minored in computers because it was the only job I could find after I graduated."

"Hmm." Luke nodded. "Yeah, I can see you in a fancy suit in a corner office, twirling your power-red tie through your fingers."

"Not me."

"No?" Luke questioned. "If it's not the corner office at the top of some high-rise, what is it you want to do with your life, Nelson?"

"You'll laugh."

Luke's brows furrowed. "Why would I do that?"

Nelson considered it for a moment. Why did he care if Luke laughed? It's not as if it would actually happen anyway; he didn't have the funds. Plus his parents would kill him if he threw away all the money they'd spent on his education. "Because it's silly."

"Man, ten years really did a number on us, didn't it?"

"What's that supposed to mean?"

"You and I never kept secrets. We told each other everything," Luke pointed out. There was a look of disappointment on his face as he stared at Nelson that caused Nelson's gut to roil with guilt.

Nelson hadn't shared everything with Luke. He'd kept some pretty big secrets when they were growing up. Still did. What he wanted to do with his life was insignificant in comparison. "It's really not a secret, Luke," Nelson finally admitted. "I'd like to own a bakery."

"Seriously?"

"Yeah."

"You mean like baking cakes and stuff, or just own it, and other people bake?"

"I love baking," Nelson responded.

"Since when? If I remember correctly, neither of us were allowed in the kitchen before dinner."

"After you left, Mom started having me help her with the cooking to keep me from moping around. I found I not only liked it, but was pretty good at it." Suddenly uncomfortable with the old feelings the memories stirred up, he looked away. He removed his napkin from his lap and dropped it on his plate. "How about we head to the bar? I could use that drink now."

"Sounds good to me. And Nelson?" Nelson lifted his eyes and met Luke's gaze. "I think a bakery is a really cool idea. You'll have to make me some goodies sometime."

Nelson nodded. It felt way too good to hear Luke say it, and the genuine smile on his face caused a rush of warmth to spread to places that had nothing to do with baking, conversations, or drinks.

Luke waved over the waiter, and Nelson pulled his wallet from his pocket, but Luke waved him off. "I got this."

"I can't—"

Luke took the folder from the waiter. "I insist."

"Honestly you don't have to."

Luke signed his name and handed it back to the waiter. "I'll write it off as a business expense. Besides, you'll just lose if we arm wrestle for it, just like you always used to."

"Hey, I beat you once," Nelson reminded him.

"Yeah because you cheated."

Nelson laughed heartily as he remembered it. The big guy didn't admit to fearing much, but Nelson knew having bugs crawl on him scared him. So a brush of toe to calf, and victory. Nelson laughed even harder at the image of Luke screaming.

"Yuck it up, Runt. I'm still paying for dinner."

"Fine, but can I at least buy you a beer?"

"Absolutely." Luke went to his feet. "Let's go."

More than likely to the great relief of the staff and other patrons of the Torch Light, Nelson and Luke headed out. Nelson was completely unapologetic for their laughter and at times loud and animated chat. The lounge was much more to Nelson's liking and far better suited for their boisterous walk down memory lane. The music was loud enough that no one paid them any attention, not a single raised brow or disapproving look.

The one drawback to the drinks flowing as easily as the conversation was the alcohol loosened Nelson's tongue and inhibitions. It also sparked his already raging libido, not the best combination.

Nelson took another big gulp of his beer. There was a lot to be said for liquid courage. "So you travel a lot, huh?"

"Too much," Luke responded. He pursed his lips and let out a heavy sigh before he downed the rest of his whiskey.

"Must get lonely. All those empty beds without someone to snuggle," Nelson hedged.

Luke shrugged. "Not really."

"Ah, a different girl in every port, huh?"

Luke tilted his head and gave Nelson an aggrieved look. "I know it's been a long time since we've seen each other, Nelson, but I'd have thought you knew me better than that."

"It's been ten years, Luke. A lot can change in that amount of time. Besides, I wasn't judging you or being mean. You're young, single, good-looking, and have a killer bod. I'm sure the girls are chasing you everywhere you go."

Luke's expression softened, and a small grin curled his top lip. "You think I'm good-looking, huh?"

"Pfft, look at you." Nelson waved his hand around, indicating all of Luke. "You don't need me to tell you how attractive you are."

Luke raised his empty glass toward the bartender and then leaned over and spoke out of the side of his mouth. "Killer bod, huh?"

The seductive tone of Luke's voice, whether real or wishful thinking on Nelson's part, sent a jolt of heat to his groin, causing his already-hard dick to twitch. Nelson shoved him away with his shoulder. "Stop fishing for compliments."

The bartender set Luke's drink down in front of him. He then nodded toward Nelson's half-empty beer, but he declined. Luke rested his elbow on the bar, turning slightly to face Nelson. "Well, you sure don't have to fish for one. I'll tell you straight up. You were always a cute kid, even if you were a runt. But…." Luke raked his eyes up and down Nelson body. "Nothing cute about you now."

"I'm not sure if that was a compliment or an insult," Nelson chuckled.

Luke picked up his glass and raised it. "Trust me, it was a compliment. You look fucking fantastic. Now you're a manly runt," he commented. He winked before taking a big gulp.

"Thanks. I think."

Nelson's cheeks heated, and he had to force his gaze away from Luke's working throat when the image of other things Luke could be swallowing down popped into Nelson's head. He gave himself an internal shake and discreetly rested his arm in his lap to hide the large bulge in his pants. Luke's nearness, his compliments, his smile, his broad shoulders, and strong stubbled jaw…. Nelson sighed. Who was he kidding? Everything about Luke turned him on. Nelson's lack of self-control, however, wasn't totally his fault.

He wasn't out to his friends and family back home, and having only recently moved, he hadn't had the opportunity or the courage to explore the gay scene in Minneapolis. It had been a very, very long time since he had anything other than his own hand wrapped around his dick. *And God, how I'd love to have something wrapped around it.* Throat suddenly dry, Nelson finished his beer in one long pull.

"You sure you don't want another one?" Luke offered.

"Nah, I better not."

"Aww, c'mon, Nelson. We're celebrating," Luke encouraged.

"Yes, but I still have to see a client in the morning, and I don't think my boss would appreciate me representing his company by showing up with red eyes and smelling of alcohol."

"You always were the smarter of the two of us." Luke glanced down at his watch. "Shit, I didn't realize it was getting so late. I have an early morning meeting too. C'mon, I'll walk you to your room and you can invite me in for one last nightcap, then I promise to be a responsible adult and let you get some sleep?"

"Sounds great."

Luke downed his drink and then turned that brilliant smile on Nelson, and he knew he was fucked. If Luke wanted to stay up drinking and chatting all night, he'd agree to it. He was young. He could pull an all-nighter as long as he switched to water. Plus he could always find another job, but when would he get another opportunity to see Luke?

Chapter Two

LUKE FLOPPED down on the couch. He stretched out his long legs and took in the room around him. His had no view and nothing but a king-size bed and small writing table with a single chair in his room. Nelson's, on the other hand, had a sliding door that looked out past a balcony to a garden and the forest beyond. In addition to the bed and writing table that were the same, the room also had a sitting area complete with couch, two leather wing chairs, and coffee table. One upgraded feature Luke didn't care about was the kitchen since he wouldn't be in town long enough to cook. Not that he would, even if he was. He didn't cook anywhere but his own kitchen. He made reservations or ordered room service when on the road.

"Wow, your room is a lot nicer than mine," Luke pointed out.

"I was pretty impressed myself. My boss is usually a tightwad, so I'm going to assume because of the last-minute arrangements, it's all he could find. Sorry, I don't have any beer." Nelson handed Luke a glass of bourbon on the rocks, then took his own and sat next to him and propped his feet up on the coffee table.

"No, this is great. Thanks."

Luke took a sip of his drink, set it on the side table, and then took the same position as Nelson. He hadn't planned on drinking anymore, really shouldn't be, especially hard liquor. He was a lightweight, beer and wine his go-to's. But he hoped the bourbon, combined with the time change and lack of sleep, would dull the fire that had flared to life when he saw Nelson in that little airport bar. To say he hadn't thought about Nelson these past ten years would be a lie. And to say he never thought about what they'd done together under covers would have been an even bigger lie. Those memories he so ferociously protected and kept entirely to himself were now floating around in his head.

During his high school years, he fooled around with a couple of guys he played football with. Although he was extremely attracted to them and had no trouble getting off, he didn't get the same emotional satisfaction as he did when he was with Nelson. In fact, no one had brought out those same types of feelings as Nelson had.

He spent plenty of time experimenting and doing some true soul searching, and in the end, Luke came to terms with the fact that he was, and always had been, attracted to both men and women. His ex-girlfriend Chelsea was a good friend before they became lovers. He cared deeply for her, their sex life was satisfying, but no way was he going to let anyone tie him down. Man or woman. He'd only been in love once, or at least he thought he was in love at thirteen, but really, what did he know at such a young age? Now sitting next to Nelson, those feelings came rushing back. He still wasn't sure if it was love, but Nelson's nearness did something to Luke that went beyond the thrill of arousal.

"I've pinched myself till I'm bruised. Keep thinking I'm dreaming, still can't believe I'm here with you," Nelson commented, pulling Luke from his thoughts.

Luke turned his head but had to look down to meet Nelson's gaze, reminding Luke of their size difference. He scooched farther down the couch. "I know. What were the chances? I hate that we lost contact. We promised to call each other every day."

Nelson nodded. "I would have kept it too, if I could have. At thirteen, me having no true concept of money, we had no idea what an expensive commitment we were making. My dad about had a coronary when he got that first bill. I spent an entire month working every day after school and every weekend to pay off that debt."

"The same reaction my dad had," Luke chuckled. "We had great plans but probably should have thought about them a little more thoroughly. Remember when we planned on joining the rodeo when we turned eighteen?"

Nelson laughed. The happy tone hit Luke right dead in the center of his chest, and he suddenly had the urge to lean over and kiss Nelson. He clamped down on the impulse. He'd been trying to get a reading on Nelson to figure out if he'd be open to having a guy hit on him, but so far hadn't been able to. Sure, he'd noticed Nelson checking him out, but couldn't tell if it was in an appreciative, sexual way or trying to get a grasp of the changes. Considering Luke was doing both when looking at Nelson, it was understandable he couldn't decide which he saw in Nelson's eyes when he looked at Luke. Anyway, didn't matter. He wasn't about to screw up their reunion by letting his dick make the decisions.

"Crazy plan considering the closest we ever came to a horse was when we went to the county fair. I still haven't ever been on a horse. You?" Nelson asked.

"What?" Luke asked in confusion, having allowed his mind to wander once again.

"I asked if you've ever been on a horse."

"Nope."

They both laughed.

Silly childhood dreams.

Luke laid his head back and turned it toward Nelson. Nelson was an extremely handsome man. It was only natural Luke found him attractive. However, while his mind was telling him not to do anything foolish, his heart overwhelmingly wanted to reconnect with Nelson on a deeper emotional level. When the strong urge to kiss Nelson hit Luke again, he pushed to his feet, needing a little distance between him and Nelson. He spotted the remote control sitting on the bedside table. "How about seeing if there are some bad B horror movies on?"

"You still into those?" Nelson asked, sounding excited.

"Of course, only now the movies we liked are classics." Luke sat on the edge of the bed, grabbed the remote, and clicked on the TV. He ran through the limited channels. "Oh shit! Look what's on," he hooted.

Nelson came to stand next to him and cracked up. "*Nightmare on Elm Street.*"

"This night just keeps getting better and better." Luke kicked his shoes off and stretched out on the bed. He patted the spot next to him. "Remember the last time we watched this together?"

"You mean you watched it while I snored," Nelson pointed out. He went around to the other side of the bed, grabbed a pillow, and tossed it to the end. To Luke's disappointment, instead of taking the spot next to him, Nelson lay on his stomach, head at the foot of the bed, and propped himself up on the pillow. "Only thing that would make this better is if we had a bag of chips and a couple of sodas."

Luke's gaze was drawn to Nelson's pert butt. *What the fuck?* Luke gave himself an internal shake and forced himself to turn away from Nelson. Luke focused on the television. On the small screen, blood fountained up out of the center of the bed, gore, screams of fear and agony, and yet Luke was turned on like he hadn't been in… well, in forever. It had to be the sheer joy of seeing Nelson again that was making Luke crazy. *That has to be it.* Thankfully the long day, combined with the alcohol, started catching up with him, and his need for sleep began to overrule his libido. He snatched up his pillow and took up the same position as Nelson, and he drifted off to sleep reliving his childhood with Wes Craven.

WITHIN MINUTES of starting the movie, small snuffling sounds coming from Luke let Nelson know he had fallen asleep. Nelson tried watching the show rather than his friend but it was nearly an impossible feat, the task made all the more difficult when Luke rolled in his sleep and pulled Nelson into a tight embrace. Nelson lay with his head against Luke's chest, listening to the steady beat of his heart, a sound that had lulled him to sleep countless times throughout his youth. It was familiar and comforting. He was complete. It only occurred to him after experiencing it again that he hadn't been truly whole in the past decade.

It made no sense. He was but a child the last time he saw Luke.

Yet the feeling was undeniable.

Nelson softly slid his hand across Luke's shoulder to the hard muscles of his bicep. Luke was much bigger, of course, more bulk of muscle, but he found the raised scar on Luke's arm he'd received from a fall out of a tree. Holy hell, had that scared the crap out of Nelson. It was bad enough watching Luke fall, but when Nelson finally scrambled to the ground, it took everything not to puke when he saw the stick embedded in Luke's flesh. Nelson was pretty sure it was at that moment, although he was only about ten, when he first realized he was in love with his best friend. He'd have happily taken Luke's place if he could have so Luke wouldn't have to suffer. Being willing to take the pain for someone, in Nelson's young mind, meant it was love.

After Luke moved away and Nelson began to heal from the loss, he convinced himself Luke was merely a first crush, Nelson's first experience with puppy love.

Now he wasn't so sure. He thought he'd gotten over Luke leaving. He'd moved on, dammit. He'd pushed those silly thoughts of conquering the world with Luke away. He was no longer a boy but a grown man, and the way Luke made his gut flutter pleasantly from a mere touch, the way his chest tightened when Luke looked at him, and the sickening feeling at the thought of Luke leaving again sure as hell felt like more than a crush.

Nelson spent the better part of the night struggling with trying to find the answer and trying to force the thoughts away. He needed sleep, and yet try as he might, he couldn't seem to shut his brain off. More importantly, knowing Luke would be going back to California and Nelson would be heading back to Minneapolis, he didn't want to miss a single heartbeat.

When the first rays of dawn crept through the window, Nelson was still listening to the strong, steady heartbeat.

WHISPERING FOLLOWED by someone gently shaking his shoulder had Nelson blinking against the harsh light until Luke's smiling face came into focus. Obviously he was finally able to fall asleep sometime after dawn. "Good morning." His voice was husky from sleep and his throat dry from too much alcohol the night before.

"I got to get a shower. You have time for breakfast before your meeting?"

"What time is it?"

"Six forty-five," Luke informed him.

Six forty-five? "Oh shit!" Nelson threw off the covers and scrambled from the bed. He scanned the area for his clothes. *Suitcase!* He rushed across the room to it and threw it open. "I have to meet my client in fifteen minutes." He grabbed an armful of clothes. "Fuck, fuck, fuck!"

"I'm going to take that as a no." Luke chuckled.

Nelson found his shave kit and tucked it under his arm. "I'm so screwed." He stopped at the bathroom door and met Luke's gaze. "Can I call you later?"

"Yeah, I'm in room 423. Let's meet for dinner instead? Say seven?"

"Great, but can we make it a little later? Not sure how long my day is going to be."

"Sure."

"Great! See you tonight." Nelson stepped into the bathroom and dropped his clothes and kit on the counter. He heard the door to his room close before he turned on the shower. He yelped when he stepped under the spray, but the cold water went a long way in forcing him to focus on what he needed to do. He set the flow to warm and washed in record time. As he dressed he ran through and rejected a multitude of excuses for his tardiness. He damn sure couldn't tell his client the truth. "I was up all night drinking with an old friend" wouldn't go over too well, he was sure of it. Nor would the naughty thoughts that had been playing in his mind as he watched Luke sleep.

"No, no, no," he chanted and turned away from the mirror. "No hard-ons, no thinking about naughty things." His dick twitched. "No!"

He sat on the edge of the bed to put his shoes on and winced. His dick wasn't about to listen, and he didn't have time to relieve a little pressure. Once he'd tied his shoes, he tilted his head back and closed his eyes. He pinched the head of his cock, gritting his teeth with the sting of pain. He tried concentrating on gross things, anything that would help get his out-of-control libido reined in, but after a few minutes, he realized the futility of it.

"Fuck it!" He pushed to his feet and grabbed his suit coat. He draped it over his arm, using it to shield the evidence of what thoughts of Luke did to him. He grabbed his room key, wallet, and headed out the door. Hopefully by the time he made it to Seattle General, he'd be more presentable.

Chapter Three

NELSON STUMBLED through the door of his hotel room. He dropped his coat on the floor, kicked off his shoes, and face-planted on the bed. He was so damn exhausted he barely had the energy to roll over, but with his nose pressed to the soft down comforter, it was either muster up the strength or suffocate. An hour and a half of sleep in two days simply wasn't enough to function on. He'd kicked ass with the crashed computer system, even if it took him twelve hours to get them back up and running. Sad thing was it should have taken half that time, but the constant interruption and questions from SG's IT department guaranteed Nelson earned his pay for the day and then some. He curled up on his side, and the instant he closed his eyes, the darkness sucked him down.

Nelson jerked awake, scanning the dark room, wildly trying to figure out where in the hell he was. It took him a second to realize he was in his hotel room, and someone banging on the door had woken him. He slid from the bed, still in a sleep-induced haze, and wiped the drool from his chin. Damn, he'd been out, like, dead for…. He glanced at the illuminated red numbers on the digital clock—ten after nine. He'd only been asleep for an hour and a half.

Without bothering to check the peephole or ask who it was, Nelson flung open the door and was instantly wide-awake when he found Luke standing there with a dimpled grin and looking too good for mere words.

Luke ruffled Nelson's hair as he stepped past him. "Now I see why you didn't answer your phone."

Nelson did his best to smooth down his bed head. "Someone kept me up past my bedtime last night," he grumbled and shut the door.

"Whatever! I slept like a champ, all warm and snuggly." Luke surveyed the room. "I see dinner hasn't been delivered yet."

"Dinner?"

"Yeah, I ordered room service for us. I had this sneaking feeling you were sleeping, so I figured you wouldn't be up for hitting the restaurant."

Nelson rummaged in his bag, looking for some clean clothes. "Ever think maybe I had dinner with my client?"

"I thought we agreed to have dinner together." Luke cocked his head. "Did you already eat?"

"No, but…" Nelson pulled out a pair of jeans and a T-shirt, tucked them under his arm, and stared at Luke, trying to come up with a witty response for his oversight. Obviously he wasn't as awake as he thought because he had nothing. "I'm starved," he finally admitted.

Luke flopped down on the couch, propped up his feet on the coffee table, and grinned smugly. "See, all the years removed, and I still know what you need."

"Mmm-hmm. If you know me so well, let's hear what you ordered for me."

"You hate most vegetables except potatoes and corn, which, by the way, I don't consider real veggies. You're a total meat, potatoes, and bread kind of guy. You dislike your foods to touch each other on your plate. You start with one thing, eat it all before moving to the next thing on your plate, and always save your most favorite—which is usually the meat—for last." Luke tapped a finger on his chin, staring up like he was looking for information in the ceiling. He suddenly snapped his fingers. "You think yogurt is disgusting—both the taste and the word—and if you smell cabbage cooking, you get physically ill." Luke's smug grin grew. "How'd I do?"

Nelson stared at him with his mouth open, completely in shock. How did Luke remember all that? Hell, to this day, his mom still couldn't remember what he liked. It wasn't a huge surprise when he'd come home from college and she'd made stew, the ingredients all swimming together, touching. Yuck! Nelson remembered eating a lot of pizza, chips, and junk when he and Luke got together. Sure, they often checked out what their moms were cooking, then decided where to eat, but honestly, Nelson couldn't remember the meals, only that Luke was always sitting next to him.

"Holy shit, I can't believe you remembered all that," Nelson remarked in awe. "But as impressed as I am, you didn't answer my question."

"I ordered a bit of everything and some wine to wash it down."

Nelson's shock grew. "You're kidding me, right? I can't afford that, and there is no way my boss is going to pick up that tab." *Way to go, big mouth.* He should have just maxed out his credit card rather than admit he was broke.

Luke waved him off. "I charged it to my room. Now will you quit worrying and go get showered? Our food will be here soon. And toss me that remote, will ya?"

"I can't let you pay for my dinner two nights in a row," Nelson insisted. "I'll cover dinner tonight."

"It's not open to discussion. Now toss me that remote," Luke repeated.

Unwilling to argue about it, Nelson picked up the remote from the bedside table and lobed it to Luke, who caught it easily. After turning the screen so they could see it from the couch, Nelson headed to the bathroom.

Beneath the hot spray of the shower, Nelson thought about the conversation he and Luke just had. Nelson remembered a lot about Luke, but what he ate obviously wasn't a priority back then. He did remember Luke always ate a lot because he seemed to be hungry all the time, but not what he ate. Nelson wondered what other minute details he missed because he'd been too busy fantasizing and drooling over Luke's hot bod.

That wasn't true. Sure, it was the one thing he remembered the most, but Nelson had been able to look past his raging hormones once in a while. He knew Luke had a big heart, had been the big man on campus yet a champion of the underdog. He was always been a great listener and always had Nelson's back.

Oh Jesus. Maybe it was hero envy he'd had and not love. What did a kid of thirteen know about love? About as much as Nelson knew at twenty-three.

A SOFT rap on the door, followed by "Room service," had Luke clicking off the TV and going to the door.

A young man in a suit complete with bow tie stood on the other side of the door with a cart piled high with silver-covered dishes. "Good evening, sir."

"Hi, c'mon in," Luke instructed. He stepped back and allowed the man to push his cart into the room.

"Where would you like me to set up?"

Luke walked over to the cart, picked up one of the silver domes, and deeply inhaled the scent of oregano and basil wafting up from the spaghetti. His stomach growled in response. "I'll take it from here," Luke informed him. He pulled a twenty from his pocket and handed it to him.

The server nodded. "Thank you, sir. Have a good evening."

Luke pulled the small table into the center of the room, pushed the cart up next to it, and placed two chairs side by side. He set the candle in the center of the table, followed by dishes, silverware, then poured them each a glass of wine.

"Something smells good."

"It's me," Luke teased. He looked up to find Nelson standing next to the bathroom door, his damp hair slicked back, his skin still flushed from his shower, looking even more delicious than the meal.

"You bathing in spaghetti sauce these days?" Nelson laughed.

"Maybe." Luke gestured toward one of the chairs. "Your dinner awaits you, sir."

"Awesome. I'm starved." Nelson sat in the chair, laid a napkin on his lap, and picked up his fork. "This looks amazing."

"Steak, potato, and bread—none of which are touching the other—for you, and spaghetti for me," Luke commented and took the seat next to Nelson. He picked up his wineglass and held it up. "To finding each other again."

Nelson picked up his glass and clinked it against Luke's. "I'll drink to that." He took a sip, and Luke couldn't help but laugh at the way Nelson wrinkled his nose.

"I told you it grows on you."

"Uh-huh. I think I'll stick to bourbon or water."

Nelson pinched off a piece of bread and popped it into his mouth. He licked his finger, causing Luke's breathing to increase, and he had to look away. Fuck, even watching Nelson eat got him revved up. He picked up his fork and twirled it in his noodles while his brain scrambled for a conversation topic to distract him for way his dick was tingling and filling.

"So tell me about this dream of yours to open a bakery. You know, I'm a decent cook myself."

Nelson finished his bite of steak before answering. "You cook?"

"Yeah, I find it kind of relaxing. Although I don't get a lot of opportunity since I'm rarely home. I should clarify I'm good with a skillet or pot, but the oven and I are not friends."

"Baking can be a bit... trying. It's all trial and error, really. I love trying to create new things, and it doesn't hurt when they work. I have a bit of a sweet tooth."

"So do I." Luke refilled his wineglass and took a large sip. "I was serious. You'll have to make me something warm and gooey."

Real or imagined, Luke caught the way Nelson swallowed hard and the way he shifted in his seat when he nodded. Luke also didn't miss the way Nelson suddenly seemed interested in the food on his plate. Was he thinking the same thing Luke was? Warm and gooey could describe what he'd enjoy lying in bed with Nelson. Probably not. He doubted anyone had their mind in the gutter as often as he did. Nelson's nearness and the hint of his freshly washed skin was enough to ensure Luke's mind stayed down in the sludge.

Luke pulled the cover off another plate. "We'll have to settle for hotel-made pastries rather than homemade, I'm afraid." He picked up the plate as well as his wineglass. "C'mon, we'll get comfy on the sofa and watch TV while enjoying these."

Nelson dropped his napkin on his plate and followed Luke.

KICKED BACK on the couch, Luke patted his belly. "Now that was a damn fine meal."

"I see you still eat like it's a sporting event."

"I'm a growing boy."

Nelson rolled his head to the side and gave Luke a disbelieving look.

"What? I am."

"Uh-huh."

A comfortable silence fell over them while they let their food digest. On TV the Red Wings were in an exciting overtime match with Vancouver, yet Luke's attention kept straying toward Nelson. He smelled so damn good from his recent shower. That smile, that look, the alcohol….

He turned his head and took another sip of his wine. No matter how hard he tried, he couldn't ignore the heat radiating off Nelson or the look of lust—real or perceived—on his handsome face. Both, either, didn't matter. All Luke knew was his skin tingled and his throat had gone dry. He took another healthy drink. No one affected him as acutely as Nelson. Perhaps it was the remembrance of youthful desires. That time in Luke's life seemed so full of wonder, exploration, and excitement.

Staring at Nelson, memories of shared sloppy kisses, fumbling fingers, and the feelings he had for Nelson came rushing back and refused to be ignored. He downed the rest of his wine, set the glass aside, and before he could think better of it, gave in to those old desires. He leaned over and pressed his lips to Nelson's. Whether it was the alcohol, the memories or true attraction, Luke wasn't sure. Apparently the reason didn't matter as he threaded his fingers through Nelson's hair and moved closer.

It was the last thing Luke had expected to do, but he couldn't deny how right it felt to be kissing Nelson again. It was as if he'd been transported back ten years to his small bedroom, and nothing in the world meant more to him than his best friend.

Luke brought up both hands to hold Nelson's face, the feeling both familiar and foreign. He'd explored every inch of Nelson's body, touched and tasted, but the stubbled jaw, the skill of the kiss—no longer sloppy and awkward—reminded Luke they were no longer children. The clink of glass on wood, then hands pressed against Luke's chest, pushing him down onto the couch. Luke was bigger, stronger, and he could stop this if he wanted to. But he must not have wanted it to stop because he lay back, Nelson nestling into him, chest to chest, groin to groin, as they continued to explore each other's mouths. Luke's hard cock twitched, and he moved a little, seeking some friction.

Nelson ended the kiss, sat back, and straddled Luke, reminiscent of the position Nelson so often took when they were in another room in another time and at another place. Luke's breath hitched when their erections rubbed against each other and saw heat flare in Nelson's eyes.

Luke settled his hands on Nelson's hips. "Damn, I always loved it when you gave me that look."

"What look?" Nelson asked. He splayed his hands on Luke's chest, rocking a little, and the lust caused those light-blue eyes to darken as his pupils dilated.

"That one. The one screaming that you like what I'm doing to you. How good I'm making you feel."

"You always made me feel good," Nelson replied. His words were a little slurred. Luke hoped it was the pleasure that caused it and not the wine.

Luke tightened his hold on Nelson's hips, encouraging him to move faster, enjoying the look of bliss on Nelson's face nearly as much as the friction on Luke's cock.

However, a moment later, Nelson was biting his bottom lip, breathing harshly through his nose, and he was digging his fingers into the muscles on Luke's chest. "You gotta slow down a little or else I'm going to blow in my pants," Nelson panted but kept rocking, thrusting his cock against Luke's. "Drive me out of my mind."

Luke slid his hands down to Nelson's thighs, pressed down hard to stop his movements. "Don't you dare. It's been far, far too long since I've had my hands on your body. Ain't no way you're coming till I've had my fill."

Nelson tried to thrust, but Luke held fast. Nelson huffed a heavy breath. "You always were pushy."

"Off," Luke demanded, shoving Nelson.

Nelson went to his feet, a frown marring his brow. Luke didn't let him question the situation for long. He stood, grabbed the hem of Nelson's shirt, yanked it over his head, and tossed it aside. Luke then bent, wrapped his arms around Nelson, and took his mouth in a blistering kiss. Luke ran his hands down the warm flesh of Nelson's back, moaning his pleasure as he slid his fingertips across every bit of skin he could reach. He explored Nelson's mouth with his tongue as greedily as he explored his flesh with his hands, only ending the kiss when he'd maneuvered them to the bed. He pushed Nelson down on top of the mattress. He pulled off his shirt before joining Nelson. Those lust-filled eyes never left him, taking in each movement. Luke dipped his head to circle one hard nipple with his tongue.

He listened to Nelson's breathing increase for a minute before hooking a finger in the waistband of Nelson's pants. "You still have far too many clothes on."

Nelson managed to kick his shoes off and rid himself of his pants and boxers, even though Luke never stopped licking and nipping at Nelson's nipples. Only when Nelson was gloriously naked did Luke roll onto his back and rid himself of shoes and pants.

Nelson watched him from beneath long lashes and took his dick in hand, stroking himself. Luke knocked his hand away. "Quit that."

"It feels good," Nelson murmured. He closed his eyes and arched up. His long, slender cock slid through his loose fist, a clear drop of precome glistening at the tip, just begging to be tasted. "You used to like to watch me stroke myself."

"Yes, well...." Luke slid down the bed and flicked out his tongue, tasting bitter sweetness. "Right now I'd rather taste you." Nelson moaned, the deep husky sound like a strike of heat to Luke's groin, so he did it again, this time opening his mouth around the head, teasing his tongue over the slit, searching out more of Nelson's delicious flavor.

Nelson vibrated beneath him, muscles tense as if he were holding back the urge to thrust into Luke's mouth. Luke wasn't having it. This was a familiar dance. Nelson had been his first kiss, his first exploration, his first crush, if one could consider the fumbling of adolescents as a relationship. Luke took more of him in. Sliding his lips down, he carefully covered his teeth as he slid his hands under Nelson's ass, urging him to move.

Nelson thrust, an audible hiss escaping him. He put both hands on Luke's head, tightening his fingers in Luke's hair painfully. "Jesus, you sure you had a girlfriend and not a boyfriend?" Nelson asked. Luke started to raise his head, but Nelson fisted Luke's hair harder still, keeping him from moving farther away. "Oh my God, I'm such an idiot. Who cares? Forget I asked."

Luke tugged slightly, loving the little sparks of pain Nelson's grip produced, then greedily sucked Nelson down. He quickly relearned what Nelson liked. When Luke licked him, Nelson made small, needy sounds, and he would jerk his hips when Luke took him deeper. The hold Nelson had in his hair now was more petting and stroking than pulling. However, when Luke pulled back, he tightened those fingers again, not allowing Luke to move away too far. It was hot as fuck, and Luke pressed his palm to his dick, needing a little friction of his own but not stroking, knowing it wouldn't take much to get off. He'd been amped up all night, and now that he was giving in to those old desires, they created new ones, brighter-burning ones. He didn't want it to end. Plus there was no way he was going to blow until he got Nelson off.

Nelson began babbling incoherently, moaning and whimpering, his hips in constant motion. Luke slid one of his hands down and wrapped his fingers around Nelson's balls, squeezing gently.

Nelson gasped and pushed Luke's head back. "I'm going to—" Nelson arched his back, then went completely still for a heartbeat. The first blast of come landed on his chest, and he shuddered and jerked through each pulse of his release.

Luke pulled his hand away from his crotch and gritted his teeth, trying to hold off the inevitable. The sight of Nelson giving in to pleasure was almost enough to make Luke blow, and he didn't want to miss a second of Nelson's pleasure. When the tension in Nelson's body relaxed and he lay there panting harshly, Luke rolled over onto his back next to him. Luke wrapped a fist around his cock, stroking it from base to tip. Heat shot down his spine, pulse racing, and he squeezed his eyes shut. Once, twice, and then he felt Nelson pushing his hand out of the way. Luke opened his eyes to find Nelson propped up on one arm, looking down at him.

Luke didn't know how he'd lasted this long, but Nelson's hand on him, jerking him, and the way Nelson was looking at him was enough to push Luke over the edge. His orgasm wrung out of him in one perfect stroke after another until spent, and his eyes fluttered closed.

"That was…. I don't even know what to say," Luke slurred. He was tingly and sleepy and just felt so fucking good he didn't want to move. Wasn't sure he could, even if he wanted to. He thought he heard Nelson grunt or say something. He might have even left the bed. Luke wasn't sure. He was floating on a high of postorgasmic bliss and alcohol and was crashing fast. The last thing he was aware of before giving in to his need for sleep was the warmth of Nelson's body against his and the smile it produced.

Chapter Four

FOR THE second time in as many days, Nelson woke to whispering, followed by someone gently shaking his shoulder. Only this time he knew exactly who it was. He opened his eyes and smiled up at Luke. It quickly fell when Nelson saw the look on Luke's face.

Nelson abruptly sat up. "What's the matter?"

"I gotta go."

"Okay. You want to meet for breakfast?"

"I can't." Luke sat on the edge of the bed. "When are you heading back to Minneapolis?"

"Not till this afternoon. When are you leaving?"

"I'm heading to the airport now."

Dread filled Nelson so thoroughly it stole his breath. It had been ten years, and they only got two days? Life could be so fucking cruel. There was still so much he wanted to ask, to know, to do.

"Hey, don't look so sad. You got my number, and this time we don't have to worry about whether our daddies will let us use their phones." Luke pressed his palm to Nelson's face, stroking his cheek with his thumb. "I'm sorry. I have to go. Now go back to sleep. I'll talk to you soon." He placed a soft kiss on Nelson's lips.

What about us? When can I see you again? Please don't leave. Nelson couldn't form words around the lump in his throat. Before he could swallow it down, Luke turned on his heel and walked out the door without a backward glance. Nelson could only sit and stare at the closed door. He was numb from head to toe. Only thing he was aware of was the tightening in his chest. He flopped back on the bed and stared unblinkingly at the ceiling. He knew this feeling; he'd experienced it once before. Emotions only Luke could bring out in him.

It had taken what seemed like forever to stop thinking about Luke all the time. However, thoughts of him never completely left Nelson. He merely tucked them away. He always hoped one day he'd see him again. Now that he had, now that his childhood dream had come true, it was reality that was fucking everything up. They lived thousands of miles apart, and after spending time with Luke again, he wanted more. So much more, but it was improbable, if not impossible. *Careful what you wish for.*

How long he lay there in that miserable state, Nelson couldn't say. It was his growling stomach and screaming bladder that forced him to get his sorry pouting ass up. Standing beneath the hot spray, scrubbing away the last scent and traces of Luke from his body, he'd never felt so alone in his life. He wasn't out to his friends and family, had no one he could share this side of himself with.

Wait. A thought began to dawn on him. Luke apparently was gay and not out either, considering he had a steady girlfriend up until recently. Nelson was in the same situation, minus the girlfriend. They'd shared so many firsts in their younger years. First day of school, first lost tooth, first sexual experience, first heartbreak. It was almost poetic that their first time coming out should be a shared experience as well. They could be the rock the other leaned on. Neither of them would be alone in this. They were a short plane ride away from the other. Who knew if they were destined to be lovers? At that moment it didn't matter. Just like when he was kid, he'd have Luke standing behind him, supporting him when he faced yet another challenge in life.

Growing up they planned to take the world by storm. It might not be the whole world they took over, but their small one they were destined to conquer. For the first time since he'd woken, the tightness in Nelson's chest eased, and he was able to smile.

As NELSON stepped through the door before his suitcase touched the floor, the phone began to ring. He ignored it. After getting up early, flying halfway across the country, which took a couple drinks and a Xanax to endure, as well as the emotional roller coaster he'd been zinging around in the past forty-eight hours, he was exhausted. He wanted nothing more than to kick off his shoes, shower, and fall into bed.

As he bent to untie he shoes, the answering machine beeped, followed by a familiar voice, and Nelson froze. "Hi, Nelson, just checking to see if you made it home safely. I'm heading out the door, but call me tomorrow, will ya?"

"Wait, I'm here." Nelson scrambled for the phone, tripping over the coffee table. Pain shot up from his toe to the top of his fool head.

"Fuck!" He righted himself, hopped across the room on one foot, and snatched up the phone. "Luke! Hello? Luke?"

The only response was a dial tone.

"Dammit!" He slammed the phone down and pulled out his wallet. He flipped through the contents until he found Luke's card. He set the wallet on the counter, pulled off his jacket, then took the phone to the couch. He dialed Luke's number, disappointed when, after five rings, the answering machine picked up. "Hi, Luke, I'm home. Sorry I missed you. Call me back."

He waited, hoping Luke would pick up, but the only thing he heard was the beep of the machine turning off. Goddammit! He ended the call, but rather than slam the phone down again, he set it down gently. He then did something he never did; he replayed Luke's message simply to hear his voice again, and then again. The only thing it accomplished was to cause him to miss Luke even more.

"Right back on the fucking emotional roller coaster you go," Nelson grumbled.

He laid his head back and propped his feet on the table. He had half a notion to try Luke's number again, but he was so tired and wasn't sure he could handle any more disappointment today. He sighed, even knowing he was being melodramatic, and closed his eyes. The insane day started to catch up with him and, although his mind was racing with thoughts of Luke, his body demanded sleep. Darkness crept up, pulling him down to a restless sleep filled with visions of Luke walking away.

The shrill sound of his phone sounded, jerking him out of his nap. He snatched up the receiver. "Hello. Luke, is that you?"

"Sorry to disappoint you, but it's just the woman who spent twenty-two hours in labor to give you life."

"Sorry, Mom, I thought you were someone else."

"Apparently. Who is this Luke person?"

"Lucas Rollins."

There was a brief pause before his mom responded. "Who?"

"Luke. You remember the Rollinses, don't you? I mean, I know you're getting old, but they did live next door to you for nearly a decade."

"Oh wow. How are the Rollinses?"

"I—"

"Before you answer that, let me tell you, I may be old, but not too old to turn you over my knee and tan your hide."

"Uh-huh, I haven't forgotten," Nelson chuckled. "But seriously I ran into Luke at the airport. He was on his way to Seattle too. His dad started a financial company, and from what I understand, has done quite well. His mom and dad are still together."

"I'm glad to hear that. I always liked Sue and Johnny. They were good people. Glad to see another couple staying together." Mom sighed. "You just don't see that often enough anymore. Do you remember Cora and Mark Hathaway? They lived one block over. Their oldest daughter used to babysit you when you were two."

"Um, no, sorry. I don't remember much from that age."

"Yes, well, I hear Mark ran off with his secretary. She's twenty-two years his junior. Poor Cora. She gave him three healthy children and nearly thirty years of her life, and he cast her aside like that."

Nelson stretched out on the couch and tucked the phone between his ear and shoulder. *Might as well get comfortable.* When Mom got on a roll, she could go on and on forever. It did no good to respond—he rarely got a word in edgewise—so he added the occasional "uh-huh" to make her think he was listening. Truth be told, he really wasn't in the mood to listen to gossip about people he hadn't seen in twenty-one years. He loved her to death, but wow, was she long-winded.

It didn't take long with Mom's familiar voice buzzing in his ear before he was drifting back off to sleep.

"Nelson, are you listening to me?"

"Uh-huh." He yawned big, not even trying to hide the sound. He pulled the afghan off the back of the couch, rolled onto his side, and covered up.

His mom sighed dramatically. "You sound exhausted. Get some sleep, and I'll call you tomorrow, and you can tell me all about your time with Luke Rollins."

Nelson grinned. *Not all of it.* "Okay. Love you, Mom. Say hi to Dad for me."

"Love you too."

Nelson hung up the phone, snuggled farther under the blanket, and gave in to his exhaustion.

Chapter Five

SITTING ON the patio, sheltered from the bright afternoon sun by a large blue-and-green market umbrella, Luke stared out toward the ocean while sipping his glass of ice water. He should be at work, in the gym, on the beach, something, anything other than sitting here brooding and willing the phone to ring.

At twenty-three he was far from old. However, seeing Nelson again transported him back to his childhood, begging the question of what he'd done that was so remarkable in the past ten years. Reuniting with his old friend reminded Luke of all the crazy plans and dreams he'd had. *We had.* They were going to join the rodeo, and just like Nelson, Luke had never even been on a horse. They were going to take on the world, and yet Luke had never even been out of the United States.

Luke wasn't ungrateful. He knew he was blessed with a good life. He had a great job, a close relationship with his parents and little brother, wonderful friends, and a nice place to live. However, he was living his dad's dream, not his own. That didn't mean he was about to give it up and go join the rodeo circuit, although he was definitely going to take horseback riding lessons, and he was most certainly going to see Nelson again. Luke wasn't sure how he was going to pull it off, but come hell or high water, they'd be together again soon. He wanted nothing more than to rebuild their relationship, but whether as best friends or more was yet to be determined. As long as they shared the same closeness they once had, he'd be happy.

The phone rang, sending a thrill racing through Luke. He picked it up before it rang a second time. "Hello?"

"Hey, Luke. It's Nelson."

"Hi! I was hoping you would call. Sorry I couldn't talk yesterday. I had a stupid meeting I couldn't get out of. And don't think I didn't beg Dad, but he can be a tough son of a bitch. Hey, I've been worried about you, you being afraid of flying and all. I hope it wasn't too terrible. How was your flight? How are you?"

"Breathe, Luke, breathe," Nelson chuckled.

Luke sat back, laughing at himself. "Sorry, I guess you can tell I'm a little excited. It's still blowing my mind that we were in the same airport at the same time and heading to the same place, no less."

"Yes, you may have mentioned that a time or three." Luke didn't even have to see Nelson to know he was rolling his eyes but was also laughing. He could hear it in his tone as he continued, "It really was our lucky day. We should have played the lottery."

"Damn, I knew I was forgetting something. Oh, well. So how are you?"

"I'm good, and so was the flight. You're right: I'm not a big fan of flying, but it went pretty smooth. I'd still much rather drive."

"Well, you know I love to fly, so I guess I'll have come to you."

There was a brief pause. "You want to come visit?"

Luke furrowed his brows when he heard the uncertainty in Nelson's voice. "Sure, why wouldn't I?"

"I… I don't know… um…. Never mind. I think it's a great idea. I'd love to have you here. I haven't been in this town long enough to meet many people, nor have I had a chance to really explore the city. We could do it together," Nelson suggested.

"That sounds awesome. Hold on, let me check my schedule, and I'll tell you when I could come."

"Okay, sure."

Luke set the phone down, then rushed into his condominium to grab his PDA. He thumbed through his calendar as he headed back outside. He flopped down on the lounger and picked up the phone. "I can be there next Friday."

Silence.

"Nelson? Did you hear me?"

"Umm…yeah. That soon?"

"Sure, I have the weekend off. We'll spend it doing some more catching up and exploring the city together. I'd hate for you to do it alone. You might get lost."

"Hardy har har."

"Luke, you home?" Colton called out.

Shit! "Hey, I have to go. My brother just walked in uninvited. I'll call you tomorrow. What time is good for you?"

"I should be home by six my time. Talk to you then, and hey, tell Colton I said hi, will ya?"

"Sure. Talk to you tomorrow." Luke hung up the phone and went to his feet. "Colton, you irritating little shit. What are you doing here?"

After a few moments, Colton's white-blond head popped around the door. "You ready?"

Luke scowled. "What the hell for?"

"Oh damn! You forgot." Colton stepped out onto the patio, slapped his leg, and hooted. "I can't wait to tell Mom."

"Dammit, what the fuck are you talking about?" Luke snapped.

"We have to pick Grandma and Grandpa up from the airport." Colton cocked his head. "You seriously don't remember?"

Luke glanced at his open calendar, and right there in black and white was the flight number and time. He'd been so distracted with thoughts of Nelson he'd pretty much ignored everything else. "No, I didn't forget," Luke lied. "What time is it?"

"It's time to go, so get the lead out. I'd prefer not to give Grandpa anything else to bitch about."

Luke snatched up his day planner and followed Colton into the condo. "Give him a break. He's old and a bit senile."

"Ha! The old coot has been cranky my whole life. There isn't a damn thing wrong with him other than he likes to grumble and complain."

Colton had a point, but Luke wasn't about to argue. He was too busy taking deep breaths and trying to clear his mind. It was going to take all his focus to keep his patience with the cranky old bastard otherwise known as Grandpa.

THE PREVIOUS two days, Nelson had found himself much as he was now, sitting on the couch, staring at the phone, waiting for it to ring. It pleased him to no end how quickly he and Luke had fallen back into their easy ways of talking, and just like when they were kids, they were able to finish each other's sentences. Yet unlike when they were kids, the sensual tone of Luke's voice was unmistakable. Also the sexual innuendos Luke was constantly sending Nelson's way were as far from childlike as it got. Who needed to win the lottery? Nelson had hit the fucking jackpot running into Luke again.

The phone rang, and the excitement cursing through Nelson ramped up to overdrive. His hand shook when he reached for the receiver. "Hello."

"Hey, Nelson." Luke's voice came through the line in a low, sexy whisper. The sound shot straight Nelson's groin.

"Hi, Luke, what's up with the whispering?"

"You like it?"

"I'm having a hard time hearing you. Speak up?"

"You used to always insist I whisper when I was lying in my bed talking to you. Seeing as I'm back in my old room at my parents' house, I thought you'd appreciate it."

"What are you doing at your parents'? I thought you told me you lived close."

"Yes, well. My grandpa and grandma are in town, and Mom thought it would be nice if we were all here. She used guilt as her tactic, using their age against me. 'This could be their last visit. Your grandpa isn't in good health.'" The suffering sigh was evident through the phone line.

"Your mom's dad?" Nelson inquired.

"The one and only."

"Oh, you poor thing, having to spend the weekend with Grandpa Joe." Nelson snickered. They were scared shitless of him when they were little, the old man always yelling and waving his cane at them. As they got older, they learned he really was a harmless thing who hated change. Funny that, for a man who'd lived seventy years—wow, eighty years now—he would have seen plenty of it.

"Stop laughing, or I'll bring him with me Friday."

"You wouldn't dare."

"No, I wouldn't. I want you all to myself." Luke dropped his voice even lower, sexier when he added, "I've been thinking about you. I was supposed to be having a nice family visit, but I couldn't get you out of my head. By the way, where are you right this minute?"

"I'm sitting on the couch, why?"

"Are you alone?"

"Yeah, why?"

"Just trying to get a mental picture of you, is all, since I can't seem to get another one out of my head."

"Is that so?"

"Mmmhmm."

"And what exactly am I doing in this mental picture you have of me?" Nelson asked.

"The way you look down at me, your face all flushed when you're straddling me."

A tingle started at the base of Nelson's spine. "That's not conducive to spending the day with your family, Luke." At least he hoped it wasn't.

"I took the opportunity of Grandpa taking a nap to take one of my own. Good thing too because I don't know if I could concentrate with how hard my cock is. It's always hard for you. You drive me to the brink of insanity." Luke's voice went a notch deeper. "I wish you were here, sprawled out across my bed, legs spread wide, your pretty cock hard and curving up toward your belly."

Nelson's breath hitched.

"Are you hard, Nelson?"

How could he not be with the images Luke was painting in his head? The sound of Luke's raspy whisper was like a touch to his heated flesh. "Yeah, thanks to you."

"Good. Wrap your hand around your cock. I want you to imagine it's my hand stroking that sweet prick."

Nelson heard the distinct sound of a slick hand stroking flesh as he unfastened his pants. He pushed them down past his hips and began doing as Luke asked.

"Squeeze it tight."

Nelson tightened his fingers further.

"God, I can't wait to see you. Want to kiss, lick, and explore every inch of your body."

Nelson's breathing increased at the thought of Luke's mouth on him, warm lips wrapped around his cock, hands stroking him as he lost himself in the ecstasy that was Luke. Nelson sped his hand up to a blur and his hips jerked.

"Want to take your cock deep into my mouth, swallow you down. Want to taste you as you come." Luke's voice was now barely a whisper, accentuated by constant moans. "Are you close? Are you imagining getting ready to fill my mouth with your hot seed?"

"Yes," he got out between panting breaths.

"Goddamn it, Colton!" Luke screamed. "Don't you know how to fucking knock?"

Nelson jerked the phone away from his ear to keep his eardrum from exploding at the roar coming through the line.

"Are you seriously having phone sex?" Nelson didn't recognize the voice but assumed it was Colton who asked and was currently laughing boisterously. Colton was only nine when Nelson and his family left, his voice back then high pitched and squeaky. Then again, it didn't take a rocket scientist to figure out it was Luke's little brother since Nelson could also hear Luke in the distance cursing Colton's name and the distinctive sound of something crashing to the floor.

"Luke?"

"I'm telling Mom," Colton hooted, followed by more banging and cursing.

Nelson released the hold on his dick as he continued to listen to the shenanigans going on at Luke's. It really wasn't conducive to orgasm. Plus it was pretty funny knowing Colton had just walked in on Luke with his dick in his hand. Nelson started to chuckle. Damn, for the first time, he was glad he never got his wish for a little brother.

He might not get to enjoy hearing Luke get off, but the fight going on was entertaining to listen to. Too bad he didn't have a beer and some popcorn. It was a hell of a show.

"Nelson? You still there?" Luke asked breathlessly.

"Uh-huh." He gritted out snorts of laughter.

"Are you seriously laughing at me right now?"

"Yes. I…I…. Oh my God. You got caught jerking off," Nelson wheezed.

"Mmmhmm, yuck it up, Mister. I'll make you pay for that when I see you Friday."

"Oh, really?"

"You bet your sweet ass I will. Now tuck your dick back in your pants. If I have to have a case of blue balls all night, it's only fair that you do too."

"Why? I don't have the threat of a little brother walking in. Thank God."

"Because I will make it worth your while if you do."

The line went dead.

Nelson shuddered. He looked down at his hard and ruddy cock. It would only take a couple of pulls and he'd be spared the same fate as Luke. He considered it for a moment, and then the image of Luke's head buried in Nelson's crotch flashed briefly. His hand didn't seem like such a great substitute anymore without Luke's sexy voice in his ear. This could prove to be the longest two days of his life.

Nelson tucked his dick back into his pants and winced. It most certainly would be a hell of a test of his restraint.

Chapter Six

STANDING IN the center of the living room, Nelson cringed at how dreary his apartment was. His furniture was a mishmash from a secondhand store, and there was no artwork or photos on the walls. It looked positively....

"It looks like shit," Nelson grumbled.

He supposed it was par for the course. He lived in this shit hole while Luke lived in a condo in Malibu. Luke had never made him feel inferior, yet Nelson on some level always had been just that: inferior. While Luke was tall, muscular, and athletic, Nelson was none of those things. While Luke was witty, outgoing, and popular, Nelson was not. Now it appeared once again the differences between them were quite stark. Nelson grew up in small-town America, Luke among the rich and beautiful. He wasn't even about to think about the differences in title or wealth. There was no comparison.

Nelson headed to the kitchen, threw open the fridge, and grabbed a beer. He greedily gulped it down much to the protest of his churning gut. He knew he was being ridiculous for being so nervous. It was Luke, for fuck's sake. He was the last person in the world who would make Nelson feel bad for his—he took another healthy drink as he took in the room—feeble surroundings.

Good Lord, he was acting like a lunatic. The stupid shit he was stressing over shouldn't matter. At least he had a roof over his head, food in the fridge, and a place to sleep. It could be worse. He could be homeless. He downed the rest of his beer, tossed the bottle in the trash, and grabbed another. He flipped on the stereo on his way to sit on the threadbare couch. Maybe a second beer would calm him the hell down. Nelson studied the bottle and nodded. "May not help, but it certainly can't hurt."

Luckily he wouldn't have to be driving or cooking. Luke had insisted on renting a car and taking Nelson to dinner. Damn good thing too since Nelson's car looked even worse than his apartment, and he hadn't yet bought much in the way of cookware. Plus it gave him a little extra time to enjoy a little liquid courage before he went and primped.

Yes, primped, and he wasn't the slightest bit sorry. Considering what transpired between them in Seattle and the interrupted phone sex, Nelson would be a fool not to take particular care of certain private areas. Mmm, maybe a hot bubble bath would be advantageous.

With a tingling sensation working down his back and a smile on his face, Nelson pushed up from the couch and headed for the bathroom. Now if he could just make it through the evening without jumping Luke's bones at the restaurant, it might just turn out to be a perfect night, one that didn't include iron bars and bail bondsmen. Most public places frowned on such acts of lewd behavior. Sitting across from Luke was going to be torture. Hopefully Luke had chosen one with long white tablecloths.

LUKE STOOD outside Nelson's apartment and took a long, deep breath and blew it out slowly. He had spent the last few minutes trying to work up the courage to knock on the door. Fuck, he had no idea why he was so nervous. His heart was practically leaping out of his chest, and sweat beaded on his brow. He felt like an awkward teen about to go on his first date. *Man, talk about reliving his childhood.* Taking another deep breath, he rolled his shoulders and reached out to knock on the door.

The door opened, and the brilliant smile blooming across Nelson's face caused Luke's toes to curl.

"Hey," Nelson greeted. He stepped back, moving just far enough to allow Luke to enter. The brush of their arms as he moved past Nelson sent a thrill down Luke's spine. He'd been wrong. It wasn't like going on a first date; it was more like a little kid on Christmas morning, and Nelson was the gift he'd been hoping for all year.

"C'mon in. Can I get you something to drink?"

Now that Luke was in Nelson's presence, a completely new kind of excitement quickly replaced the nervous jitters. "Yeah, beer if you've got it."

"Two beers coming up." Nelson waved his arm and ushered Luke into the living room. "Make yourself at home."

Luke didn't miss the way Nelson averted his eyes or the pink that bloomed across his cheeks. Luke stepped into the small, sparsely furnished apartment, the walls a dingy yellow. The tan couch was threadbare, and the tables were a mismatch of wood and plastic. It was clean but sad, really, no photos or anything on the walls. Cold and impersonal. The solemn feelings the room created washed away instantly when Luke saw Nelson coming in with beers in his hand.

Luke's breath hitched as he noticed the way Nelson's jeans hugged his firm thighs, the stretch of his gray T-shirt across his chest and flat stomach. However, it was the look of happiness on Nelson's face and the way his hazel eyes shone with it that had Luke's heart speeding up. Nelson was a vision that made Luke's thoughts rush past playfully naughty, careening out of control toward the sweat-slick bodies-pounding-together zone. He briefly closed his eyes to dispel the image, but not before they caused an involuntary moan to pass his lips.

"You okay?" Nelson stepped forward and held out a beer. "You looked a little lost for a minute there." Nelson's upper lip twitched in slight amusement.

Luke took the offered beer and bowed his head, hiding his heated cheeks. Guess it was his turn for embarrassing moments. *For fuck sake, have a little control*, he chided himself. "Yeah, I'm good. Just zoned for a minute."

It was the wrong kind of zone to be in when standing in front of his walking wet dream. The loose jeans he'd chosen to wear did little to hide his growing erection. He needed to get them out of Nelson's apartment and to the restaurant before his desires overwhelmed him. Nelson no doubt wouldn't mind, if Luke was reading the look of lust in Nelson's eyes correctly. But Luke was all about the anticipation, letting the need build. And he was fucking starving. He needed to get them somewhere there wasn't a bed, a couch, the floor. He groaned in frustration. The thrum of blood in his swollen shaft reminded him just how achingly long it had been. Christ! Why was he punishing himself? Better question, how was he going to survive until dessert?

He turned with the pretense of checking out his surroundings while casually sipping his beer. He tried to will his growing arousal down. It was going to be a long dinner, a very long, very painful one if he couldn't control his hunger. And that hunger couldn't be sated with anything that would be on the menu at Tifton's. Maybe a quick trip to a private stall would at least make it endurable.

When he turned back around, Nelson was taking a long pull from his beer. Luke's eyes narrowed in on the way those lush lips pressed against the opening of the bottle, and the throb increased. The threads of his control began to unravel, nearly shredding when Nelson lowered his beer and licked his lips. *That's it. I'm only human.*

He downed his beer in one long pull and set it on the side table. "Ready?"

Nelson looked at him in confusion. "Uh, yeah, I guess. I thought we'd hang out for a bit."

LUKE HAD no clue why he wasn't just giving in to his desires and Nelson's, which were clearly obvious in the way Nelson kept raking his eyes up and down Luke's body and the way he'd lick his lips when doing so. If he were a smart man, he'd say fuck it and sample a sweet little appetizer, better known as Nelson, first. *Because you have reservations.* Oh, right. He'd chosen Tifton after doing a little research on the place; he found it catered to the gay community. He wouldn't have to worry about offending anyone if dinner became *romantic*. He wanted to woo Nelson, and not just with his dick. Nelson meant far more to him than that. Besides, if he played his cards right, it would be the first of many romantic dinners he'd share with Nelson.

"We can chat over dinner. You wouldn't want us to be late for our reservation, would you?"

"Well...." Nelson raked his eyes up and down Luke's body one more time, then huffed a breath. "No, I don't suppose we should."

"Good. Let's go, then." Luke grabbed Nelson's hand and led him to the door. He really should work on his restraint, but the best he could do at the moment was get them away from the temptation the solitude of the apartment was creating.

THE HOST greeted them warmly, showed them to their table, and, once they were seated, he handed them each a menu. "Tonight's special is prime-cut filet with choice of Cajun lobster tail or Alaskan king crab legs, chicken marsala with lemon, butter, and parsley, and our featured appetizer is Maryland crab cakes with lobster bisque sauce." The server filled their water glasses.

They ordered drinks, Nelson a beer and Luke a glass of red wine. Luke waited until the host moved away before asking, "Everything sounded amazing. Have you ever been here before?"

Nelson set his menu down on the table. "On my salary? Fat chance of that." He glanced around the room. "This is the second time you've taken me to a swanky place. You could have warned me, and I'd have worn something more appropriate."

"I would think the only way you could be more appropriate for my taste would be if you were naked."

Nelson blushed. "I don't suggest you start filling me with those mental images, or we may not make it to the main course."

"I will try to control my strolling in the gutter."

"At least till we are back at my place." Nelson gave him a shy smile, his cheeks tinting pink.

Luke smiled broadly, a thrill racing through him. "Deal," he said, reaching out and laying a hand over Nelson's.

"We should probably check out what they have to offer," Nelson responded softly. His blush deepened, and he tried to hide it behind his menu. Nelson peeked up from behind his menu. "You know what I'm really in the mood for, so behave."

"I will try my best." Luke picked up his menu with a smug smile. It seemed they were both on the same track, and he doubted any of the food choices at Tifton's could compare to the delicious anticipation.

"You mentioned you hadn't ever explored Minneapolis. Anything in particular you want to see or places you want to go while you're here?" Nelson inquired.

Having decided what to order, Luke set his menu aside. "I'm only here for the weekend, so I don't really have much time to explore the city." *Especially since I doubt I'll want to leave your apartment after tonight.*

Nelson's face fell. "Oh, I thought you were here till Wednesday."

"I did plan on it, but there was a last-minute change of plans I only learned of this morning. I fly to Miami on Sunday night."

The server came and set down their drinks. "Good evening, gentlemen. Are you ready to order?"

"Yes, I'll have the chicken Alfredo, and my companion will have...." Luke nodded to Nelson.

"Oh, umm.... Sorry." Nelson looked stunned for a moment but recovered quickly. "I'll have prime rib, medium rare, please."

"Very good."

The server picked up the menus and walked away before Luke spoke again. "I am really sorry if I've ruined your plans. I swear, if I could get out of it, I would," Luke assured him.

Nelson waved it off. "It's no big deal." He smiled before taking a drink of his beer. Luke didn't miss the disappointment in Nelson's eyes before he turned to look around the room. "This place is quite something, isn't it?"

Luke laid his hand on Nelson's forearm and waited until Nelson looked at him. "Yes, it is, and so are you. We'll just have to cram a lot into the time I do have, and it's not like I won't be back."

Nelson nodded, and this time the smile did reach his eyes. "I've always been a fan of quality rather than quantity."

"Yes, well, perhaps one day, we'll have both." Nelson's grin grew wider still. It looked good on him, making his handsome face all the more so. It was an expression Luke hoped to always keep on Nelson's face.

The dark cloud lifted enough that their conversation turned light and happy while they ate. Luke was distracted more than once as he watched Nelson eat. Nelson was a sensualist, and it was obvious food gave him pleasure. Luke couldn't remember the last time he'd enjoyed someone's company so much or been so turned on by simply watching them eat. Even so, the physical attraction, though significant, was only a small part of what turned him on. Nelson was a very handsome man, and it pleased Luke to no end Nelson hadn't let his looks turn him cocky. He'd met many men, not nearly as hot as Nelson, who were completely full of themselves. Just like he was as a young teen, Nelson was humble and seemed completely unaware of how beautiful he was.

Nelson pushed his empty plate away with a huge sigh. "I give. I can't eat another bite."

The way Nelson reached down and rubbed his flat stomach drew Luke's gaze. With his long fingers, he caressed the firm muscles beneath the cotton of his shirt.

"I was thinking we should order some dessert," Luke suggested. "I'm sure it won't be as good as yours, but getting something warm and messy here would keep you out of the kitchen and…" He let his voice drop to a deeper level. "Give you more opportunity to show me your bedroom."

"I like warm." Nelson looked up at him from under his thick lashes. "And messy."

The visual of Nelson's naked body flashed behind Luke's eyes. He met Nelson's gaze, and the flutter in his stomach created a pleasant tickling. He continued to stare into those expressive hazel eyes as he flushed with sexual heat. Luke deliberately let the tip of his tongue moisten his dry lips. A shiver raced down his spine as he watched Nelson swallow hard and squirm in his seat.

Nelson quickly darted his eyes to their surroundings before meeting Luke's with an embarrassed look. "Maybe we should settle for an after-dinner drink."

It was charming how easily Nelson blushed, and every time he turned his sweet smile on Luke, the arousal would fuse with tenderness. He ordered two coffees and continued to stare at him while Nelson took in the room around them. Everything about Nelson fascinated him, from his humble demeanor to the way he got excited and talked with his hands when he was passionate about something. Nelson had been such a good soul, and it pleased Luke to discover he still was and had depth to his character.

Luke thanked the server as she set two mugs of coffee down on the table, but he couldn't take his eyes from Nelson. Taking his mug, Luke leaned back in his chair and asked, "Have you ever thought of visiting California?" before taking a sip of his coffee.

"Sure, thought about it all the time after you left," Nelson replied, then sipped his own coffee. "But I finally gave up on that dream."

"One should never give up on their dreams, Nelson."

"I don't know if I have," Nelson said with a shrug. "I think they've just changed, become more realistic."

"I don't think visiting California is unrealistic. I'd love for you to come stay with me. I know Mom and Dad, and especially Colton, would love to see you again."

"Oh. My. God. That reminds me, how did Colton fare?"

Luke cocked his head. "What do you mean?"

Nelson started laughing so hard he shook his mug, causing the hot coffee to splash onto his hand. "Ow, crap!" Nelson set his mug down and shook his hand before wiping up the mess with his napkin. His eyes still danced with laughter. "You know, after you beat the crap out of him. Sounded like one hell of a scrap."

"Oh!" Luke laughed too. "He came out unscathed but with the promise of my boot up his ass if he ever did that again."

"I suspect he won't be letting you live that down anytime soon." Nelson snickered. "Does he know it was me you were talking to?"

Luke waved a dismissive hand. "It never came up. I was too busy teaching the little shit a lesson."

"Ah, then there is no chance that my cheeks will burn off if I ever see him again. Perhaps my job will bring me out that way one day."

"I think we should make it a priority. Do you have any vacation time coming up?"

Nelson ducked his head, sipping his coffee, and shrugged again. "Not for another six months. So about that dessert?" Nelson asked, changing the subject quickly.

The subject wasn't over. He'd have to compare his calendar with Nelson's. Maybe they could figure out a way to get him to California for a long weekend. They'd figure it out. But at the moment, other things were much more pressing. Luke waggled his brows. "You want something a little sweet?"

"Yes, and warm and messy too."

The way Nelson was suddenly looking at him with a come-hither look in his eyes, Luke couldn't help but take the bait. "Warm, sweet, and messy is a personal favorite of mine," he purred.

"Really?" Nelson asked as he leaned closer to Luke. "What else is on that list of personal favorites?"

"Hard." He leaned in. He came within inches of Nelson's mouth. "Tight."

"We have that in common," Nelson murmured in a breathy tone.

Luke leaned in the last couple of inches until their lips were nearly touching. "Fast?"

"Sometimes," Nelson responded. "Though other times nice and slow has its appeal."

They sat there suspended for a long moment. Neither of them moved forward that last mere breath of distance. The sexual desire arching in the air between them sent Luke's heart rate into a rapid beat.

A throat cleared, and both he and Nelson jumped at the sound, sitting back in their chairs. Luke looked up at the knowing but pleased smile on the server's face.

"Can I get you gentleman anything else?" she asked as she began clearing the empty plates from the table.

"No, thank you," Nelson said, sounding a little flustered. "Everything was wonderful, but I'm stuffed to the gills."

"How about you, sir? Would you care for anything else?" she asked, turning her attention to Luke.

A wicked thought popped into his mind. "No, thank you. I think I'll be having mine at home." He winked at Nelson.

The server giggled, left the bill, and scurried away.

"I can't believe you just said that."

"Too much information?" Luke asked with a sly grin.

"Not for me," Nelson announced. "I'm ready when you are."

By the time they made it back to Nelson's apartment, Luke was shaking with need. Nelson's warm hand on his thigh, the heated sidelong glances thrown his way, and his spicy scent filling his small car had Luke wild with lust. He was damned lucky he hadn't lost control of his car. The instant they stepped into the apartment, Luke had Nelson's lean body pushed up against the closed door.

"Fuck, I have wanted to do this all night." Luke groaned as he took Nelson's face in his hands and brought their mouths together.

There was nothing soft about the kiss. It was hard and fierce, full of pent-up tension and need. Luke licked and nibbled at Nelson's lips as he pulled the lithe body tight against his own.

Nelson wrapped an arm around Luke's waist, encouraging him to deepen the kiss. Luke probed at Nelson's mouth until he groaned, opening and allowing him entrance to the warm heat. Nelson's flavor exploded across Luke's tongue, and he had to lock down his trembling knees from the intensity of the kiss.

He slid his hands into Nelson's hair, tilted his head back farther, and plunged his tongue into the depths of his mouth. The kiss became feral, a clash of tongues and lips, both fighting to win dominance.

The sounds of passion filled the room, the deep moans making a perfect kind of melody. Luke ground his hard shaft against Nelson's hardness, causing Nelson to cry out. Luke pulled the moan inside, demanded more as he rolled his hips. He frantically humped against the bulging erection and tight belly pressed against him. Without warning, Luke was suddenly teetering on the verge of exploding.

"Jesus," Luke panted, drawing large gasps of air into his lungs as he broke the kiss. His heart hammered as he fought to get his body back under control. *Fuck, that was close.* The last thing he wanted was to come in his pants like some damn teenager, not when he had a creature like Nelson in his arms.

Nelson closed his eyes and bit down on his lip. His skin flushed, and he trembled slightly as he breathed deeply through his nose. Good to know Nelson was as deeply affected as he was.

Luke leaned back in and playfully nipped at Nelson's kiss-swollen lips. He tightened his hold on Nelson and steered them away from the door until the backs of his calves encountered the couch. He twisted and fell onto the couch with Nelson stretched out beneath him.

"Where were we?" Luke murmured against Nelson's mouth.

"Right here," Nelson moaned in reply as he wrapped his arms around Luke's neck and sucked at his lips.

Situating himself more firmly between Nelson's spread legs, he leaned back enough to access the waistband of Nelson's jeans, popped the button, and eased down the zipper carefully. A harsh moan from deep in his chest escaped as the wet tip of Nelson's cock pushed up out of his boxers. Nelson's arousal slicked the way as he ran the tip of one finger across the leaking slit. His mouth watered.

"Is this all for me?" he murmured.

"Oh fuck yeah," Nelson groaned. He jerked his hips, pushing harder against Luke's hand. "Luke, you keep teasing me, and I might just lose my fucking mind."

"We can't have that," Luke said. He rolled his hips again, enjoying the stimulating friction a bit longer.

"Luke, please."

Luke growled at the need in Nelson's voice. His own cock pulsed hard against the stiff denim. A strangled gasp escaped Nelson as Luke wrapped a hand firmly around Nelson's long, slender shaft. He stroked Nelson in long, firm pulls, heat radiating against his palm.

"So gorgeous," he whispered, voice thick with need.

Luke lowered his head, never losing contact with those incredible eyes as he placed a soft kiss to Nelson's lips. Luke continued to stroke Nelson at a slow, steady pace. He wanted Nelson with an all-consuming need, but he was in no hurry for it to end. He wanted to savor each precious moment.

"How about we move this to my bedroom?" Nelson offered, his tone husky, seductive, and so fucking sexy it curled Luke's toes.

Luke rolled to his feet and pulled Nelson to his. "I thought you'd never ask," Luke drawled and took Nelson's mouth in a blistering kiss.

Chapter Seven

SOMEHOW THEY managed to move to the bedroom without ever breaking the kiss. Nelson bucked against the hard ridge of solid muscle the instant their bodies came in contact. Luke thrust his hips in an answering call.

"Fuck, Nelson. I have to have you," Luke moaned as he bit at Nelson's mouth. Tiny nips of Luke's teeth against his lips sent out delicious sparks of pain.

Nelson tried to think past the lust. He could count on one hand how many lovers he'd had. Though he wasn't a virgin, he'd only bottomed once. It hurt like hell, and the thought of doing it again caused his arousal to wane. However, being in Luke's arms, having Luke's mouth on his, felt so damn good. God, how many times had he dreamed of being with Luke like this? Still, the nervous churning in his gut had him rethinking his fantasy.

Luke didn't give him a chance to dwell on it. As Luke explored his mouth with his tongue, Nelson's mind shut down the ability to form rational thought, his body awash in a mixture of sensations.

Nelson slid his hands beneath Luke's shirt, wanting to feel skin against his fingertips, muscles flexing beneath his hands as he explored his heated flesh.

Luke broke the kiss long enough to let Nelson pull the shirt over his head. He reclaimed Nelson's mouth once the shirt was free and falling to the floor.

They both laughed into the kiss as they fumbled with buttons and zippers. Neither being willing to break the connection made removing clothing difficult, but somehow, they managed. Nelson had never laughed through a kiss before, and he liked the way it vibrated against his lips, loved the sounds Luke made.

Luke managed to get their jeans down past their hips. Nelson's hard shaft leaped into Luke's hand, and he rocked his hips, seeking out more of the perfect friction of a warm palm against his cock. Luke wrapped his fist around their pricks and began to pull slowly from base to tip and back down again.

Throwing his head back, Nelson moaned as Luke broke the kiss and brushed his lips along Nelson's jaw and down the side of his neck. Luke's deep, husky voice rasped in his ear. "So fucking hot. Love the feel of your cock against mine." Luke sped up his hand as the precome steadily dripped from their cocks, easing the way. "Want to feel you come all over me. Feel your cock throb against mine. C'mon, Nelson, show me how good it is."

Nelson could only groan his agreement. The slide of his prick against Luke's as he jerked them harder and faster made Nelson's balls draw up tight against his body. He dug his fingers into Luke's shoulders, clutching them in a death grip as his knees buckled. Luke's hand on his cock and naughty words against his neck sent him to the edge. He didn't want it to end. He fought against the orgasm running down his spine. Just when he thought he might draw it out a few minutes longer, Luke bit down on his neck and then began sucking greedily.

The intensity of his orgasm ripped through every cell in his body and exploded in a shower of liquid heat. He heard Luke growl his name as an accompanying heat joined his. He could only rock through the convulsions of the aftershock. It took all his might to stay standing, to keep from falling to his knees.

Nelson looked down at the mess they created. Jeans disheveled, shirts thrown about the bedroom. He looked back up and met stunned blue eyes. He leaned in and laughed against Luke's lips. "Now that's what I call the perfect after-dinner treat."

"You certainly gave me what I asked for." Luke looked down his body, then met Nelson's gaze, a mischief grin curling his upper lip. "Definitely warm and messy."

"Definitely." Nelson ran a single finger across the head of Luke's cock, causing him to shudder.

Luke grabbed on to Nelson's hips, pushed him toward the bed. "And just think, that was merely a sample."

They shucked their pants and briefs, then fell onto the bed in a tangle of arms and legs. Then it was joyous skin on skin, Luke's weight perfect on top of him.

Luke covered his mouth, pushing in his tongue and exploring, seeking out every hidden area as if Luke were claiming him. The kiss deepened until the only flavor in Nelson's mouth was Luke.

Grabbing on to the back of Luke's neck, he gave back as good as he got. He frantically thrust his hips. It was all-consuming, yet still not enough. He needed more. More skin, more weight, more Luke. The mixture of Luke's mouth, the heat of his skin, and the perfect slide of hardening cocks. The pleasure grew too big to contain, overflowing from his mouth in a series of moans and whimpers. Nelson could only hold on and float on a raging sea of pleasure.

"Need you now," Luke panted as he broke the kiss. "God, want to feel you inside me so fucking bad." His mouth moved down Nelson's chin, across his jaw.

Taken aback, Nelson stilled briefly. He'd have thought for sure, considering Luke's size and domineering personality, he'd also be a dominant lover. Then again, Luke had a soft side to him as well. Oh hell, didn't matter now. The last shred of unease washed out of Nelson. He was practically fucking giddy with excitement as he scrambled from beneath Luke.

Nelson yanked open the drawer and pulled out a bottle of lube and a condom he'd purchased in anticipation of Luke's visit. He dropped the condom on Luke's chest before snapping open the top on the lube. He kneeled between Luke's thighs and slid slick fingers between his asscheeks as he kneaded Luke's inner thigh with his other hand, encouraging him to spread farther. Nelson worked a finger past the tight muscles of his opening. Nelson struggled to go slow. Had he not already gotten off once, he'd be coming again, simply from the way Luke was looking at him with such want and need shining in his eyes and the way his tight ass clamped down on Nelson's finger. God, he couldn't wait to bury himself deep inside Luke's body.

"So fucking tight," Nelson groaned. He slid a second finger in and began scissoring them, stretching Luke further. It took forever and no time at all for Luke's body to begin to relax, and Nelson moved his fingers easily in and out of Luke's ass.

Luke fumbled with the condom, struggling to tear open the foil package, rocking his body as he pushed himself farther onto Nelson's invading fingers. A guttural sound poured from Luke, and his eyes fluttered shut. Nelson took the condom from him, rolled it on his hard shaft one-handed as he continued to pleasure and tease Luke with his fingers. Thank God one of them still had enough brain cells left to do more than squirm and moan.

Nelson moved up, guiding his slick cock to Luke's ass. He removed his fingers and began slowly filling him. The delicious friction from Luke's tight ass around his cock had Nelson's eyes rolling back in his head. "Oh God, Luke, so fucking tight."

Luke nodded his agreement and thrust his hips up, an unspoken plea to get Nelson to fill him.

Nelson nuzzled the side of Luke's neck, his body trembling with the restraint it took not to thrust and rut like an animal like he wanted. Instead he pushed in slowly, moving inch by painstaking inch until Nelson was in danger of losing his mind.

Luke wrapped his long legs tightly around Nelson's waist, encouraging him. "Fuck, I love the way you're stretching me. More, God, Nelson. More." He arched his back as he tightened his legs around Nelson's waist, his body begging Nelson to go deeper.

Nelson growled, then pushed in to the hilt in one hard thrust. The deep rumbling sound the movement pulled from Luke sent a fire racing to Nelson's aching cock.

Nelson rolled his hips, barely pulling out of Luke before pushing back in. They melded together from head to toe, their bodies never losing contact as they moved perfectly in a lovers' dance.

"This isn't going to last long. You feel too good." Nelson reached up and grabbed Luke's biceps, encouraging him to put his arms up over his head. "Gotta just do it." Nelson gripped the thick muscles, digging in his blunt fingers, and started moving faster. "So fucking good."

"Do it. Oh fuck, just like that." Luke thrust his hips up, spurring Nelson on.

Nelson was so close, just a little more, and he'd fall over into pure bliss. He slid his right hand between their bodies, wrapped it around Luke's cock, and stroked it in time with every thrust. Luke's prick leaked a steady stream of precome.

"That's it, Luke. Come for me. Let me feel it." Nelson shifted position on the next thrust, aiming for Luke's sweet spot. The howl of pleasure that escaped Luke let Nelson know he'd hit it, and he thrust again over and over.

Luke moaned Nelson's name as jet after jet of hot seed covered their stomachs and chests. Just as the last drop seeped from Luke's body, Nelson thrust one last time, then stiffened, breath held as he teetered on the edge.

Then he was throwing his head back, crying out as a thrill rushed through him *and* he filled the condom deep inside Luke's ass.

He floated on the high, completely satisfied, and then collapsed onto Luke's chest, breathing harshly and feeling so fucking good he tingled from head to toe.

Once his heart rate had slowed, as well as his breathing, Nelson reluctantly rolled off Luke.

"Hey, where are you going?"

"I like warm and messy, but cold and crusty, not so much." He headed toward the bathroom and stood near the door. "You coming?"

"I already did twice. Jesus, Nelson, what do you think I am? A machine?"

Nelson shook his head but refrained from rolling his eyes. "Okay, you stay right there and stick to the sheets. I'm going to take a shower."

Luke was up and out of bed, crowding Nelson into the shower before he could even set the taps.

STILL WARM and damp, Nelson lay stretched out on this bed, his head resting on Luke's chest, staring unblinkingly into the dark room.

"Luke?" Nelson whispered, keeping his voice low in case the slow, steady rise and fall of Luke's chest meant he'd fallen asleep.

"Yeah?"

"I was just thinking there must have been something in the water back at Fillmore Middle School."

"Why is that?" Luke inquired.

"Well, you and I are gay, Monty Tomas last year admitted to me he is gay, and I heard a rumor that a couple of girls who went to school with us are lesbians."

"Maybe." Luke chuckled. "Except I'm not gay."

Nelson ran his fingertips down the hard ridges of Luke's stomach and ran the tip of his pinky finger along the head of Luke's cock. "I don't know, Luke. I'm thinking if anyone sees us right now, they may disagree with you."

A shudder went through Luke, and he pushed Nelson's hand away. "That tickles." He pulled Nelson into a tight embrace and pinned his hand under Luke's bicep. "And I'd have to argue that fact. I'm not gay. I'm bisexual."

Nelson chewed on that tidbit of information. He'd only known one other person who claimed to be bisexual but later admitted he only said that to test the waters before coming out as gay. Nelson had a hard time comprehending it. How could someone be sexually attracted to both men and women? He certainly wasn't an expert on the subject since he couldn't understand why anyone would be sexually attracted to a woman. Seemed to him it would make life a whole lot more difficult. Could Luke commit to one sex when he also desired the other? Trying to figure it out made his head hurt.

"Do your parents know you're bisexual?" Nelson finally asked.

"Yeah. Mom is cool with it. Dad's having a bit harder time accepting it, but he wants me happy, so he doesn't say much. Although I'm sure he is secretly hoping I'll settle down with a nice girl."

"So it's not hiding behind a more accepted label," Nelson surmised aloud.

"I don't think it's a more accepted label. Actually I think it's harder to tell people I'm bi. I get grief from both sides." Luke laid his hand on Nelson's cheek. "I'm not hiding behind anything. I think I know my own mind and heart. What about you?"

"No, I'm not out to my parents. Or anyone else, for that matter," Nelson huffed.

"I'm sorry to hear that, but I meant do you know your own mind and heart?" Luke clarified.

"I—" Nelson snapped his mouth shut before he finished his sentence since he'd be wrong in answering to the affirmative. He was sure about his sexuality, but that was about the only thing he was sure of. "That's a good question," Nelson admitted. "And if I wasn't so tired, I might give it some thought."

Luke kissed his nose. "Go to sleep. We can talk about it in the morning." He rolled until he was once again on his back, bringing Nelson with him.

Nelson settled against Luke, listening to the steady rhythm of his heart. For quite some time. Nelson lay there thinking about Luke's question without knowing how to answer it. He was tired. His body was sated and exhausted, but his brain was wide-awake. Did he know his own mind? His own heart?

Chapter Eight

A COOL breeze blew through the trees as Nelson walked along the bike trail, which wound its way around Center Park. He felt almost cocky with Luke at his side. Nelson couldn't remember ever being as happy as he was at this moment, doing something so mundane as taking a walk. It was nuts. He'd been afraid for so long to come out to his family and coworkers, and now it seemed he didn't give a shit who knew. He was so damn proud to have Luke in his life and in his bed. Nelson wanted to fucking scream it to the world. The only thing keeping him from doing it was Luke wouldn't be at his side tomorrow.

Half a continent separated them, and once Luke was gone, Nelson would be alone once again. He wasn't ready to deal with all the issues he might have to face by coming out by himself. He was a coward at heart. Plus he needed his job. He couldn't take the risk. He looked over at Luke, who was scanning the trees. He was so handsome, so wonderful. Nelson so badly wanted to take a risk, but once again, the coward in him reared up, and instead of taking Luke's hand like Nelson wanted to, he shoved his hands in his pockets to keep from giving in to the strong urge.

"This is the one thing I miss most," Luke commented while he continued to look at the trees with a serene expression on his face.

"What's that?"

"The changing of the seasons," Luke explained without looking away from the canopy of trees. "Especially fall. I haven't been to a cider mill or pumpkin farm in over ten years." Luke looked down and met Nelson's gaze. "Remember the corn maze?"

Nelson chuckled. "How can I forget? You darted off into the corn, leaving me alone to navigate the thing by myself."

"I did not. I kept my eye on you."

"Yeah, so you could jump out and scare the holy hell out of me just before I made it to the end." Nelson swatted Luke's arm. "I nearly pissed my pants."

"You should have seen your face. Dude, it was priceless!" Luke hooted. "I thought you were a big fan of Jason."

"I liked *Friday the 13th* just fine, but that didn't mean I wanted to meet the psycho, and in a cornfield all alone, no less. Where in the hell did you get that damn mask, anyway?"

"Bought it at Woolworths. I can't believe you didn't know something was up. Record heat wave for October, and there I was with a coat on, sweating my ass off." Luke rustled Nelson's hair and started to walk again. "You were always so oblivious."

"That's because I was too busy checking out your ass," Nelson blurted before thinking better of it.

"Seriously? You thought about doing me even back then?"

"You know I did," Nelson huffed. "While you and the other guys were chasing girls, I was too focused on my attraction to you and trying not to end up in hell to be worried about girls."

"And do you still think you're going to hell?" Luke asked.

Nelson shrugged. "Don't really know, but I don't worry about it as much as I did when I was a kid. I have more important things to worry about these days than whether my mortal soul is damned to hell."

Luke arched a brow. "Yeah? Like what?"

Eating and paying rent. He didn't say it out loud but shrugged again. "You know... life. I figure I should be focused on the here and now rather than always worrying about what's going to happen to me when I die. Need to make it through this life first."

"You still go to church?"

"Nope, much to my mom's dismay. You?"

Luke shook his head. An older couple who looked to be in their seventies, maybe even eighties, stepped out from around the bend. The gentleman was hunched slightly, a cane in his right hand, his wife's hand in his other. *How sweet.* Nelson had no idea how long the couple had been together, but he liked to think it had been all their lives and to still be in love, holding hands during their golden years.

Nelson nodded and smiled at them as they passed. Once he and Luke rounded the corner and were out of earshot, Nelson looked up at Luke. "You know, I think I wouldn't mind going to hell if I had that on earth."

"What's that?" Luke inquired, but from the knowing smile on his face, Nelson was pretty sure Luke knew what he was talking about. Still, he clarified it for Luke.

"To find someone to grow old with who you still want to hold hands with, even at that age."

"Ever think maybe she was holding his hand to keep him from falling and breaking a hip?"

"Wow."

"What?" Luke asked, trying to sound innocent. "It's a very real possibility."

"Such a romantic, you are," Nelson chided lightly.

"Hey, I was being romantic. Holding his hand to make sure he didn't fall was sweet. I bet she even helps him up in the morning and hands him his teeth. Oh, or maybe they share a denture cup. I can't imagine getting any more personal and romantic than that."

"You're done." Nelson wrinkled his nose. He then shuddered when the images Luke was planting popped into Nelson's head. "Way to ruin my fantasy of growing old together and achieving the coveted happily ever after. Thanks a lot."

Luke slung his arm over Nelson's shoulder. "You're welcome."

Nelson took the close contact to exact a little revenge for the tarnishing of his fantasy. He dug his fingers into Luke's side, going for the sensitive spot he knew was just above Luke's hipbones. Nelson wriggled his fingers and was rewarded with a pleasing yelp from Luke seconds before he spun out of Nelson's reach.

"You are so asking for it, Runt," Luke warned.

Nelson broke into a dead run. "Got to catch me first, Brobdingnagian," Nelson called without looking back. His shoes ate up the pavement as he sprinted along the path, Luke right on his heels.

Nelson fared better than he had when Luke chased him as a kid. While Luke had a longer stride, he was bulky, heavy with muscle, and had a difficult time weaving around the course Nelson set. Nelson dodged around trash cans, leaped over park benches, spun around a bush, all the while laughing. He broke out of the bike bath and raced across the open field. That decision was his downfall. Before he even realized what was happening, his feet left the ground as big arms wrapped around his biceps and chest. He was effectively pinned, barely able to wriggle as Luke tightened his hold to nearly crushing pressure.

"Uncle!" Nelson yelled. "I give. I give!"

"I should spank your ass for making me chase you," Luke panted.

Luke's warm breath tickled Nelson's right ear. He shuddered, then froze as that tingling sensation wormed its way through his body on a fast track to his crotch. Christ, a little rough housing, the thought of a hard swat on his ass, and he was popping a fucking boner. He really did have it bad for Luke.

Luke was apparently keen on Nelson's reaction to the thought of Luke spanking him because he went dead still for a split second, then flicked the tip of his tongue out to tease the shell of Nelson's ear. "You like that idea, don't you, Runt?"

"What?" Nelson asked, feigning innocence.

"You know damn well what I'm talking about," Luke growled. "I may just have to turn you over my knee when we get back to your place."

Nelson's breath hitched.

A football came whizzing by just inches from Nelson's other ear, saving him from having to respond to the tantalizing offer. A stranger jogged toward them, and Luke set Nelson back on his feet.

"Sorry about that," the stranger called as he went to retrieve his ball.

"No problem," Nelson responded. Only then did he notice the group of guys standing around with yellow flags hanging from their belts, staring at him and Luke. He was so hell-bent on outrunning Luke, Nelson hadn't realized he had run straight into the path of a flag football game.

"Oh shit. It's me who should be apologizing to you and your friends. I didn't mean to interrupt your game," Nelson said.

The stranger walked over to them, tossing his ball, a large smile on his face. "I have to admit it kind of freaked me out for a minute. I thought the big guy here"—he stabbed his thumb in Luke's direction—"was going to take you out."

"I would have too," Luke chuckled. He held out his hand. "I'm Luke, and this is my annoying best friend, Nelson."

"Nice to meet you both. I'm Trent." He shook Nelson's hand, then Luke's.

"You got room for two more players? Nelson and I used to be pretty good, back in the day."

"Speak for yourself," Nelson mumbled. He hadn't played football since Luke moved away, and he wasn't that good back then. He wasn't totally out of shape. It was just…. Well, he wasn't in the greatest shape either. Thanks to good genes, he was naturally thin, but too many long hours sitting at a desk had left him a little soft.

"The more the merrier. C'mon, I'll introduce you to the guys," Trent offered.

INTRODUCTIONS WERE made, but Nelson knew he'd never remember the names of all eight guys from Minnesota University, so he didn't even try. However, as the game got underway and Nelson hit the grass face-first with a couple of meaty guys on his back, he was acutely aware of the fact they were all members of the university rugby team.

He hoisted himself up with a groan, wiped the grass from his pants, and adjusted his shirt. "Flag football my ass," he grumbled.

"What was that, Runt?" Luke asked, looking way too fucking happy.

It was that look of happiness that had Nelson shaking his head and dropping back down into position to prepare for the hike of the ball. "Let's do this."

An hour later, his body covered in bruises, every muscle in Nelson's body screamed, even some he didn't even know he had. His sweat-soaked clothes clung to him, and he was huffing and puffing like a lifelong smoker. He might not have been any better at the game when he was younger, but he'd had a hell of a lot more stamina. He really needed to reconsider joining the gym.

The ball hiked, and the next second, Nelson was flying backward, pain radiating across his ass and spine. He sat up in time to see one of the guys from the opposing team sprinting toward the goal line for the win. Nelson flopped back onto the ground. He had nothing left in the tank. He closed his eyes and focused on slowing his racing heart and panting breath. Maybe the guys would be busy celebrating, and he could get a nap.

"Damn, we almost had them. Losing by one point sucks," Luke grumbled.

"Mmmhmm." Something brushed gently against Nelson's cheek, and he opened his eyes to find Luke grinning at him. "I thought I'd just lie here and take a bit of a nap."

"I've got a better idea. How about we head back to your place, take a shower, and nap on a soft mattress?"

"Nah, I'm good right here." Nelson's eyes started to flutter closed.

"Okay, suit yourself, but you'll miss out on the body massage I was going to give you."

Nelson jumped to his feet. "On second thought...."

Luke laughed, and after saying their goodbyes, they headed back to Nelson's place, Nelson's steps quick and with purpose, the aches he'd felt only moments ago, quiet. The excitement of having Luke's strong hands on him, massaging him, easing him, obviously was one hell of a pain reliever.

"I'll get the shower started," Nelson offered the instant they walked through the door. He kicked off his tennis shoes and whipped off his sweat-soaked shirt.

"You keep doing that, and we won't make it to the shower."

Nelson stopped midstep and turned to look at Luke. "Do what?"

Luke raised his brows, his gaze settling on Nelson's exposed chest. "That," he said.

"Well, I'm certainly not going to shower in my clothes." And seriously? Like he cared if Luke took him here and now. He unbuttoned his shorts and took a step toward the bathroom. The ache in his thighs reminded him why it wouldn't be a good idea to add carpet burns to his poor abused and bruised body. On second thought…. He moved his hand away from his waistband and quickened his steps.

Nelson flipped on the taps and barely had time to get beneath the flow of warm water before Luke crowded in behind him. "Wow, you're quick."

Luke wrapped his arms around Nelson, splayed his hands on Nelson's chest, and pulled him close. "Yeah, when I want something really bad, I am."

Nelson groaned, surprised at how quickly the arousal surged through him with Luke's cock pressed against his ass.

Luke slid his hand down, moving his palm easily across Nelson's stomach until his fingers brushed against the head of his cock. "You're not as banged up as you let on, I see."

"Luckily it's the one part of my body that didn't get bruised. Plus it has a mind of its own. I think it kind of likes you," Nelson teased. He thrust up against Luke's hand. "Yeah, it likes you, alright."

"Then we better get you washed up so I can give my little buddy some personal attention."

Nelson looked down at his hardening cock, then tilted his head to meet Luke's gaze. "It's not that little."

Luke wrapped his fist around Nelson's shaft, pumping it a few times until he'd pulled a needy sound from Nelson. "You're right. It's perfect." He kissed Nelson's jaw, and then much to Nelson's disappointment, released him and stepped back.

"Hey, I was enjoying that," Nelson grumbled playfully.

"I'll make it up to you,"

"I'm holding you to that." Nelson turned and tipped his head back beneath the hot spray, letting the water rinse away some of the sweat and grime from his hair. Luke grabbed the shampoo from the shelf and poured a dollop into his palm. Before he could set the bottle down, Nelson took it from him. "I'll do you if you do me?"

Luke waggled his brows. "Now you're talking, and trust me, it's me who will be holding you to that."

Nelson squeezed a good amount of shampoo on Luke's head and lathered it up. "I was talking about washing each other, you goof."

Luke scrubbed his fingers through Nelson's hair. "I wasn't."

Chapter Nine

LUKE STOOD next to the bed, clicking the snap top to the lotion open and closed, taking a few moments to enjoy the sight before him. Lying facedown, Nelson had his cheek resting on his folded arms. His skin was still flushed and glistening from their recent shower. A single drop of water ran from Nelson's hair down between his shoulder blades, a trail Luke had only moments before followed with his mouth. The taste of Nelson's clean skin still lingered on Luke's tongue.

"What are you looking at?" Nelson asked, sounding sleepy.

"You."

"You can look all you want while you're giving me that full-body massage you promised."

"I always keep my promises, and I plan on working out every kink and sore muscle." Luke ran the tip of his finger lightly across Nelson's firm pert asscheek. "Some more than others."

"Is that so?"

"Oh yeah," Luke assured him. He climbed onto the bed and straddled Nelson's thighs. He snapped open the lotion and poured a line down Nelson's spine.

"Hey!" Nelson yelped.

"Oh, I'm sorry. Was that cold?"

"You know it was," Nelson grumbled, still squirming beneath him.

Nelson's movements caused Luke's cock to brush against the crease of Nelson's ass setting off a tingling sensation in Luke's groin. "You keep moving like that and I may not get to all your muscles."

Nelson went still for a few ticks of the clock, then rose slightly to look over his shoulder at Luke. There was a thoughtful expression on his face, and Luke wasn't sure which one he wanted more. Skipping the massage and going right to the fucking sounded pretty damn good. However, letting the anticipation build while exploring Nelson's body sounded awesome too. Hell, either way, it was a win-win situation.

They continued to stare at each other for a brief time, then Nelson laid his head back down and relaxed against the mattress. "I am all yours, masseur."

Win-win.

Luke ran the palm of his right hand down Nelson's spine, picking up some of the warmed lotion. He rubbed his hands together before spreading them against Nelson's back and began working the lotion into his trapezoids and deltoids, kneading the tightness out with a circular motion of his thumbs. Each time Luke hit a spot that made Nelson groan or grunt, he made a mental note of it. Those where the areas that would need the most care.

Only the tiny noises Nelson made from time to time interrupted the silence. It was peaceful and soothing, and yet the heat of Nelson's body, the smoothness of his creamy skin, ignited sparks along Luke's nerve endings. If he focused too much on what touching Nelson's body was doing to his libido, he'd be saying fuck it—literally.

"This feels a lot different than when we did it when we were kids," Luke commented, needing a distraction.

"I should hope so. I was a scrawny kid."

"You're still a runt," Luke teased. "But now you're a muscular runt."

"Some of us weren't blessed with the Brobdingnagian gene. Ow... ouch."

Luke froze his thumb over a spot that was beginning to turn purple on Nelson's right hip. He felt a hard knot just below the skin. "Going to have to work this out. Grit your teeth."

Luke pressed his thumb against the knot firmly. Nelson cried out, his body tense for a few heartbeats while Luke worked to make the muscle relax. It took several moments before it gave way, and Nelson began to relax.

"Goddamn, that hurt," Nelson panted.

"Sorry, but I had to. It would have hurt much worse later."

"I could have done later," Nelson grumbled.

"You'll thank me tomorrow," he assured him. Luke shifted farther down Nelson's legs to straddle his calves, giving the muscles of his thighs the same attention he'd given Nelson's back. He found a couple of knots but no bruising. He massaged and inspected Nelson's calves as well. Satisfied, he went up on his knees. "Roll over."

"I don't wanna. I'm comfortable."

Luke considered swatting Nelson's ass to get him to comply but instead leaned forward and licked a path from the top of Nelson's ass crack up his spine. "C'mon, I promise to make it worth your while."

Nelson shuddered. "But I'd have to move, and then you couldn't do that again."

Luke did it again and was rewarded with another shudder from Nelson. "There, I did it again. Now roll over and let me do it to the other side."

"Now there's an offer I can't refuse." Nelson rolled onto his back, his long, slender cock standing tall and erect.

"Hmm, I guess you were enjoying what I was doing to you."

"You didn't need to see my dick to know that," Nelson countered. He crossed his wrists over his chest, taking up a Pharaoh pose.

"Arms over your head," Luke suggested.

Nelson waggled his brows. "You going to tie me to the bedposts?"

"Only if you want me to, baby."

Nelson tucked his hands beneath his head. "Maybe another time."

"Seriously?"

"Sure. I know you wouldn't hurt me, and I think it might be kind of fun."

Luke picked up the bottle of lotion and poured a good amount into his palm. This time he rubbed his hands together, warming the lotion before laying his hands on Nelson's chest and kneading his pecs. "You ever let anyone do that to you?"

"Nope. You?"

Luke shook his head. "Thought about it, but it's one of those topics I wasn't sure how to approach with a one-night stand. Believe it or not, I can be a little shy."

Nelson's eyes went wide. "You?"

"Yeah, me. At least when it comes to asking a stranger if I can tie him or her up. That could be taken two ways, ya know. Either very sexy or 'you fucking perv.'"

"You were with Charlotte for quite a while. How come you didn't ever ask her?"

"She wasn't the adventurous type." Luke pinched Nelson's nipple, making him squirm. "I don't want to talk about her or anyone else right now. I want to focus on the here and now. Me and you."

Nelson's smile warmed Luke all the way down to his toes. "That works for me."

THE DUAL sensation surging through Nelson was driving him mad. Luke was working Nelson's sore muscles with his warm hands , turning part of him into a big pile of contented goo. Yet at the same time, those same ministrations were making his cock ache with need. Each time Luke's fingers got close to Nelson's cock, Nelson wanted to beg Luke to stroke it, suck it, anything to relieve some of the pressure that was building. But then Luke would move to a hip, a thigh, a calf, working out each tense muscle, and Nelson would melt into the mattress again.

However, soon enough the madness eased, and Nelson didn't have to beg because Luke moved farther down Nelson's body and wrapped his fist around Nelson's prick. He began stroking it from base to tip. Luke's tongue left a wet trail across the inside of Nelson's thigh, and he forgot all about madness, sore muscles, and melting. His only thought was how badly he wanted that perfect warm mouth on him. "How about you put that tongue where your hand is at?" Nelson suggested.

"How about both?"

Nelson's hips snapped of their own accord as Luke placed a soft kiss to the tip of his cock. Luke looked up at him with heated eyes as he continued to stoke Nelson slowly, snaking out his tongue to tease the tip each time he slid his hand down to the base. A pearl of precome seeped from the small slit, and Luke lapped it up.

"I'd say your cock likes the idea as well," Luke murmured and licked his lips. He took Nelson's erection into his mouth, flicking his tongue along the underside as he slowly sucked Nelson's shaft farther into his mouth. A shudder went through Nelson as Luke took him deep, moving his hand down to caress and squeeze Nelson's balls.

When his cock hit the back of Luke's throat, Luke hummed his approval, and Nelson felt the vibration shoot up his spine, and his hands flew to Luke's head, threading his fingers into his hair, holding on. "Fuck yeah, Luke, suck me." He snapped his hips forward, the urge to move too strong to ignore. Luke released his hold on Nelson's sac, taking Nelson's hips in his big meaty hands, encouraging him to thrust harder and take what he wanted, what he needed.

Oh, and how he needed. He thrust deep into that warm, wet mouth, rutting and groaning, and holy fuck, it felt so goddamn good. Luke slid his hands back to Nelson's ass, lifting him until Nelson had to plant his knees on the bed. In this new position, Nelson used the power in his legs to thrust even harder, Luke encouraging him with his hands as well as the moans and grunts pouring from him. Luke teased the underside of Nelson's prick with the tip of his tongue each time he pulled out before slamming back in. On the next snap of his hips, Luke swallowed, and his throat constricted around the head of Nelson's shaft.

His orgasm suddenly raced through him like a runaway train. Nelson didn't know where the brakes were and was powerless to use them, even if he did know where they were. "I.... Fuck...." Nelson's words turned into more of an incoherent animalistic growl, and he was coming, pumping his release down Luke's throat hard and fast.

Luke apparently didn't mind that Nelson hadn't warned him. He swallowed down every drop and then lapped at Nelson, his tongue almost gentle against his still-pulsing prick. Luke pulled back, letting Nelson's softening cock slide from his mouth. Licking his lips, he placed one last kiss on the tip.

Nelson glanced down with heavy-lidded eyes to watch Luke slide up Nelson's body until they were face-to-face. Luke leaned forward, nibbling on Nelson's lips before diving in for a deep, tongue-probing kiss. He tasted himself on Luke's tongue. The mix of his own essence and Luke's unique flavor made his flagging cock twitch as if it were seriously thinking how quickly it could be ready for another go-round. Luke kissed him senseless, leaving him panting for more.

"Damn, that was good," Nelson complimented. "Both the blow job and the body massage."

"You're welcome."

"I'm pretty sure the mattress and I have become one. Don't think I could move if I wanted to."

Luke sat back on his calves, exposing his hard prick. He looked down at it, then arched a brow at Nelson. "Your mouth seems to be moving just fine."

"Yes, it is. You move up here, and I'll show you just how fine it can move."

"Oh fuck yeah," Luke crowed. He moved up to straddle Nelson's chest. He wrapped his hand around his dick and guided it toward Nelson's mouth. "Open up, baby."

Nelson tilted his head up, opened wide, and true to his word showed Luke just how damn fine his mouth was.

Chapter Ten

THEY SAID all good things must come to an end. Nelson wanted to kick the *they* who came up with that shit. Why the hell did good things have to end? What a stupid fucking rule. Lying in bed watching Luke pack his duffel bag, the ache in Nelson's chest was nearly as painful as the muscles in his legs and back. He wasn't ready for it to end. He wasn't ready to say goodbye.

"You sure you can't stay tonight?"

Luke gave him a sad smile. "I already looked for alternative flights and no go, nothing that would get me back in time to meet my client in the morning."

Nelson sighed dramatically. He rolled onto his side, and the sigh turned into a groan as pain shot from his lower back all the way down to his toes. "I'm not even sure I'll be worth a damn tonight, anyway. I don't think there is a place on me that isn't aching, throbbing, or on fire."

Luke sat on the edge of the mattress. He ran a gentle hand over Nelson's hip. "I never thought the game would be that rough. I did try to make it up to you with a body massage."

Nelson laid his hand on Luke's. "I'm sure I'd be even in worse shape if you hadn't given me one. Besides, it's my own fault. I can't believe I've let myself get so soft. First thing tomorrow morning, I'm joining a gym and pumping some iron."

"If I had more time, I'd let you pump my iron," Luke said slyly.

"Lord, that's a horrible pun," Nelson groaned. "But if I wasn't dying, I might take you up on the offer."

"You're not dying. You always were a bit of a drama queen."

Nelson lifted his arm to swat at Luke but dropped it back down when spark of pain bloomed across his elbow. God, not only was he a drama queen, he was a bit of a pansy. So totally not traits becoming to a man who wanted nothing more than to be at Luke's side and his equal. "Okay, my demise may not be imminent. Can I get a raincheck on pumping your iron?"

"Absolutely." Luke pressed a gentle kiss to Nelson's lips. "I'll call you tomorrow."

"I can see you to the airport."

"Thanks, but that's not necessary. Get some rest." Luke kissed him again and spoke against Nelson's lips. "You're going to need it for the next time I come."

Luke started to rise, but Nelson stopped him by grabbing his forearm. "When?"

"As soon as I can."

Warmth spread through Nelson, and he was almost giddy. Sure, he'd like to have a date to look forward to, but Luke saying he was coming back as soon as he could, that he planned on coming back at all, gave Nelson hope that perhaps their reunion might finally fulfill Nelson's longtime fantasy of having a relationship beyond friendship with Luke. Nelson released his hold on Luke and pushed up to sit on the side of the bed. "I'll be looking forward to it."

Luke picked up his duffel and shouldered it. "Me too. I'll call you tomorrow."

The warmth that had spread through Nelson seeped from his body, leaving him cold when Luke walked out of the bedroom, followed by the sound of the front door opening and closing. Nelson rested his forearms on his knees and hung his head. He really should be disgusted with himself. He was a fucking drama queen. But dammit, being with Luke was amazing, the best kind of high. When he wasn't around, it flat-out sucked big-time.

Long after Luke left, Nelson finally dragged out of bed and headed for the shower. He set the taps and let the warm, pulsing water ease some of the tension from his aching joints and muscles. His mind was blank, thoughts numb. He placed his hands against the tile wall. He stayed beneath the warm flow for a long time until the water began to cool. He grabbed the soap and rushed to wash, but ended up gritting his teeth when he had to rinse with cold water.

Goose bumps bloomed, and he was shivering by the time he stepped out of the shower. He grabbed a towel, fastened it around his waist, then grabbed another and wrapped it around his shoulders. He found himself standing in the kitchen, water dripping down his body and pooling on the floor. He couldn't remember why he'd gone in there. He opened the fridge, then the cupboard, but still the reason why he was there eluded him. His head and heart were a mess.

Giving up on the why, he tromped over to the couch, dropped his wet towels on the floor, and snuggled beneath the afghan. He found the remote under the pillow and flipped on the TV. He spent a considerable amount of time clicking through channels, disinterested in everything. He finally settled on a rerun, and with an aggravated huff, he tossed the remote on the floor.

He spent the rest of the day on the couch trying to pay attention to the shows playing. However, his thoughts kept wandering to Luke, and he couldn't rightly say what he watched.

It was strange: one moment he was walking on sunshine, then the day turned dark and cold after Luke left, as if he'd taken the sunshine with him. Which, Nelson supposed, Luke had. Snuggling deeper beneath his blanket, Nelson alternated between blinking at the screen and dozing.

The next day he didn't feel all that much better. He tried keeping the promise he'd made to himself and checked out the local gym. He stood outside watching people go in and out, but finally decided he was too sore to work out. Besides, with as distracted as he was, he'd probably drop the dumbbells and break something like a foot.

He was a whiny mess when he let himself into his apartment. He was being silly, but he couldn't help it. Having Luke with him had been wonderful. Someone to talk to, to laugh with, and a warm body to hold while he slept. Now he was acutely aware of Luke's absence, and it reminded him how lonely he was. Once again, he found himself dependent on Luke for his happiness, and that scared the shit out of Nelson. The last time he'd done that hadn't ended well.

"God, you're pathetic," he chastised himself.

He started for the fridge, hoping a good meal and a stiff drink would help him get out of his funk. Perhaps if he ate and got some sleep, he'd be able to deal with his emotional issues. And if not, maybe he could take a class on Grow the Fuck Up 101. The idea made him chuckle.

The phone rang, and he made a mad dash for it, snatching it up before it could ring a second time. "Hi! I was hoping you would call."

"You did? And just pray tell, why were you hoping I'd call?" his mom asked.

Nelson scrunched up his face and closed his eyes briefly. "Oh, sorry, thought you were someone else," Nelson replied, trying to keep the disappointment out of his voice and failing miserably.

"You keep doing that, and I'm going to get a complex. Let me guess, you were hoping it was Luke again?"

"Yeah, I mean, I'm glad you called, Mom. It's just, he left yesterday, and I wanted to make sure he had a good flight home."

"He came all the way from California to see you?"

"Yup. Had a great weekend too. I'm a bit sore, but other than that, it was fun. Did a lot of catching up."

"Sore? Are you hurt?" his mom asked, sounding concerned.

"It's nothing serious. We went to the park and came across some guys playing football and joined in. I'm not any better now than I was as a kid. Ended eating dirt more than once," Nelson chuckled.

"Yes, well, you never were what I would call graceful. I'm glad you're making friends. Listen, I don't want you to get alarmed."

Uh-oh. That didn't sound good. Anytime Mom said that, it was always bad news. "What's the matter? Are you okay?"

"Yes, I'm fine, but your dad has to have a procedure—"

Yup, alarm was setting in and kicking up his pulse. "Is he sick? What kind of procedure?"

"If you wouldn't interrupt me, I'd tell you."

When his mom stayed silent, Nelson blurted, "Fine, just tell me."

"He's been experiencing some chest pains, and apparently his stress test didn't go so well. They want to do a heart cath. Now the doctor assured us it was no big deal. But you know how your father is. He'd like you to be here, if at all possible."

"Of course. When is it?"

"Next Tuesday," Mom informed him.

"I'll talk to my boss in the morning. I'm sure it won't be an issue getting the time off work."

"Thank you, son. Now I don't expect you to go in debt, so I'll make all the arrangements."

"It's okay, I plan on driving."

"Nonsense, you'll spend more time on the road than time with us."

"But Mom, I ha—"

"Yes, yes, I know you hate flying, but you're much safer in a plane than in a car. Time you got used to it."

"But—"

"I have to go. I'll call you tomorrow with your itinerary. Bye, Nelson. Love you."

Before Nelson could protest further, the line went dead. Goddammit. Now he was worried and pissed. First, whatever was going on with his dad was much more serious than Mom was letting on, or Dad wouldn't want Nelson to come home. Second, he hated to fly, and he wasn't a child. He could make his own plans. Plan that didn't include being thirty thousand feet off the ground.

Well, he had been looking for a distraction. He sure the hell got his wish this time.

Chapter Eleven

GETTING TIME off work wasn't an issue. Nelson would only be gone a couple of days, and since his folks had a phone line and a computer, he could deal with most problems that might arise from home. The flight was the issue. *It's only an hour-and-a-half flight*, Mom said. *It's safer than driving*, she said. Not once did she mention the storm or the turbulence. Nelson clutched the armrest in a white-knuckle grip as the plane dipped and shook. The kid who'd been kicking the back of his seat for the past hour was now screaming bloody murder at an ear-piercing tone. It was probably a good thing Nelson couldn't breathe or pry his fingers from the armrest, or he might just scar the kid for life.

Heart hammering, sweat pouring down his temples, Nelson closed his eyes, praying the flight would end soon and preferably not with him ending up in a pine box. He'd been hoping for a distraction to keep his mind off Luke, but this damn sure wasn't what he had in mind. It didn't help. It only added to the stress and uncertainty.

Luke had called the day after he returned to California, sounding happy and excited about planning their next visit. Nelson had left several messages on Luke's answering machine, but over the last week, he'd only spoken with Luke twice. Once a brief call from Luke to tell Nelson he was busy with work, a second time, Nelson did all the talking, and Luke barely said a word. Luke assured him he was just busy at work, but Nelson couldn't help but think there was more to it than that. Luke had been distracted, and if Nelson wasn't mistaken, there was a hint of sadness or maybe fear in Luke's tone. Whatever it was, Luke would surely tell Nelson when he was ready. For the moment Nelson had his own concerns to deal with, namely getting through his dad's heart cath with a favorable outcome.

Hair sticking up, hands aching and legs shaking, Nelson stepped off the plane. At the end of the jetway, Mom stood waving with a broad smile on her face.

"You look like hell," she said by way of greeting.

Nelson gave her a hug, just as much for the affection as the support. "That was the worst flight ever."

Mom patted his back. "Still a big ol' baby, I see."

"Seriously, Mom, that was horrible."

"Mmhmm." She rolled her eyes. "C'mon, let's get your luggage, and we'll go home and make dinner for your dad."

"I don't have any luggage, only my carry-on. And honestly, Mom. You're going to make me cook dinner after what I just went through? What I need is a drink and to be pampered."

"Not going to happen," Mom said confidently. "Besides, this is about your dad, not you."

"Wow. Way to make me feel loved."

"Oh, hush, Nelson. You know baking helps you relax. Now let's go."

There was always something about coming home that transported Nelson back to being a child. Perhaps it was sleeping in the same room that hadn't changed since he left for college. Or it could have been the way his mom constantly reminded him to pick up his shoes, wash his hands, or swatted him for putting his feet on the coffee table. Walking into the living room and seeing his dad sitting in his recliner looking pale and fragile reminded him how far removed he was from his youth.

"Hi, Dad, how are you?" Nelson asked, sitting in the other recliner.

"I've been better. Good to see you, son. How's Minneapolis?"

Nelson silently cringed at how weak his dad's voice was. "It's fine, which I wish I could say for you. What's going on?"

"Ah, my ticker's acting up. It's no big deal."

Nelson heard the lie in the statement and saw the worry etched in the lines around his dad's eyes. Being a police officer, his dad had always been a tough, strapping man. He was still in damn good shape for fifty-six. He had a head full of hair. Surprisingly, considering the stress of his profession, he had very little gray. There was always an air of authority that swirled around his dad. His posture and demeanor were always confident. To see him now looking so pale and weak hurt Nelson's heart.

"It looks like a big deal," Nelson insisted. "Why did they make you wait a week for this procedure? Why aren't you in the hospital?"

"You sound like your mother," Dad huffed.

"Good, at least there is one person in this house that has some sense."

"Simmer down, son. I'm sure the doctor knows what he's doing. You two always have been worrywarts. Tomorrow I'll have the cath, be good as gold."

Worrywart or not, Nelson wanted to scream and demand someone do something now. He hated seeing his dad like this. He also knew it would do no damn good. He felt helpless. He could only imagine what his mom was going through. Still, his dad might sound confident, but Nelson knew he was scared. There was no point in stressing him out any further arguing and complaining about things that wouldn't change. Best thing Nelson could do was try to keep his dad's mind off tomorrow.

"Mom asked me to help her cook dinner. Anything in particular you want?"

"Anything that isn't on the heart-smart diet," Dad replied. "I don't know how people survive without cream sauces and bacon," Dad grumbled. "And don't even get me started on an existence without doughnuts."

"Whatever. You're the only cop I know who eats granola rather than doughnuts, but I'll see what I can do about the bacon." Nelson pushed to his feet. "You need anything before I go?"

"Nope, got all I need right here," he exclaimed, holding up the remote.

Nelson walked into the kitchen to find his mom standing at the sink washing her hands, staring out the window.

"He looks worse than I expected," he said, coming to stand next to her. "You could have warned me. Or, Christ, Mom, I should have been here sooner."

"I didn't want to alarm you."

"Dammit!" he blurted. She gave him that look that could strike fear into him, and he lowered his voice. "Sorry, but I'm a bit frazzled and a whole lot worried. And from the expression on Dad's face, he's worried too."

Mom nodded. "He is, but he's also stubborn. The doctor wanted him in the hospital last week, but your dad refused. He claimed he had some loose ends to tie up at work."

"And you didn't hog-tie his butt and deliver him to the ER?" Mom was the only person on the planet his dad would back down from. It made no sense, and the anger quickly trumped the worry.

Mom's eyes flashed a fiery green. "You don't think I didn't try? Your father wouldn't be swayed. The best thing I can do for him right now is keep him calm and not add to his stress." She pointed a finger at him. "And that's exactly what you're going to do as well. Now wash your hands, and let's get dinner started."

Properly chastised and now with a heavy dose of guilt for upsetting his mom, Nelson did as he was told. He stared out into the backyard, taking slow, deep breaths to get the raging emotions under control. He'd spent his entire life looking up to his dad, always saw him as larger-than-life. He knew he'd disappointed his dad when he decided not to follow in his footsteps, choosing to study business instead of joining the force. It was another reason he never told his dad that he was gay. He couldn't stand to see that look of disappointment in his eyes again. The thought of no longer having Dad in his life—it was too horrible to think about. A lump formed in his throat. Tears formed at the back of his eyes, but he blinked them away.

This wasn't about him right now. He needed to keep calm and his emotions in check. The last thing he wanted to do was make this any more difficult for Mom or Dad. He took a few more moments to get himself together, then turned off the taps, grabbed the dish towel, and turned to face his mom while drying his hands.

"Dad wants bacon for dinner." He was pleased his voice was even considering the turmoil waging war inside.

"That's not going to happen. I was thinking about roasted chicken and a nice salad."

Nelson turned and leaned against the sink while he dried his hands. "How about we compromise? We'll make him happy, and only you and I will know he's eating healthy."

"I'm listening."

"We make him a BLT and chips."

Mom gawked at him. "Have you lost your ever-lovin' mind? He can't eat that."

"Sure he can. We'll use lean turkey bacon. I know a brand that you'd swear was regular smoked pig fat. Whole-wheat bread. Lettuce and tomato are both good for him, and instead of potato chips, we do a side of kale chips or veggie chips." Mom stared at him for a long moment. Nelson could tell by the expression on her face she was skeptical. "Trust me, it will be healthy. You just come up with an equally healthy dessert."

"Okay, I have some fresh fruit. I'm sure I can whip up something."

"Great. I'll run to the store. Do you need anything?"

"No, I'm good. The keys are hanging by the door."

Nelson pecked her on the cheek. "Be back soon."

RESTING HIS back against the headboard in his childhood room, Nelson rubbed his overly full stomach. Dinner was a hit, Dad winking at him and grinning as he polished off the second half of his BLT. Mom's fresh-fruit salad with Cool Whip and drizzled with dark chocolate had everyone smiling. Now if Nelson could only feel as good about his dad's health. He was crazy with worry, and if he could just talk to Luke, maybe he could take his mind off the heart cath.

Nelson glanced at the phone again, but it mocked him with its silence. It wasn't only his dad Nelson was worried about, but Luke too. He'd been so distant the last time they spoke. Nelson had no idea what was going on, but he had a really bad feeling about it. Only he couldn't put his finger on why.

He checked the phone to make sure the ringer was on, then grabbed a magazine and scootched down in the bed. Maybe reading about duck calls and big bucks in *Outdoor Life* would take his mind off everything. But after reading the first paragraph on an article about wildlife preservation three times, he knew it was useless. He slung the magazine to the floor and stared at the ceiling. It was going to be a long night and even longer day tomorrow.

Nelson was just about to doze off when his new cell chimed. He checked the display, smiled, and answered the phone. "Hi, Luke."

"Hey, how's your dad?"

"He doesn't look real good. I'm worried," Nelson admitted.

"I'm sorry to hear that. Is he in the hospital?"

"No, that's why I'm so worried. He should be, but he's so damn stubborn."

"Well, now we know who you get it from," Luke said.

"Whatever. He's lucky his heart cath is scheduled for tomorrow, or I'd personally escort him to the ER tonight."

"That bad, huh?" Luke asked with true concern in his tone.

"I've never seen him so weak."

"I'm sorry to hear that."

Nelson had hoped Luke would be able to take his mind off his dad's health, but as the silence stretched out between them, he had another problem to worry about. "Is everything okay, Luke?"

"Yeah, why do you ask?"

"I don't know. You've just seemed… distant the last couple of times we talked."

"I've had a lot on my mind."

"Anything you want to share? I'm a really good listener," Nelson told him.

"Thanks, but you have enough to worry about right now. I have to run. I just wanted to make sure you made it safely and see how your dad was doing. Call me after the cath, okay?"

"Okay, but—"

"Sorry, have to go."

The line went dead.

Nelson stared at his cell phone for a long moment. What in the world was going on with Luke? They'd gone from long conversations with lots of laughter to short no-nonsense talks. Was Luke purposely trying to pull away from him? And if so, why? If Luke were really worried about the shit Nelson was dealing with, he wouldn't be adding to his stress. There was certainly something going on. There was a sadness in Luke's tone as of late, which of course sent Nelson scrambling to find an answer. Was it Nelson he wasn't happy with? Had Luke decided he'd made a mistake and didn't want to rekindle their relationship? Was it yet another sexual experiment, and now that he'd gotten what he wanted, he was trying to cool things down between them? Scenarios ran through Nelson's mind in rapid succession, each one getting worse until Nelson was convinced Luke was ending their relationship.

"Goddamn it, I don't need this stress!"

His dad's health needed to be his main concern right now, and he wasn't going to be any good to him or his mom tomorrow if he was up all night worrying about things he couldn't change. Nelson slid from bed and headed to the kitchen. A stiff drink and a warm bath should help. Hell, even if it didn't, it would still be better than lying in bed, staring at the ceiling.

Chapter Twelve

NELSON SNATCHED the phone up on the first ring. "Hello?"

"Nelson, it's Chuck Goldberg. How's your dad doing?"

Nelson swallowed down his disappointment at the caller being his boss instead of Luke. "He's doing much better, sir. Thank you for asking. What can I do for you?"

"Jackson has had a family emergency, and I need you to take over a new installation for him."

"Absolutely." Nelson wasn't a big fan of new installations—they were a major pain in the butt—but anything would be better than sitting at home, fretting over Luke's silence.

"Glad to hear that. I'll have my secretary call you with your itinerary."

"My itinerary, sir?"

"You do know what that is, don't you?" Chuck asked. He sounded annoyed, so Nelson snapped down the witty retort that wanted out.

"I apologize, I should have asked where I was going."

"LA. Gotta run. Miss Elliot will be calling shortly." The phone went dead.

Nelson set the receiver back on its cradle and frowned. "LA?" As in Los Angeles, California? His first reaction was excitement. It meant he would be closer to Luke and might have an opportunity to see him. Immediately after excitement came dread and panic. He'd have to fly. The thought made him nauseous.

He didn't have time to dwell on it when the phone rang again. "Wow. That was quick." He grabbed his planner and a pen so he'd be prepared for the information Miss Elliot would be giving him.

"Hi, this is Nelson."

"Hi, this is Luke."

"Oh… umm… hey," Nelson stuttered. "I was expecting someone else."

"I hope you're not too disappointed."

"Don't be ridiculous. I'd much rather talk to you than my boss's secretary. How have you been?"

"Okay."

There was a long silence. Nelson expected the normally talkative Luke to say more, but he didn't. "Is everything alright?"

"Yeah, it's fine. I was calling to find out what your schedule is this week. I was hoping we could get a chance to see each other."

"When you called, I was waiting to hear back from the office with my itinerary. Apparently I'm going to LA, but I have no idea when I leave or how long I will be gone. I'm going to assume it will be soon since my boss asked instead of his secretary."

"Even better. I could meet you there."

Nelson's excitement was back in full force. Sure, he'd have to fly, which totally sucked, but instead of a job waiting for him at the end of his journey, Luke would be there. "That makes flying almost bearable."

"Fantastic. Can you give me a call as soon as you have the details?"

"Sure."

There was another long pause, and Nelson wanted to ask again if everything was alright. Before he got the chance, Luke said, "I have to go. Talk to you soon."

"Okay," Nelson responded, trying to keep the disappointment out of his voice.

"And Nelson?"

"Yeah?"

"Everything will be fine."

Nelson stared at the phone long after Luke hung up, trying to figure out exactly what Luke meant. Did he mean the flight, or was there a deeper meaning? Whether *everything would be fine* or not, Luke's statement did little to ease Nelson's increasing panicked state or the dread that had settled in his belly.

NELSON HADN'T expected to have a car on its way to his apartment when Miss Elliot called. Then again, he supposed having mere minutes to pack was probably better than sitting around fretting about the trip. Plus, he'd have a couple of days to see Luke before he had to meet with the client on Monday. A mad dash to the airport, six hours of drinking, and three and a half hours of white knuckling through the skies, and he finally touched down in LA. His legs were wobbly as he made it down the tarmac. He had the strong urge to drop to his knees and kiss the ground.

Then it was the urge to push those in front of him out of the way and run when he spotted Luke waiting for him.

Luke wore a pair of khaki shorts, a white short-sleeved button-up shirt opened at the neck to show off the deep-olive tone of his chest, and leather sandals. He looked good, damn good, and the sight of him kicked Nelson's pulse up a notch. He wanted nothing more than to wrap his arms around Luke, kiss that handsome face, but he restrained himself, settling on a small wave.

"Hi."

"Hey, Nelson. How was your flight?"

"Sucked, but I didn't puke or try skydiving, so I guess there is that," he teased.

Luke shoved his hands into his pockets and looked around at everything but Nelson. "Glad to hear it. Do we need to stop by baggage claim?"

"No, I was able to pack everything I needed in my carry-on." He patted his duffel bag.

"Cool, let's go. Are you hungry? Or would you rather I take you straight to your hotel so you can shower or rest?"

Nelson frowned. Luke still wasn't looking at him. He wanted to ask what was going on, but in the middle of a busy airport wasn't the best place to talk. "I could eat, but if you have something you need to do, I can order room service."

"I know of a great steak house that's on the way to the hotel."

Nelson had to quicken his steps to keep up with Luke's longer strides. He didn't say anything further, and Nelson had the strange feeling he wasn't going to like what Luke would say if Nelson asked what was wrong. There was definitely a change in Luke's demeanor since the last time they were together. Luke avoided eye contact, walked stiffly, and Nelson hadn't seen the playful smile he was used to seeing.

LUKE THOUGHT he'd been dealing with some of the hardest shit of his life, that it couldn't possibly get any harder. He was wrong. Seeing Nelson step off the plane, it hit Luke the hardest was yet to come. He'd thought he'd resolved himself, was confident in his decision, yet the urge to pull Nelson into a tight embrace and never let go made him realize he hadn't resolved shit. Still, it didn't change his plans, only made it more difficult to embrace those plans wholeheartedly. Hopefully in time it would get easier.

The ride to the restaurant was quiet and uncomfortable, Luke lost in his own thoughts, but not so much that he was unaware of the tension rolling off Nelson. Luke knew Nelson was aware of the change in Luke and was probably thinking worst-case scenarios. Luke could ease his curiosity, but to do so would be to cause him pain. Luke wasn't quite ready to do that, even if on some level, he knew prolonging it was cruel.

"How is your dad doing?" Luke asked simply to end the painful silence.

"He's doing great. I talked to Mom this morning, and he's driving her nuts wanting to go back to work."

"Already? Are the doctors going to allow that?"

"No, they won't clear him for another couple weeks. I don't know how poor Mom is going to deal with him that long."

"Yeah, but it's a good sign he's a pain in the ass."

"True," Nelson chuckled.

The silence returned, Luke unsure of what else to say. Thankfully he was pulling into the parking lot of the restaurant. The silence between them continued to stretch out into the steak house, through ordering their meals, and by the time the waiter brought Luke a beer, he was sure it was going to choke them both. He planned on waiting until they were alone back at Nelson's hotel room, but he could no longer stand the tension between them or the unsure look in Nelson's eyes.

Luke took a long pull from his beer before saying, "I have a confession to make."

Nelson visibly stiffened, his expression wary. "I have a feeling I'm going to need a drink for this." He downed his bourbon, then waved to the waiter.

"I don't know that it would help," Luke replied. Nevertheless he took another big drink of his beer before continuing. "I lied. It wasn't work that had me so distracted. It was Charlotte."

"Your ex?"

"Yeah. She's pregnant."

How wide Nelson's eye went would have been comical if the reason behind the reaction weren't so upsetting. "Yours?"

Luke pursed his lips and nodded, his only response since the waiter arrived at their table.

"Can I help you, sir?"

Nelson held up his empty glass to the waiter. "Hit me again. In fact, bring me two."

"Yes, sir."

Nelson waited until the waiter moved away before he looked at Luke. "I'm trying to picture you as a dad." He shook his head. "Wow."

"Pretty much my reaction too. I guess I should have been less concerned about being a husband and more about being a father." It was two weeks since Charlotte told him, and he was still having a hard time saying it, let alone believing it.

"Okay, this isn't as bad as I thought it was. I knew there was something going on, and I kept thinking I had done something wrong, that you and I...." Nelson gestured back and forth between them with his hand. "You know, having second thoughts about us."

"I questioned my feelings for you when we were younger because I didn't understand them. But I can assure you, as an adult, I have never doubted them." Unable to hold Nelson's gaze, Luke looked down at the beer bottle in his hand. "It makes it all the harder."

The waiter returned with Nelson's drinks and set them on the table. "Would you care for another beer, sir?"

Luke shook his head without looking up.

Once again Nelson waited until the waiter moved away before speaking. "Makes what all the harder?"

"Breaking my promise to you," Luke mumbled, barely able to say the words.

"Your promise? You never promised you wouldn't be a father," Nelson pointed out.

Luke took a deep breath and blew it out slowly, then took another as he tried to muster up the courage to meet Nelson's gaze. It took several more seconds before he could do it. "I'm getting married."

"Oh."

The devastation on Nelson's face was painfully evident. It didn't matter there was no commitment, no spoken relationship beyond friendship between the two of them. They had been working on building something more, and just like that, Luke pulled the rug from beneath Nelson. It wasn't only Nelson who was feeling its effects. Luke's fucking chest hurt, and it felt wrong. Hell, it was wrong, but there was nothing he could do to change it.

"I...." Luke's voice cracked. He swallowed down the lump of emotion that had welled up in his throat. "The last thing I want to do is hurt you."

"Then why are you?" Nelson demanded. "I thought there was something growing between us. Something real, something...." He shook his head and looked away.

"There is something real between us. Something I wish we could explore and see where it would go."

"Then why are you marrying her if you want a relationship with me?"

"I have to," Luke said sadly.

"You don't have to do anything you don't want to. Do you love her?"

"She's a good person."

"That's not what I asked," Nelson snapped. "I asked if you loved her?"

"No," Luke admitted. "But I care about her a lot."

"Then why are you marrying her?"

"I know this is hard. I have barely slept or eaten in two weeks trying to figure out what to do. It only got worse once I made my decision because it made me sick to my stomach when I thought about telling you."

"Is everything okay here?"

Luke looked away from Nelson toward the hostess, then around the room to see several people staring at them. Only then did he realize how loud they must have been. "Yes, we're fine."

"Speak for yourself," Nelson grumbled. He pushed out of his chair and threw some money on the table. "Could you please cancel my order? I'm no longer hungry."

Before Luke could stop him, Nelson was heading for the door. Luke pulled two one-hundred-dollar bills from his wallet and handed them to the hostess. "This should cover anything we ordered." He hurried to catch up with Nelson.

Chapter Thirteen

I'M GETTING married. The weight of the words crushed down on Nelson like a ton of bricks, constricting his lungs and leaving him trembling. It took every bit of his willpower to keep his feet moving and to hold back the tears that threatened. He knew something was going on and worried Luke would end their relationship. Hearing those three little words dashed any hope he'd had that Luke wouldn't.

"Nelson! Wait up."

Nelson kept walking even though he had no idea where he was or where he was going. He didn't dare stop, didn't dare turn around for fear the tentative hold he had on his emotions would be ripped away. He wasn't going to cry, dammit. He wasn't!

"C'mon, Nelson, wait."

Luke's voice grew closer, but Nelson didn't stop, didn't turn around. One foot in front of the other. He rounded the corner, and a hand landed on his shoulder. He shrugged it off.

"Dammit, Nelson. Just get in the car so we can talk about this."

"There is nothing to talk about. You're getting married," Nelson spat.

"Oh, so because I'm getting married, we can no longer be friends?"

The statement was enough that the anger burned away the sadness, and he spun around. "Friends! Friends! Is that what you thought I was when I had my dick up your ass?" Nelson asked. He didn't care who heard him.

"Yes, I did," Luke countered. "I mean, was I hoping for more, that our relationship would grow into a lifelong commitment? You're damn right I did. But fucking life happens, Nelson. I'm not going to apologize for trying to do the right thing for my child."

"And that means being in a loveless marriage?" Nelson pushed out his chest and stepped close to Luke. He glared at him. "Way to teach your kid a lesson in settling for less than it all."

Luke didn't back down, towering over Nelson and returning the angry gaze. "It's a better lesson than teaching them that it's okay to run from their responsibilities. That it's okay to be a weekend parent!"

"Why do you have to be a weekend parent? You could fight for custody!" Nelson's voice rose with each word until he was screaming.

"You know damn good and well dads don't have any rights when it comes to raising a child on their own. If the mom is alive, the judge sides with them every time."

"Because you've tried, right?" Goddammit, this was not how he wanted to spend his limited time with Luke. Screaming and bickering in public. But he couldn't help it. He had either to lash out or cry. Anger seemed a whole lot easier to deal with at the moment.

"For what, Nelson? Fight to take my child away from his or her mother and choose someone who is too fucking afraid to tell anyone he's gay? Is that what you want me to do? Is that my choice?" Luke roared. "A loveless marriage or a closeted coward?"

Nelson narrowed his eyes, his breathing as fast as his racing heart. He curled his hands into fists to keep from punching Luke in his damn jaw. An angry tear escaped. He'd be damned if he'd stand here and cry in front of Luke, no matter whether the tears were filled with anger or sorrow. "I'm done." Nelson spun on his heels and stomped away, barreling into someone standing in his way.

"Watch it, you little pansy faggot."

Nelson stopped dead in his tracks. "What did you just call me?"

The stranger, a middle-aged man with a comb-over and a disgusted expression on his plump face, took a step toward Nelson. "You heard me. Why don't you take your nasty faggot lovers' quarrel someplace else?"

Before Nelson could react, the stranger shoved Nelson, sending him stumbling back. He hit the brick wall with such force he bit his tongue, but he didn't feel any pain, only pure hot rage. "Motherfucker!" He lunged at the bastard.

Instead of getting his hands around the man's neck like he wanted to, Nelson hit another wall, this one made of muscle. Nelson tried to scramble around Luke, but Luke grabbed him, keeping Nelson behind him.

"Sir, if you know what's good for you, you'll move on down the road before I release my friend here. He's not as patient and polite as I am." Luke's words might have been polite, but the deathly serious tone of his voice even had Nelson hesitating for a split second.

Nelson caught up quick enough. "I don't need you to fight my battles." He tried to pull free, but Luke held fast. "Goddammit, let me go!"

The stranger apparently reasoned he had better do as Luke had instructed because he scurried down the sidewalk like the little cockroach he was.

Nelson finally freed himself from Luke. "I told you I don't need you to fight my battles," he spat.

"I wasn't fighting your battles. I was keeping your feisty little ass from going to jail."

"It would have been worth it! I'll be damned if I'm going to let anyone talk to me that way."

Luke grabbed Nelson's arms, holding tight. Nelson glared up at him. "It's not worth it. I know words can hurt, but if you retaliate, you're stooping to his level. You'll end up with a record and probably paying that prick for the rest of your life after he sues you. In the end he'll have won. Is that really what you want?"

Nelson held on to his rage, just fucking vibrating. He wanted to chase the guy down and teach him some manners—with a fist—but somehow Luke's logic penetrated Nelson's anger. Or maybe it was the threat of not only becoming a felon, but a broke felon, that stopped him. He needed an outlet, and since he couldn't spew his ire at the stranger, he turned it on Luke. "I hate you."

"Aww, little man, you don't hate me."

"Yes, I do, and stop calling me that!" And damn if those tears of rage didn't start to fall again. He angrily wiped at them, huffing and puffing and shaking and so damn ready to shatter.

Luke, apparently oblivious to Nelson's rage, let out a heavy sigh and wrapped his arms around Nelson. "I'm so sorry," he whispered. "You've gotta believe me, Nelson. I didn't want this."

Nelson remained rigid. He heard the sincerity in Luke's voice, but the anger refused to dissipate. It wasn't fair. So long he had dreamed of finding Luke again, hoping, and finally had those prayers answered, only to see them snatched away. It was a cruel joke.

"Please believe me. If I could change it for you, I would, but I can't."

Tired in his head. Tired in his heart. So damn tired his anger seeped from him, leaving him exhausted and numb. "I know."

And he did. Now that he didn't have the rage fueling his reactions, reason was beginning to return. It still sucked big-time, but part of him understood what Luke was doing. Luke was always a stand-up kind of guy, always tried to do the right thing. It was one of the attributes of his character that Nelson loved the most.

"C'mon, let me take you back to your hotel room."

Nelson nodded, the fight in him gone, and allowed Luke to lead him to his car.

LUKE HAD begged Nelson to let him drive him back to his hotel room, but now that he was standing inside, alone with Nelson, Luke wasn't sure why he insisted on being here. The devastated look on Nelson's face, and knowing there was nothing he could say to make it better, rendered him speechless.

He'd broken a promise and Nelson's heart. How the hell was he supposed to make up for that? He couldn't. Luke knew he should leave, walk away, and give Nelson time to process it all. But Luke couldn't. Maybe he was a selfish bastard, but he couldn't help but think if he did walk, he might never see Nelson again. He couldn't let that happen.

"I'm…. Do… I…?" Luke huffed a frustrated breath and slumped down in a chair. "Tell me what I can do or say to make this better."

Nelson stood next to the window, looking out, his arms across his chest. "Nothing you can do."

"But I want to try. I want you in my life. I know that's probably selfish as hell, but I want us to continue to be friends." God. Just saying that felt wrong. Luke hung his head in his hands. His chest constricted as if there were a vise squeezing his heart. "I have no right to ask that of you."

"No, you don't," Nelson replied curtly. He let out a heavy sigh. "But I get it. I do." Luke heard Nelson moving across the room. Luke tilted his head, his cheek resting in his palm, and watched as Nelson sat in the only other chair in the room. He still looked sad, but there was resolve in his eyes. "You're going to be a great dad."

"I don't want to be a dad," Luke whispered. "I'm not ready."

"Well, you should have thought about that before you had unprotected sex," Nelson pointed out. He didn't sound accusatory but matter-of-fact.

Luke snapped his head up. "I didn't. I swear! Charlotte was on the pill, but from what she told me, when she'd had to take an antibiotic for bronchitis, it rendered her pill ineffective."

"Or she simply didn't take them."

Luke shook his head. "I'm not trying to make excuses, Nelson. I swear it. But she was pretty devastated when she found out. She's still upset and scared. She's a dancer and had dreams of joining an international troupe. I don't think she did this on purpose."

"Didn't you say she had been talking marriage?"

"Yeah, she wanted to get married. Problem was she loved me more than I did her. Don't get me wrong, I care about her; she's a great friend. But kids?" Luke ran his hands through his hair. "No, neither of us wanted this, but it's going to happen. I have to do what I think is right even if that means hurting you and me."

"I'm hungry."

Luke blinked at Nelson. He had thought Nelson would have a lot to say on the subject, but thinking about food wasn't on the list. "Umm... okay. Do you want me to take you back out?"

Nelson pushed to his feet and walked over to the bed. He picked up the phone. "I'm going to order room service. Do you want anything?"

The way Luke's gut was churning, he wasn't sure he could eat, but he'd at least have something to concentrate on when they talked, rather than having to look at the hurt in Nelson's eyes. "Sure. Cheeseburger and fries. Oh, and a Coke."

Nelson put in their order. After setting the phone back on the cradle, he flittered from one thing in the room to another, ignoring Luke. Luke wanted to ask what was going on in Nelson's head, but the thoughtful expression on Nelson's face silenced Luke. Nelson no doubt needed some time to process what was going on. He was curious to know how Nelson would deal, considering Luke had had a couple weeks to think about what was going on and what his future would hold.

On one hand, the thought of a little human being he'd helped create was pretty awesome. However, beyond that, everything else about it scared him shitless. He was resolved in his decision, knew in his heart, his very soul, he was making the right decision for the child. He also knew that decision had been made at the sacrifice of his and Nelson's happiness together.

"You want something to drink? There's only water or coffee. They don't have a mini bar in the room."

"No, thank you. I'll wait for my Coke."

"Oh right, we ordered food," Nelson said with a nod. It spoke volumes to how distracted Nelson was.

"Are we going to talk about this?"

"Not until I've had some food. I don't think I can handle this on an empty stomach. Besides, I need it to absorb some of the alcohol. This is serious shit we have to talk about."

"Yes, it is."

Luke felt somewhat better that Nelson did plan on talking to him. He'd been afraid Nelson would kick his ass to the curb and never speak to him again. At some level he believed there was a very real possibility Nelson still might. Luke would need to tread lightly and not push Nelson too hard.

For twenty minutes the tension in the room increased. Nelson continued to flitter around, fidgeting and looking generally uncomfortable. For the first time in their lives, they couldn't seem to find that easy way they'd always had with each other. While tension had surfaced briefly the minute they met again in that airport, then it was as if they'd never been apart. Now it all seemed to be gone, and that hurt Luke's heart even more than losing Nelson as a lover.

Luke jerked when he heard a sharp rap on the door. Nelson obviously was startled too since he nearly tripped midpace. "I got it." He rushed to the door and slung it open, startling the poor guy with the food cart.

"Good evening, sir."

Nelson stepped back to allow the man entrance, tipped him, and thanked him. Nelson then began rearranging the furniture to allow the cart to sit between the two chairs, all the while never looking at Luke or speaking. Luke wet his dry mouth with a swig of Coke, then lifted the silver dome from his plate. His gut roiled at the thought of food, even though it smelled delicious and he hadn't eaten since the day before. Nelson had ordered grilled chicken and apparently wasn't having the same difficulties as Luke since he was digging in and eating heartily.

"So, have you thought about what you're going to name your kid?" Nelson asked around a big bite of food.

The question caught Luke off guard once again. "No, I'm still trying to wrap my mind around the fact that I'm going to have a kid."

"I've always liked the name Freddie."

"Umm... no."

"How about Jason?"

"Nelson! I'm not naming my kid after a psycho movie character. Jesus, it will be scarred for life." Luke chuckled.

"So Carrie is out too?"

"Yes!"

Nelson shrugged and stuffed another large bite in his mouth. Luke picked up a fry and munched on it while he tried to figure out why Nelson was suddenly joking about a very not-so-humorous situation.

"Are you going to have a big wedding?"

"We're not having a wedding. Going to the justice of the peace, and our parents will be witnesses."

"That's probably a good idea. It takes months to plan a proper wedding. Since you're wanting to tie the knot before the oven timer goes off on the bun, I don't see anything wrong with going to the justice of the peace. The outcome is the same, and it saves a ton of money. Which in your case is a really good thing. It's expensive raising kids. Trust me, I know this because my dad used to remind me all the time."

Nelson continued to chatter away about the expense of kids, but Luke really wasn't listening. Hearing Nelson talk about such things instead of what Luke viewed as the bigger picture—them—was maddening.

When he could stand it no longer, he asked, "What are you doing?"

Nelson stopped with his fork halfway to his mouth, looked at it, then at Luke. "It's called eating."

"You know exactly what I mean. You're rambling on about my kid and marriage and avoiding what the hell you really want to say."

Nelson tilted his head. "And just what is it you think I should be talking about?"

"Us."

"What about us? You want me to beg you not to marry her? Start praying again and asking God to fix your mistake? You seem to know what it is you're looking for, so you tell me what you want me to talk about. Better yet, you just start the fucking conversation, and I'll join in."

"There's that fire," Luke pointed out.

Nelson glared at him. "Fuck you, Luke. I'm teetering on the edge of crying like a fucking baby or diving headfirst into rage and punching you in the face. I don't suggest you tip me in either direction. Not right now." He pointed his fork at Luke. "Now eat your fucking dinner and tell me about the financial portfolio you plan on putting together for this kid."

"Before I do, can I at least ask if we're going to stay friends?"

Nelson stared at him for a moment, then tapped his finger against his chin like he had to think about the answer. Luke held his breath. He was a selfish bastard, that had already been established, but dammit, he didn't want to lose Nelson.

After what seemed like forever, Nelson finally gave Luke a small smile. "Only if you eat all your dinner."

Chapter Fourteen

ALONE IN bed in his dark hotel room, Nelson finally gave in to his heartbreak and let the tears fall freely. He'd lost Luke, and it wasn't fair. He cried for the injustice, for what could have been, should have been. Luke had convinced him it was fate that brought them both to the airport at the same time, fate that had them traveling to the same destination, and fate that they were both single.

"Well, fuck you, fate!"

If there truly was a thing as fate and destiny, then they were cruel bitches. How could they bring him and Luke back together, only to rip them apart? It was beyond unfair; it was downright wrong.

Now just like the promises they made to each other at thirteen, it would be made with good intentions. The difference was Nelson was no longer a child. He knew how the world worked. He wished he still viewed it through the innocent eyes of youth, then maybe the stricture around his heart would ease and he'd be able to take a full breath. Maybe he wouldn't be lying in the dark, soaking his pillow with his tears. But he wasn't naive. He was a grown man, and no matter how much he wished otherwise, he knew he would lose Luke.

Luke was about to become a husband and a father; both roles would demand much of his time and effort. If that wasn't enough to keep Nelson and Luke apart, there was also family, jobs, and nearly an entire continent between them.

Regular phone calls would become fewer and fewer, as would the occasional trips, until they stopped all together. And those were the easy things that would keep them apart. The larger issue was Nelson was and always had been in love with Luke. How the hell was he going to keep it together seeing Luke and Charlotte together, knowing she had what Nelson wanted? That she was sharing her life and her bed with Luke. Knowing Luke came home to her each day. There was little solace in it being a loveless marriage. Luke admitted he and Charlotte were friends.

He cared for and respected her, even admired her. To Nelson it sounded like the perfect foundation to build a strong marriage.

Nelson rolled onto his side and hugged his pillow. He needed sleep. He had an early appointment with his client, then had agreed to meet Luke afterward. He was having a hard enough time dealing with everything. It would be even harder without sleep. However, each time Nelson closed his eyes, he'd see Luke's face, and images of him and Luke together would pop into his head and remind him once again of what he was losing.

Nelson opened his eyes and stared off into the darkness, wishing like hell he could find the off switch to his brain. He spent the entire evening searching but never found it. At 5:00 a.m., he gave up, sat up in bed, reached for the phone, and called the one person he knew would listen.

"Hello, Mom."

"What's wrong?"

"Can't a guy call his mom to say hello?"

"Of course he can, but you're not just any guy, you're my son, and I know when something is wrong. So spill it," she demanded.

"I don't really want to talk about it. I'd rather you tell me how you and Dad are doing." Dammit, why did she have to know him so well? He wanted a distraction, didn't want to think about the pain in his heart. He didn't want to talk about life without Luke. Hell, he didn't want to talk about his problems at all. He wanted to be in his mom's kitchen, mixing and measuring and sharing silly stories and laughter.

"I'm good. Your dad is getting stronger every day and is starting to drive me nuts."

"That's a good sign."

"Yes, it is," Mom agreed. "So now how can we make you good?"

"I am, really."

"Don't lie to your mother. What happened?"

Mom apparently wasn't going to let it drop. He'd made a mistake calling her when he was so upset. He knew there was no point arguing, and he wasn't crazy enough to hang up. "I was just having one of my pity parties and wishing you and I were baking."

"It would be nice if you were here, but even though you're not, I'm going to ask you the question I'd ask if you were standing in front of me. What happened today to get you down?"

"Luke's going to be a daddy, and he's getting married," Nelson blurted.

There was a slight pause before Mom said, "He's a little young, but from what you told me, he's financially secure. I would think you'd be happy for him. Do you not like his girlfriend?"

"I don't know her, but I'm sure she's a great girl. Luke's a great guy. He'll be a great dad and husband."

"But?" Mom hedged.

"But what?"

"You say one thing, but the emotions don't match the words. I can hear the sadness in your voice. Are you afraid you're going to lose him again?"

"Yes."

"And this is different than when you were thirteen?"

A tear rolled down Nelson's cheek. "Yes."

"Because you can no longer brush it off as a childhood crush?"

Nelson started to protest, but Luke's accusation came rushing back: *Choose someone who is too fucking afraid to tell anyone he's gay?* It was on the tip of his tongue to tell his mom, but he couldn't. It wasn't the kind of thing someone told their mom over the phone. So instead of answering her question, or worse, lying, he said, "You know what, I'm being silly. I'm overly tired. I'm sure things will be back to normal after I've had some sleep."

"Will you stop loving him after you've had some sleep?"

Nelson paused, teetering on the edge. Before he could figure out what to say, his mom continued.

"You know, son, I've always believed there was much more going on between you and Luke when you were younger. In the years that followed, I've been even more convinced. I've never heard you talk about a girl like you did Luke. I had a feeling you might be gay but never asked you about it. I figured you would tell me when the time was right."

Nelson closed his eyes and blew out a steadying breath. "I didn't want you to find out like this," he whispered.

"I'm hurt that you couldn't tell me this before, but you do know I'll love you no matter what, right?"

"Yes."

"And your dad will too," she assured him.

Nelson's eyes flew open. "You can't tell him."

"I won't, but you will. It may take him a while for it to sink in, but he loves you. He has a right to know, and more importantly, he needs to know you trust him."

"I will, but I don't want to do it over the phone. Jesus, I didn't want to tell *you* over the phone. That's not why I called."

"No, you called to tell me your best friend, the man you love, is getting married, and you're heartbroken. You called because you knew your mom is always there to lend a shoulder to cry on."

Nelson didn't even try to hold back the tears any longer. They flowed freely onto his mother's strong shoulder.

THE EVENING hadn't gone as Luke had planned, which really wasn't a huge surprise. He was an idiot to think it would go any other way than ending on a sad note. After Nelson feigned a headache and asked Luke to leave, Luke spent the entire evening walking along the beach. He teetered between rushing back to Nelson, snatching him up, and running away with him, to despair over not being able to do so. He found himself still wandering the shore aimlessly when the sun began to crest the horizon.

Luke climbed to the top of a mound of sand and sat. A front-row seat to watch the sunrise. He bent his legs and wrapped his arms around them, his chin resting on his knees. The soothing sound of the gulls and rolling waves should have been relaxing, yet he was rigid, muscles tense. He should have been exhausted by not having slept in nearly twenty-four hours, but sleep was the last thing on his mind. He was too consumed with Nelson and the sadness he'd witnessed in his eyes to focus on anything else.

"How the fuck did I get myself into this?" he grumbled. Of course, the empty beach didn't respond.

His dad was over the moon he and Charlotte were getting married, his mom bursting with giddiness she was going to be a grandma, as was Charlotte's mom. However, they seemed to be the only ones excited about it. Even Charlotte herself had reservations about the marriage, and she was less than thrilled about becoming a mom at this point in her life. Still, they were resolved to make the best of the situation and were committed to what was best for the child.

"My child." Luke sighed heavily.

Finally, when the sun had fully risen, Luke pushed to his feet and strolled back to his car. He had a few errands to run before he could go home and shower. Hopefully it would be enough to keep his mind off Nelson until seeing him later. Luke knew the futility of the wish but still hoped.

Two hours later he stepped through his front door, dropped the keys on the table as well as the marriage application he picked up from the county clerk's office. Any other day this would have caused his nerves to zing, having to pick up the paperwork to tie the knot, but today, it just felt so wrong.

He showered, shaved, and dressed robotically. The rest of the day trudged on in a haze until Luke found himself outside Nelson's hotel door. It was crazy. He was excited to see Nelson and yet dreading it with every ounce of his being. He'd fight to make sure it didn't happen, yet the feeling lingered that this would be the last time he and Nelson would be together. Blowing out a heavy breath and plastering a fake smile on his face, Luke reached out and knocked.

It took several tense moments of Luke wondering if Nelson would open the door and let him in. The profound relief he felt when Nelson did in fact answer the door was a testament to just how messed up Luke's emotions were.

"Hi, c'mon in," Nelson said. He stepped out of the way to allow Luke to enter.

At first glance Luke wondered if Nelson was having as difficult a time as he was by the wide grin on Nelson's face. Then Luke spotted the dark circles beneath Nelson's eyes and knew that wasn't the case. Nelson could fake the smile, but the eyes didn't lie.

"How are you?" Luke asked, trying to keep the conversation light, then realized too late what a stupid question it was.

"I'm fine," he said. The lie was in how strange Nelson's voice sounded. It was strained, sad. A little too quiet. Nothing followed except tense silence, and he was avoiding eye contact. "The day went well, and I'm all packed for the airport."

The dread Luke had been feeling for days exploded. It cut off his breath, his chest squeezing his heart painfully. His heart was pounding, and he had to lock down his knees to keep the shaking from causing him to land on his ass. "You're leaving today? I thought...."

"I know, but the installation went smoothly, and my boss needs me in Houston ASAP."

Breathe.

Luke choked down the lump of panic constricting his throat. "I hoped we'd have more time." Dammit, he needed more time with Nelson. Needed to talk to him. To make this right. "Is there any way to postpone it at least for another day?"

"No," Nelson whispered, the sadness in his voice apparent.

Luke looked around the room, the bed made and Nelson's duffel bag next to the door. So that was it. Nelson was leaving. In that moment of absolute despair, Luke was in pain like he'd never experienced. The only thing keeping him from completely losing it was his unwavering conviction he would not lose Nelson. "How much time do we have?"

Nelson glanced down at his watch. "About an hour."

"Jesus."

"Does it really matter?" Nelson asked. He sat in one of the leather chairs.

"Yeah, it matters," Luke insisted. He took the other chair across from Nelson and laid his hand on Nelson's forearm. "You just got here. I want to spend time with you."

Nelson looked down at Luke's hand, hesitated for a moment, then pulled his arm free. "I think it's for the best that I go." He looked up and met Luke's gaze. "I'm not really doing that good right now."

"I know, and it's my fault. I want to make this right."

"I just need time."

Luke clasped his hands and laid them in his lap to help fight the urge to reach across the table again. It hurt his heart, his very fucking soul, that Nelson couldn't seem to stand Luke's touch. "You know, I didn't mean it when I called you a coward. I was angry and frustrated, but that's no excuse. I'm sorry. I shouldn't have said that."

"It's true. I am afraid to tell people I'm gay, so why apologize?" Nelson countered.

"Because it had nothing to do with the decisions I've made. It's not about you or me, but about my child. I need you to know that."

Nelson ran his hands along the side of his head, clasping them behind his head. "I'm not an idiot, Luke. I get it. I even understand it and think you're doing the right thing. Does that make it easier? No, but I'm trying to deal. I need some time to change gears and adjust to our new reality."

Luke's first reaction was to argue his point, to scream or hit or cry or something. Anything but give up. However, it would serve no purpose. Nelson needed time, and Luke would only make things worse if he tried to push Nelson before he was ready to talk. "Will you make me a promise?" Nelson arched a brow. "I know, we don't have a stellar record keeping them, but this one is an easy one."

Nelson looked skeptical but said, "I'm listening."

"After you've worked through it all, talk to me. Don't just hide and never speak to me again. If you decide you don't want to be friends, that you never want to see me again, I need to know. Can you do that?"

"Yes."

Nelson didn't hesitate in his response, and Luke had to hope that meant he would do as asked rather than saying it to get Luke to shut up. It bothered Luke that he wasn't sure which one it was, but he had no other choice than to accept Nelson's affirmation. "Thank you. Now that's settled, can I buy you dinner before you leave?"

Nelson shook his head. "I'll have a liquid diet when I get to the airport. Makes traveling easier."

Luke swallowed down his sigh. "Can I at least give you a ride?"

Again Nelson shook his head. "My company already arranged a car for me." He glanced down at his watch. "In fact, they should be here any time."

"I—" Luke snapped his mouth shut before he could insist. He had no right to demand anything from Nelson. No right at all. Luke hung his head. "Were you even going to say goodbye?" he whispered.

"I asked you to come, didn't I?"

"I don't know. I'm not sure of anything anymore," he admitted. He remembered talking to Nelson, remembered the urgency in seeing Nelson, but couldn't remember if Nelson had asked him to come or if he'd forced himself on Nelson. Luke had only known he had to see him.

But then it didn't matter because the phone rang, and Luke heard him say, "Thank you, I'll be right down," and the stricture that had been around Luke's heart all day tightened to a nearly unbearable degree. Nothing but loss and pain registered; he was gripped by it so completely the room around him darkened and went silent.

The only thing that was able to penetrate Luke's misery was a warm hand on his shoulder and Nelson's sad voice. "I have to go."

Before Nelson could slip away, Luke jumped to his feet and pulled Nelson into a tight embrace. He buried his head in Nelson's neck, the tears refusing to be held back a second longer. "I love you," he mouthed. He didn't dare say it out loud, he couldn't. It would only make what he was doing to Nelson all the more cruel.

Luke clung to Nelson like a lifeline. He knew the minute Nelson walked out the door, he'd be taking Luke's heart with him, and he had no idea how the hell he was supposed to live without one, only knew he had to.

"I have to go," Nelson repeated. But he was holding Luke just as tightly.

It was several long moments before Luke could get himself under control enough to let him go. He placed a soft kiss below Nelson's ear, then released him, turning quickly to hide his wet cheeks. "Have a safe trip."

There was a brief silence, and Luke held his breath, holding back the sob that threatened. When he was sure he wouldn't be able to stay on his feet a second longer, he heard the door open. "I'll call you."

As the door closed, Luke let out a breath, and with it a sob that came from his very soul. With no longer any reason to stay strong, he fell to his knees and gave in to his grief.

Chapter Fifteen

ALTHOUGH HE'D been expecting it, the shrill ring of his phone caused Nelson to jump, and he dropped his bottle of beer. "Fuck," he grumbled. He snatched up the bottle and raced to grab a rag. "I'm coming, hold on." He dropped the fizzing mess into the sink and the rag on the one on the floor, and then picked up the phone. "Hello."

"Hi, son, it's Dad."

Nelson's breath hitched. He'd been expecting his mom to call, but to hear his dad's voice caused panic to skitter down his spine. Mom had assured him she wouldn't say anything to Dad, but she'd gone back on her word, if Dad was calling. He rarely ever called.

"Hi, Dad," Nelson responded warily. "How are you feeling?"

"I'm as healthy as a horse, but I hear you're not doing as well. What's going on?"

"Huh? I'm not sick," Nelson insisted. Heartbroken? Yes. An emotional mess? Yes, but not physically sick. That would just be the nail in his coffin.

"Oh, then what's going on? Your mom said she was worried about you. Is it work? Do you need money?"

It was on the tip of his tongue to tell his dad, but between the bombshell Luke had dropped on him and the one he'd dropped on Mom, he was at his limit of the emotional turmoil he could handle for the week. Hell, he'd had enough to last a fucking year. "No, Dad, I don't need any money, but thanks for asking. I've been traveling a lot and I'm just worn out." It wasn't a complete lie. He was exhausted. "Hey, and since when do you call? You usually make Mom do it, then yell from the other room to ask questions or to tell me something."

"I hate talking on the phone. Seems like that's all I do at work anymore. Usually it's someone yelling at me, or I'm yelling at them."

"I know, so why the call?"

"I'm worried about you," Dad admitted.

"Wow, is someone becoming an old softie in his old age?" Nelson teased.

"I'm far from old and even farther from soft. But I admit this last scare had me realizing I'm but a mortal man."

His dad had always been a bit gruff and a man of few words. However, Nelson always knew there was a softer side to him. He'd seen it in the way he'd look at Mom, the way he touched her, and the way he was utterly devoted to his wife and son. But for Dad to admit a weakness spoke volumes of how his heart issues had affected him.

"You're much more than mortal," Nelson finally said.

"Yes, well. So everything is really okay?"

"It will be once I get caught up on some sleep." At least that was Nelson's hope. Everything was harder to deal with when tired. He grabbed another beer from the fridge, popped the top, and slumped down on the couch.

"Little early for alcohol, isn't it?"

Instinctively Nelson scanned the area. "How in the heck do you know what I'm drinking?"

"I'm a cop. One of the requirements is a gift of observation," his dad pointed out. "Above that, the sound of a beer bottle being opened is pretty distinctive."

"And with that I am reminded why I was never able to get away with anything as a kid." Nelson tipped up his bottle and took a long pull.

"So, are you going to tell me what has your mom so worried and baking up a storm? Mind you, normally her being in the kitchen wouldn't bother me, but she keeps making things I like and giving them away. It's torture, son."

"It's no one thing, Dad, honestly. I was complaining to Mom about how much the traveling sucks, that I hate this apartment, and may have mentioned the lack of friends or family here. I shouldn't have whined, but you know when I'm tired, I get cranky and start feeling sorry for myself." Not one word of it was a lie. Nelson had complained to his mom about all of it, and he did tend to enjoy a good pity party from time to time.

"Move home," Dad said curtly.

"Excuse me?"

"Move home."

Nelson froze with his beer halfway to his mouth. "And do what? Live with you and work at the Save-a-Lot? Mow lawns?"

"Whatever you want, Nelson, as long as it makes you happy."

"Who are you and what have you done with my dad?"

Dad made one of his signature long-suffering sighs. "I'm serious, son. If you're so miserable that you're drinking before noon and not sleeping, then you need to make some changes."

Nelson sipped on his beer while considering what his dad had said. Neither Mom nor Dad wanted him to move to Minneapolis. It was his idea, partially based on wanting to spread his wings and be independent, but it was also a bit of guilt. Mom and Dad had sacrificed to put Nelson through college. They were the only reason he wasn't strapped to a huge debt. He figured the very least he could do for them was get a job and start paying his own way. When he was unable to find a job back home, he expanded the search and jumped at the first offer. He'd regretted his hasty decision ever since.

"Nelson? You still there?" Dad asked, pulling Nelson from his musings.

"Yeah, I'm here. I was just thinking about what you said."

"And?"

"And I'll give it some thought."

"Good. I better get off here. Your mom is standing in the doorway about to burst for wanting to talk to you."

"Okay. Thanks for the talk."

"I hope you really will think about it and you're not saying that only to pacify me."

"Of course he is," Mom said, her voice close to the phone. "Now give me that."

"Pushy woman," Dad grumbled. Nelson could hear the fondness in his dad's voice, and apparently he'd given in to her demand because when he said, "—and don't you be trying to influence him one way or the other—" it was from a distance.

"You really should come home."

"Mom! I can't believe you told him," Nelson shouted rather than respond to her statement. "You promised you wouldn't say anything."

"Young man, I suggest you lower your voice," she chastised. "I did no such thing."

"Then why is he calling me?" Nelson asked with skepticism. Why else would his dad call?

"Did he ask you about your sexuality?" Mom countered.

"No, but…"

"Then that's not why he was calling you. Your dad had a hell of a scare. He's been much more aware of his mortality and wondering about the legacy he leaves behind."

"But—"

"Do you really want to talk about this right now? He'll be back any minute, and I won't lie to him again when he asks me what we're talking about."

Nelson downed the rest of his beer. He tucked the phone between his ear and shoulder and picked at the label on the empty bottle. "He asked me to move home."

"Yes, I was aware that he was going to. How do you feel about it?"

"My first instinct is to tell my boss I quit, leave my crap behind, and start driving. But I don't know how much that has to do with it being the right choice for me, or if I'm allowing my heartbreak to influence me."

"I'm sure it has a bit to do with both," Mom said gently. "You've been there for months and haven't said one positive thing about it. You hate your job. You have no friends or family there, and right now, you need them."

Nelson blew out a heavy breath. She was right, of course. She always was. Still, things were happening too fast, and he needed time to think about what the move would mean. What he'd do once he moved back home and had time to resolve his issues of feeling like a failure both in being on his own and his love life. He just needed time and another beer.

He pushed to his feet and headed to the fridge. "I'm going to sleep on it."

"Good idea. I know you'll make the right decision."

"Thanks, Mom." He sure wished he had her confidence.

"And Nelson?"

"Yeah?"

"I love you."

"I love you too. Talk to you tomorrow."

Nelson hung up the phone and returned to the couch with his beer. He popped the top and took a long pull. He had no clue what was the right thing to do, but part of him already knew he'd be moving home, pride, independence, and Minneapolis be damned.

Chapter Sixteen

DRESSED IN a simple but elegant white dress, blonde hair curled and cascading down her slim back, Charlotte was the vision of beauty. However, it was the uncertainty in her pale blue eyes that spoke the loudest to Luke. He knew the feeling all too well. The justice of the peace was reading from her small book, their parents standing next to them with smiles on their faces, his soon-to-be wife and mother of his child at his side, yet Luke's thoughts and heart were halfway across the country. He wished he could feel better about his decision, wished he could put thoughts of Nelson out of his head at least long enough to make it through his wedding vows, but no matter how he tried, he couldn't. This wasn't what he was supposed to be doing today. He shouldn't be setting out on a journey with Charlotte. He shouldn't be an expectant dad, and he sure as hell shouldn't be this far away from Nelson.

Yet he was, and all the praying and wishing wouldn't change it.

Luke locked down his trembling legs, fought the urge to run, and said, "I do."

"By the power bestowed upon me by the state of California, I now pronounce you husband and wife."

Luke's stomach knotted painfully, and his chest tightened while he tried to remember how to breathe.

"You may kiss the bride."

Luke plastered a small smile on his face and pressed his lips to Charlotte's.

His dad patted Luke's back; his mom beamed. Charlotte's mom was crying as she hugged her. Even her dad looked pleased. Sadly neither Luke nor Charlotte were as happy as their families. Charlotte hated the fact Luke was only marrying her because of the child. Not that she was any happier about the fact there was a child. But it was what it was, and the only thing they could do was try to make the best of a bad situation.

"Are we all riding together or separately?" his mom asked.

"We can all squeeze into the Cadillac," Charlotte's dad offered.

Luke took Charlotte's hand in his. "You guys go ahead. We'll follow you."

"Are you sure? It's really not a big deal. We can drive you back to your car after dinner," Charlotte's dad assured him.

Luke didn't have to protest again as Charlotte's mom piped up. "Let the lovebirds be alone for a moment." She leaned over and kissed her daughter's cheek. "See you at L'Étoile."

Luke could have kissed his new mother-in-law just then. The way he was sweating and his gut roiling, the thought of being jammed into the car with the rest of them made him nauseous. All he had to do was make it through their dinner "celebration," then he'd be free.

Like you'll ever really be free again.

Luke swallowed down the idea as it left a bitter taste in his mouth and a burning in his gut, but he was determined to make the best of it.

LUKE PEEKED in on Charlotte. She was lying on her side, hand tucked beneath her cheek, and appeared to be sleeping. He eased the bedroom door closed and walked quietly to his office. Once behind his closed door, he sat at the desk and picked up the phone. He didn't dial the familiar number right away, struggling with wanting to hear Nelson's voice and knowing it was selfish. What the hell was he supposed to say? *Hi, just got married and wanted to tell you all about it. How it made me feel sick so I can make you feel even worse for breaking your heart.*

Luke set the phone back on the cradle and leaned back in his chair. This was pure fucking torture. Several more times he picked up the receiver and set it down again. After playing the game for a few more minutes, Luke slammed the phone down and jumped to his feet. He needed to move, to pace, or run or scream or....

He needed to talk to Nelson, was what he needed.

"Goddammit," he growled. He plopped his ass back down in the chair, snatched up the phone, and stabbed the buttons angrily.

The phone rang several times, and Luke was about to hang up when he heard Nelson's sleepy voice. "Hello?"

"Hey, Nelson, it's Luke."

"Luke? Is everything okay?"

No. "Yeah, just wanted to chat."

"Dude, it's two o'clock. I was sleeping."

Only then did Luke glance at his watch and realize it was midnight and he'd forgotten about the time change. "I'm sorry. I didn't realize it was so late."

Nelson must have heard something in Luke's voice because he suddenly sounded much more awake. "What's wrong?"

"Nothing," he lied. "I hadn't talked to you in a few days and was thinking about you, is all." The second part was the truth. Hell, he'd done little else but think about Nelson, and he had a sneaking suspicion he always would. It was simply one of the sacrifices he'd have to learn to live with.

"Why don't I believe you?" Nelson asked.

"What? I was thinking about you," Luke insisted.

There was a long pause, and Luke was beginning to think Nelson had fallen back asleep, but then he heard a rustling sound and Nelson sigh. "Please tell me it wasn't today."

"What?" Luke asked in confusion.

"Did you get married today?"

Luke hesitated, wanted to say no, but couldn't form the word. He wasn't sure why. He'd been getting pretty good at lying to Nelson and to himself, but he found himself nodding and saying, "Yes."

"You shouldn't have called me. You should be with your wife."

"I—"

"You made your choice, now go lie with it," Nelson said, his tone snappish.

Before Luke could apologize or explain or say anything, the line went dead. Luke squeezed his eyes shut and ran his hand over his face. Dammit, he knew he shouldn't have called Nelson, knew it was selfish, but he guessed he didn't care about Nelson's feelings or anyone's but his own. Of all the things he wanted to share with Nelson, not once had Luke thought he'd be sharing his wedding day with him. He was truly and utterly fucked-up in the head.

Luke returned the phone to its cradle. He pulled open the desk drawer and pulled out a bottle of bourbon he'd hidden there. He didn't even bother with a glass, took a long pull straight from the bottle. He tried to concentrate on the burn the alcohol caused in his belly rather than the ache in his chest. His wedding night and he was sitting alone in his office, unable to make himself walk down the hall to his wife when all he wanted to do was hop on a plane and go to the one person who could ease the ache.

Life was so unfair. He took another big drink and then another. Maybe he could drink the ache away.

Chapter Seventeen

"PLEASE CALL me back. I really could use a friend right now."

Nelson stared at the answering machine, wavering between wanting to snub Luke once again and giving in to the pleading sound of Luke's voice. Nelson had endured this battle several times over the past few months. The audacity of Luke calling him on his wedding night had made it easy to ignore Luke's calls for the first month. However, it became increasingly difficult. The few times he'd given in and talked to Luke, the conversations were forced and awkward, mainly about the weather, jobs, entertainment. They never spoke of family, friends, or the future because, really? What was the point? There was no future for them, at least not one that included the two of them being together.

Nelson might understand why Luke had done what he had in marrying Charlotte, but he was still bitter about it. He was jealous as hell of Charlotte and pissed beyond all reason at Luke. Most days he couldn't control those feelings, and so it was best not to speak to Luke. If he were a smart man, he'd cut all ties with Luke, if for no other reason than his sanity. But as painful as it was to talk to Luke at times, the thought of never speaking to him again was pure agony.

The pleading in Luke's voice had Nelson picking up the receiver and dialing Luke's number. Nelson was officially a masochist, a total glutton for punishment.

"Hello?"

"Hey, Luke, it's Nelson." He was surprised how even his tone was considering he wanted to scream every time he heard Luke's voice.

"I was beginning to think you weren't going to call me back."

"I just got home. I've been a little busy."

"Doing what?"

Nelson's first thought was to tell Luke it was none of his business. He was in one of his moods and had been an idiot to call in the first place. *God! Why do I keep doing this to myself?* He swallowed down the sigh that threatened. "I've been packing. I'm moving home next week."

"Wow? Really?" Luke asked, sounding stunned. "When did you decide this?"

Nelson shrugged even though he knew Luke wouldn't see the gesture. "I've been considering it for a while. Dad put in a good word at the prison for me, and I got a position in their IT department."

"Are you going to live with your parents?"

"Yeah, for now." Nelson tucked the phone in the crook of his neck and washed his hands before heading to the fridge to see if there was anything edible within. Not finding anything but old bologna and a beer, he settled on the beer. He popped the top and took a healthy swig. "So what's up? You sounded a little sad when you left the message."

"Not really sad," Luke responded.

There was a long pause, and Nelson knew he wasn't going to like what he was about to hear. Knowing Luke always paused before dropping another bomb on him. Nelson downed the rest of the beer and braced himself.

"Charlotte had the baby this morning."

"What? I thought she wasn't due for another two months?"

"She wasn't. The baby is eight weeks premature, and they had to put her on a ventilator. She's so tiny. I'm scared, Nelson."

Nelson's heart went out to Luke. Being a father wasn't on Luke's bucket list, but he was, and Nelson could hear the fear in his tone. Guilt assaulted Nelson. How many times had he tried to wish the baby away, prayed something would happen so he and Luke could be together? He hadn't wanted to hurt the baby, just wished it hadn't happened. Now the tiny little thing was struggling to live, and Nelson prayed like hell she would be okay.

"I'm so sorry, Luke. What are the doctors saying about her condition?" *A little girl, wow.* She would have Luke wrapped around her finger, Nelson was sure of it.

"They said she has a good fighting chance. They put her on the ventilator because she was breathing fast, and they wanted her to rest. But I don't know, Nelson. I feel so fucking helpless. She's hooked up to all these tubes and machines. I can't hold her or do a damn thing to make this right."

"Hey, she's made of that good Rollinses stock. She'll be fine," Nelson assured him, although he really had no idea. Eight weeks early seemed like an awful lot, but what did he know about pregnancy and babies? Zilch.

"This is my fault," Luke whispered.

"How is Charlotte going into labor early your fault? Unless you pushed her down the stairs or something. You didn't, did you?"

Luke missed the teasing tone in Nelson's voice or chose to ignore it because he said, "I can't tell you how many times I wished I wasn't going to be a father, that I could get a do-over, and now...." Luke's voice cracked on a sob. "I didn't mean like this."

Luke's guilt mirrored Nelson's. Nelson had done and said the same thing, but he knew logically God wasn't answering the prayers of a jilted lover or a scared man who wasn't looking to become a father or husband. Nelson was sure, if there was a God, he had much more important things to worry about. "You listen to me, Lucas Rollins. You did nothing to cause this. Now you need to dry your tears, man up, and be there for.... What did you name her?"

"Nellie."

"Nellie needs you, and that must be your focus. You can whine about your guilt later. How is Charlotte doing?"

Luke sniffed, then cleared his throat. "She's on a lot of pain medications after her C-section, so she's resting comfortably right now."

"Are your mom and dad there?"

"Yeah."

"Good. Your poor mom is probably a wreck right now. You two need to lean on each other."

"I wish you were here," Luke whispered. He sounded so lost it broke Nelson's heart.

"I wish I could be there too," Nelson admitted. And he meant it. With Nellie struggling to breathe and Luke's tears, Nelson wasn't so selfish as to put his own feelings above theirs. Luke needed a friend, and the very least Nelson could do was try to be one. "Is there anything you need?"

Nelson could have sworn he heard Luke whisper, "You," but he couldn't be sure. "I could use a couple hours of sleep."

"Sorry, bud, can't help you there. I haven't even figured out how to shut off my brain long enough to get a couple hours of my own."

"Another thing I'm sure is my fault," Luke muttered.

"Stop that! What did I just tell you?"

"I don't know," Luke said, sounding defeated.

"Ugh. You're such a pain in the ass. You know damn good and well what I said. Now you go focus on sending Nellie positive vibes and call me later."

"Yeah, okay," Luke, replied sounding hesitant.

"Call me and keep me updated," Nelson said and then hung up the phone before Luke could respond.

There really was nothing Nelson could do to make this right, and although Luke wanted him there, Nelson knew in his heart it would be a really bad idea to go. There were too many unresolved feelings between them. The last thing Nellie, Charlotte, or anyone else needed was the tension that would surely be swirling around Nelson and Luke. It sucked that he couldn't be there for his friend, but then again, it sucked they were in this situation in the first place. He'd had a moment of clarity and wouldn't do anything to make a bad situation worse.

LUKE HUNG up the phone, pulled a handkerchief from his pocket, and wiped his cheeks and eyes. He wasn't sure if he wanted to fall to his knees and cry or punch a wall while screaming how fucking unfair life was. The conflict rolled through him like a tidal wave, slamming into his mind, gut, heart, his very soul, leaving him unsteady on his feet. He pressed his back to the wall, slid down it, and wrapped his arms around his legs.

The first time he laid eyes on Nellie, he knew in that second he could love someone as much as he loved Nelson. Nellie was so tiny, so vulnerable, and needed him; of this he was sure. Looking into her dark eyes, seeing her tiny little hand clutching his pinkie finger, cemented his conviction to do right by her. Sacrificing his own happiness for hers seemed like such a small sacrifice in that moment. However, the instant he heard Nelson's voice, the battle raged once again.

Luke wasn't sure how long he could continue to keep fighting. It was a war he couldn't win. And what about Nelson? How fair was it to him? What about when Nelson found someone else? It would fucking shred Luke's soul to know Nelson was with someone else. Yet how the hell could he hold it against Nelson when he had a wife and child at home? If he could only have his cake and eat it too, he'd be married to Charlotte in name only and keep Nelson as his best friend and lover.

Problem was Luke hated cake, and he might be a selfish son of a bitch, but he wasn't so cruel as to ask that of either of them. The final blow to Nelson's heart would have been to even ask it.

Luke let out a heavy sigh and scrubbed his hands over his face. At twenty-three he shouldn't be facing so many difficult choices. He laid his forehead on his knees and closed his eyes. There really was only one choice he could make, one that would save everyone a lot of unnecessary pain and anguish. Luke might not be able to eat cake, but dammit, he could do the right thing for those he loved.

He had to let Nelson go.

Chapter Eighteen

FIFTEEN MESSAGES—LUKE never returned Nelson's calls.

Chapter Nineteen

No word from Luke.

Chapter Twenty

STILL NO word from Luke.

Chapter Twenty-One

FUCK YOU, LUCAS ROLLINS!

Chapter Twenty-Two

Present Day, 2015

TURNING THE order form from side to side, Nelson squinted, trying to read it. No good. He snatched up his reading glasses from the counter and tried again but still was unable to make out the chicken scratch. In disgust Nelson threw it on the counter, closed his eyes, and did his best not to grind his molars down. It was the final cake of the wedding season, he reminded himself. Last one, then he'd be free and clear of Doug.

Eight years he and Doug had been together, building Nel-D into a thriving business. Well, they'd been together that long, but it was Nelson who made the bakery into the thriving business it was. People came from all over Michigan and beyond to have Nelson create a cake for their special day. Doug, on the other hand, was too busy either flirting with the employees or holing up in the office working on his novel to be bothered with Nel-D.

The deal done, one more cake, then the bakery would close its doors for six weeks. Paperwork was notarized and filed, lawyers paid, assets split, and when the doors reopened, it would do so with a new name, a single owner, and a whole lot less stress for Nelson.

"But first I need to know what the hell this says." Nelson snatched up the order form and went in search of Doug.

The bakery was quiet when Nelson walked through the kitchen. It was the calm before the storm. No one would be in for another hour. However, Nelson loved being here alone. It gave him time to get his thoughts together, enjoy his coffee, and set up a game plan for the day. Being a morning person, Doug also arrived early, but he'd head straight for the office. His excuse to write down the thoughts that came to him in the night. The rest of the day, Doug was rarely seen unless he was hungry or it was time to go home.

"Novelist hard at work, my ass," Nelson snickered.

He had a lot of respect for those who aspired to be authors, really, he did. It took a lot of courage to send your words and thoughts out into the world for others to read. Doug, on the other hand, had yet to write a single thing he could share with others, let alone submit, in the past eight years. More times than not, when Nelson would pop into the office, Doug would be on Facebook, Tumblr, Twitter, or surfing internet porn. Research and promoting, he'd claimed. But in eight years, that research and promo hadn't helped Doug complete a single story. It was a damn good thing they opened Nel-D a year after they met, or neither of them would be eating or have a roof over their head.

Doug sat behind the desk, glasses perched on his thin nose, silver hair tussled at his temples as if he'd been running his fingers through it. What stopped Nelson in his tracks, beyond the fact Doug was typing, was he had at least three days of growth on his jaw. Doug always shaved morning and night, even when Nelson begged him to try the rugged look.

"Rough weekend?" Nelson asked.

Doug jerked back in his chair, his hand instantly going to his heart as a look of shock crossed his face. "Jesus H. Christ. You scared the hell out of me."

"Sorry, I figured you'd have heard me grumbling from the other room."

Doug pushed his glasses up onto his forehead and closed his laptop. "I was deep into my story," he explained.

"Yeah? How's it going?"

"I picked up a story I had started years ago. It's really flowing. I guess I just needed some time away from it."

"I've heard that before," Nelson mumbled.

"What was that?"

"I said it's a good thing you're typing it," he lied—sort of. He shoved the order form at Doug. "Your handwriting sucks. What the hell does this say?"

"Hey, I write better than most doctors," Doug protested.

"Barely, but I can't read their writing either."

Doug studied the paper. "It's the Heinz cake."

"I'm aware of that since I asked you to take the order." Damn lawyers. *Heaven forbid they work around my schedule.* It didn't matter that he had something to do or that he'd have to leave the paperwork to Mr. Chicken Scratch.

Doug handed the order form back to Nelson along with a pen. "Have a seat, and I'll translate it for you."

Nelson took the chair on the opposite side of the desk and wrote as Doug spoke. Nelson was amazed Doug could remember what he wrote weeks ago. The crap on the form certainly didn't in any way resemble actual words, and the symbols and scratching didn't correlate with what he was saying in the slightest. Doug would make a great spy writer. Problem was, no one but him could decipher the crap.

Once Doug was done rambling, Nelson set the pen down and took the paper from the notebook, folded it, and slid it into his shirt pocket. "I have no idea how you did that, but thanks."

"It's a gift," Doug said with a wink. Nelson shook his head and started to rise. "Any chance you've reconsidered relocating?"

"Any chance you've reconsidered the split in assets?" Nelson countered.

Doug frowned. "Why would I do that? I was half the business. I'm rightfully entitled to half the profits."

"Well, then, there's your answer," Nelson said curtly.

"This is my hometown, and I'd really prefer not to run into you all the time."

"I doubt there is much chance of that with you being so busy with your research and all."

"C'mon, Nelson, be fair."

Be fair? The idea would be laughable if Doug's idea of fair weren't so hard to choke down. Nelson couldn't afford to reestablish his company in a new town. The cost of moving away from Saugatuck and acquiring a new building would bankrupt him. Besides, he'd given in on losing the name since it was Doug's idea to name it Nel-D. If he kept it, he'd have to pay Doug future royalties from the brand name, and there was no way in hell Nelson was going to give him another dime. Doug was already getting way more than he had earned. *Asshole.*

"I'm being more than fair," Nelson assured him.

"Dammit, Nelson. Why do you have to always be so difficult?"

"Oh, I don't know, Doug. Maybe because I've worked my balls off for eight years doing eighty percent of the work, only to give you fifty percent. You're already getting more than you deserve."

"That's bullshit and you know it. I may not have done the physical work you've done, but it's because of me you even came to Saugatuck. It was my connections that brought in the first customers. It was me who got you this building for a steal."

"And while I appreciate those things, it was eight fucking years ago! What have you done since?"

"We agreed I'd have writing time—"

"Beating a dead horse here, Doug. How about we just try and accept what we've already agreed to and walk away, if not friends, then at least cordial, shall we?"

"Do you really believe that's possible? You broke my heart. How am I supposed to move on when I'm constantly reminded of what could have been every time I see this place?" Doug waved his hand around the room. "If only you had worked less on this place and more on our relationship—"

Nelson stabbed a warning finger in Doug's direction. "Don't you dare say it. We've been over and over it. It's another dead horse." Nelson stood behind his argument that, had Doug helped him around Nel-D, he wouldn't have had to work sixteen-hour days and would have had more time to spend with Doug. Nelson was so fucking over this shit. He went to his feet. "I'll let you get back to your story."

"Nelson, please," Doug whined. He scrambled out of his chair to stand between Nelson and the door. "I never thought you would take it this far. Can we please just talk about it? Let's go out and have some dinner and drinks and talk."

Nelson tilted his head and gawked at Doug. "The check we made out to the attorney didn't clue you in as to how serious I was? We don't need dinner or drinks, and we sure as hell don't need to do any more talking. Everything is settled. Just leave it alone." He tried to move around Doug, but Doug blocked him again.

"Baby, I'm not eating, I'm not sleeping. I need you. I miss you."

Doug reached out, but Nelson spun out of his grasp, irritation fueling his movements. "Stop it. Just fucking stop it!" He put his hands on his hips and glared at Doug. "For years I've asked you for help, but you refused. I begged you to stop flirting with every Tom, Dick, and Harry; you refused. I implored you to go to counseling with me; you refused. So you know what? It's my turn to refuse you. Now get the fuck out of my way."

Doug obviously knew he'd pushed Nelson too far because he sighed dramatically and stepped aside.

Nelson stormed out of the room. *One more goddamn cake! Last fucking one!* Was it too much to ask that he'd be able to do it in peace? Apparently so because…. Ugh! Why did Doug have to start this shit again now?

Nelson knew long ago things with Doug weren't going to work. The seed of resentment was planted early on, and each year it was watered, fertilized, and cultivated until it bloomed into hate. He should have left years ago, but hadn't, and that was his biggest regret. The way he felt about Doug was as much Nelson's fault as it was Doug's. He never should have let it get to this point.

"Morning, Nelson."

Startled, Nelson jerked to a halt, then stumbled back.

"Whoa there," Grady called out and rushed to catch Nelson before he fell on his ass.

Grady missed, but luckily for Nelson, he grabbed the counter at the last second, allowing him to get his feet beneath him. "Holy shit, Grady. You about took me out."

"Pfft. I simply said good morning." Grady cocked his head. "Let me guess: you were talking to Doug?"

"That obvious, huh?"

"He's the only one I know who can get you to do that sourpuss face."

Only man who can make my fucking blood boil too. Nelson pulled the slip of paper from his pocket and handed it to Grady. "I don't want to talk about him. You mind getting the batter started on this? I need a cup of coffee."

Grady took the paper. He gave Nelson a sympathetic smile. "Not much longer, and relief is in sight."

"God, I hope so," Nelson responded. "Be right back. You want anything?"

"Nah, I'm good. Take your time."

Nelson patted Grady's shoulder as he passed. Grady Parker was a hulk of a man. The first time Nelson met him, he was struck by how much Grady looked like a supersized Martin Short. Only difference was Grady kept his long hair pulled back into a ponytail. Otherwise Grady was Short on steroids.

Grady also might have hands built for hard labor, or boxing or lifting cars or something as strenuous, but he had a soft touch. The delicate flowers and piped lace he could create were awe-inspiring. Grady had come to work for Nelson when he was sixteen, but in only five short years, he'd moved up the ranks from prep to Nelson's right-hand man and confidant. If only Doug had half the ambition Grady did, they'd have been twice as successful. Either that or if Grady were gay and a few years older, he'd have made one hell of a boyfriend and partner.

Nelson sighed. Such was his luck. He grabbed his mug, poured out the cold coffee, and refilled it. He blew on the steaming brew before taking a tentative sip. "Yeah, such is my luck."

It seemed he was born under an unlucky love sign. Those he wanted were out of his reach, and those who wanted him.... Nelson took another sip. "Eh." It was what it was, and no amount of wishing, bellyaching, or tears would change a damn thing. And really? Who was he to complain? He had great friends, loving parents, and a thriving business. He was certainly better off than most. So why was it his life felt so empty and unfulfilling?

Nelson spent a bit longer enjoying his pity party and finishing his coffee before he got his ass in gear to join Grady.

"One more cake," he reminded himself. He so had this.

Chapter Twenty-Three

BILLOWING PALE blue sheers swayed across the back wall as if they were dancing to the soft music that played from overhead speakers. Hundreds of round tables covered with white linen stood around the room sporting bows the same pale blue as the sheers. Vases of complementary yellow, white, and darker-blue flowers adorned the center of each table. Perhaps Nelson was becoming a bit jaded, but it looked the same as hundreds of other wedding receptions he'd viewed. Or perhaps it was the fact each reception represented hours and hours of work, and he was simply too exhausted to truly appreciate the beauty.

Across the room Nelson spotted the cake table and steered toward it. Moving a hundred-pound cake with two towers, archways, bridges, and enough sugar flowers to cause a hundred men to eat themselves straight toward diabetes was a hell of a feat. However, he and Grady had been here before. They worked easily together like a well-oiled machine. It also certainly didn't hurt that Grady was strong as an ox.

"How come no one ever sets the cake table near a door?" Grady grumbled.

"Aww, what fun would there be in that?" Nelson countered, his voice a little strained beneath the weight of the cake.

The instant they set the cake down, Grady shook his arms out. "Who gives a shit about fun? Easy would be nice for a change."

"Let's get this set up, and I'll buy you dinner at the pub."

Grady sighed dramatically. "Great, they get champagne and prime rib, and I get a greasy burger and flat beer."

Nelson rolled his eyes. "You hate champagne."

"I know, but I need something to bitch about."

"You can bitch about the pay I take out of your check when we get nailed for not having this thing ready in time for the little bride and groom to slice and dice."

It was Grady's turn to roll his eyes. Grady knew it was nothing but an idle threat. Nelson often teased Grady that he'd get a lot more work done if he weren't so busy flapping his jaws. Truth was, even though

Nelson preferred to focus and listen to music while he worked, now he couldn't imagine working without Grady rambling on and on about the weirdest shit that made absolutely no sense.

They got busy assembling the cake and connecting the towers by way of delicate—in Nelson's opinion, tacky—plastic bridges. They fell into a steady rhythm, but it didn't last long.

"Fuck," Grady grumbled under his breath.

"What's the matter?"

Grady held up a portion of the bridge. "Any chance we can glue this back together?"

"Might not have time to dry."

"Fuck," Grady grumbled again.

"Don't sweat it, big guy. I figured your thick and meaty fingers might have a problem with something so delicate, so I brought extra."

"Ha! You're normally the one who breaks shit."

"Sorry, can't hear you," Nelson tossed over his shoulder. "I'm too busy running errands for you."

"That'll be the day," Grady called.

Nelson pushed through the door, laughing. Poor Grady was always having to put his work aside to run to get one thing or another Nelson had forgotten.

Outside Nelson jogged to the van. He rummaged through the box of supplies and found what he was looking for. He slid out of the van, slammed the cargo door, turned, and slammed into a brick wall, breaking the piece he'd just retrieved.

"Son of a bitch," Nelson yelped.

"Hey, watch where you're going," a husky voice grumbled.

Pissed, Nelson stepped back and thrust the broken bridge at the man. "Look—" The words died in Nelson's throat as he tilted his head back and met the man's gaze.

Time seemed to stop as they stared at each other. Nelson scarcely breathed for fear the vision before him would disappear. Wheat-colored hair, darker now, sprinkled with silver, laugh lines more prominent at the corner of wide blue eyes, as were the dark circles beneath them. Arms and chest still heavy with muscle, larger-than-life presence. Yet it was the face that held Nelson's attention. The last time he'd seen it, it was behind a wall of tears, and yet it was crystal clear in his mind.

Luke.

"Well, I'll be damned. We seem to meet in the strangest places," Luke finally said, breaking the silence.

"It seems we do," Nelson responded. He was surprised his voice came out even and strong past his constricted throat.

"How long has it been?"

Seventeen years, three months, and a countless number of hours, give or take. "A long time. What brings you to Saugatuck?"

"Colton is getting married." Luke scrunched up his face. "Are you here for his wedding? How did you know?"

A vise tightened around Nelson's chest. At one time he'd thought himself part of Luke's world and vice versa, yet it had been years. Colton was still a teenager the last time Nelson saw him, and it was ridiculous he felt slighted by that long-ago relationship. He swallowed down his disappointment where it belonged. "Let me guess: he's marrying a girl name Heinz?"

"Yes! Do you know her?"

"No, but I met her once. She hired me to create her cake." Nelson looked down at the broken bridge. "In fact, I just came out to grab something I needed to complete it."

"You live here?"

Nelson nodded. "I… I'd love to stay and chat, but I'm on a pretty tight schedule to get this done before the party."

Luke furrowed his brows. "You're not coming? I'd love to have the chance to catch up on old times."

I wasn't invited. Nelson clamped down on the response. He wasn't a child anymore, and he no longer played the drama card. "You have a party to attend, and I have a mess to clean—"

Grady burst out the door. "What the hell is keeping you?"

"Sorry, be right there," Nelson assured him.

"Well, hurry up, I need your help."

Nelson nodded, and Grady went back into the hall. "I better get going. It was good seeing you." Emotions he thought he'd long ago buried came rushing to the surface, and Nelson turned away for fear Luke would be able to read them on his face.

"Dammit, I have to run too. They're waiting for me to take photos." Luke laid his hand on Nelson's shoulder. "I'm staying at the Waterside Inn. Room twenty. Come by later or tomorrow or…." After a few seconds of silence, Nelson looked back over his shoulder and met Luke's gaze.

"On second thought, meet me here, say at eight. I know Colton would love to see you again."

"I don't know," Nelson said hesitantly.

"Please. If you won't do it for me, then do it for Colton. Just one drink with an old friend on his wedding day."

Nelson saw the pleading in Luke's eyes, and before he could come up with a good excuse not to, he found himself nodding. "One drink."

"Great. I'll see you then."

Nelson stood dumbfounded, staring at the empty parking lot long after Luke disappeared. Their relationship had ended on a bitter note. After months of waiting by the phone, Nelson had vowed he couldn't do it anymore. He had to put Luke and his feelings behind him. Had let go of his anger in order to heal, but not without great difficulty. The constant longing, wishing, tears, anger nearly drove him to insanity. Removing Luke from his life was one of the hardest things he'd ever had to do. It took him months after that last phone call to get himself up and start living again. It took him years to finally put that part of his life behind him and get to a place in his life where he was ready to open himself up for love. And he had. He'd loved Doug and, in some small way, supposed he still did, but he never loved him the way he did Luke.

Nelson stumbled back against the van as the full weight of that statement slammed into him. Christ, had he unknowingly sabotaged his relationship? When Doug accused him of being closed off, was it true? Did he really have a thick wall around his heart and hold a part of himself back as Doug suggested? Nelson ran his fingers through his hair and let out a heavy breath. His mind raced to so many different thoughts, emotions running through him, leaving him trembling, and there was a very real possibility he might puke or fall down or both.

He wanted to scream, to let out the tidal wave raging inside him before he exploded. He'd never really dealt with the loss of Luke, simply learned to move on. He pushed those feeling so far down, locking them behind a wall, he was afraid of what would happen if he were to allow those feelings out. How long he stayed in that stunned state, trying to get a grasp on what he was feeling, Nelson wasn't sure. Seeing Luke again caused so many suppressed feelings to rush to the surface, which by themselves would have been difficult to deal with. However, combining them at the end of his longtime relationship with Doug was like a one-two sucker punch to Nelson's heart and gut.

"Nelson!"

Nelson blinked at Grady, who was standing at the door. His face was red with anger.

"What the fuck are you doing? You do realize we have ten minutes to finish, right?"

Nelson blinked again. *Wedding. Cake. Right.* He pushed away from the van, whipped open the doors, and grabbed another piece of bridge work. "Sorry, I got distracted," he said. He slammed the door and jogged toward Grady.

"How do you get distracted in a fucking parking lot?" Grady's voice was tight with irritation. However, he must have seen something off with Nelson because his angry expression quickly disappeared, replaced with one of concern. "What's wrong?"

Nelson handed Grady the cake piece. "What do you mean?"

"Your pupils are blown and you're as white as a ghost."

"I think I just saw one."

"Seriously?"

"Yeah, I'll tell you about it later." Nelson gave Grady a shove. "Let's get this cake finished first."

STANDING OUTSIDE the reception hall, Nelson stood rooted next to his car, his legs refusing to respond, and he could only stare at the door. The smorgasbord of emotions he'd been dealing with all afternoon increased with the addition of nervousness. As it took the forefront, he not only had to hold down the nausea, clamp down on the shaking, but now he had to remember how to fucking breathe.

"Why in the hell did I agree to come?" Nelson mouthed.

Because you're a glutton for punishment, the little voice in his head responded.

"Are you talking to yourself?" Grady asked.

"Maybe," Nelson grumbled.

"You're losing it, man."

No, he'd already lost it and was on the fast track to the looney bin. Nelson fidgeted with his bow tie, tucked in his shirt, smoothed down his pants, and then his hair.

Grady patted Nelson's back. "Too late, you already lost it."

Nelson looked up at Grady. "Will you come visit me?"

"Sure, I'll even bring you a file in your cake."

"How am I supposed to use a file if I'm wearing a straightjacket?"

"Good point," Grady chuckled. "Guess I'll just bring a bib to catch your drool while you watch me eat cake."

"Thanks. You're such a good friend." The fact that Grady agreed to change his plans and come to the reception with Nelson was proof of that. He promised Grady they would only stay for one drink, then Nelson would pick up the tab at the pub.

Grady waved toward the door. "So are we going to do this or say screw it and head to the pub instead?"

Obviously, it was the former because, instead of running like he should, Nelson took one last deep breath, opened the door, and went inside. Loud thumping dance music, flashing lights, and a roar of voices laughing and talking. He was thankful for Grady's presence at his back and the thick crowd. Part of Nelson hoped he would be able to see Colton, say hello, congratulate him on his nuptials, and get the hell out of there. Another part of him—the masochistic part—wanted to see Luke.

Stepping through the entryway, the masochistic part of him got its wish. Luke stood directly in Nelson's path a mere ten feet away. He was talking with a man whose back was to Nelson, but Nelson only spent a second wondering who the man was who had Luke smiling. It was the tall blonde Luke had his arm around that caught Nelson's attention. She was gorgeous, her dimpled smile almost as brilliant as Luke's. She was way too young and way too gorgeous to be Charlotte. The young lady had to be Luke's midlife crisis. Nelson bet Luke had a candy-apple-red sports car to chauffer her around in. Probably to school.

The idea both disgusted Nelson and made him laugh at the ridiculousness of it. He never would have pegged Luke to be the kind of guy who'd have an issue with his age. Then again, what did he really know about Luke? Absolutely nothing considering he hadn't seen him in seventeen years. The good-hearted boy was gone. The wide dimpled grin was gone, and in its place was a handsome man who obviously struggled with entering his forties.

Luke spoke animatedly to the man standing in front of him, and then suddenly his gaze landed on Nelson and his eyes went wide. "Nelson!" Luke waved him over.

The man standing in front of Luke turned around, and Nelson immediately recognized Colton. The slender baby face had been replaced by a ruggedly handsome one. He was the dark to Luke's light coloring, but the resemblance was undeniable.

"Nelson, wow, so great to see you. Glad you could come," Colton greeted.

"Great seeing you too," Nelson responded. He held out his hand, but Colton pushed it aside and pulled Nelson into a hug.

"Man, Luke said he ran into you, and I was like, no fucking way." Colton pulled back to look at Nelson. "And you like seriously made my cake? Dude! It's awesome, and holy hell, what are the chances that Missy would know you?" Colton tilted his head. "When did you move to Saugatuck? And when in the hell did you start making cakes? I thought you were some computer geek or something."

Nelson started to laugh; he couldn't help it. Colton not only looked like his older brother, he rambled on and on like him too.

Colton went silent for a moment, then burst out laughing. "Sorry. Guess I should have given you a chance to answer the first question before hitting you with another one."

"It's okay," Nelson chuckled. "I used to get that all the time."

"I know you're not talking about me," Luke protested, but the teasing smile left no doubt as to his guilt. His smile lessened as his gaze settled on Grady, who was standing behind Nelson.

Nelson turned to Colton. "Shit, sorry, this is Grady," he said, stabbing his thumb over his shoulder toward Grady. "I hope you don't mind that I invited him along. I should have asked first."

"Hell, the more the merrier, I always say." Colton held out his hand. "Colton Rollins."

Grady reached around Nelson and accepted Colton's hand. "Nice to meet you. Grady Durham."

Nelson pointed toward Luke. "And that's his brother, Luke."

Grady and Luke shook hands, and from the expression on Luke's face, Nelson could tell he was sizing Grady up. For what reason, Nelson didn't know. But he didn't have long to contemplate it when Luke pointed to the woman standing next to him and said, "This is my daughter, Nellie."

Nelson was sure his jaw was sitting on the floor as he gawked at the stunning woman. Nelson had only seen one picture of her when she was a newborn. She was a little curly-haired cutie with huge blue eyes, and now she was all grown up, and rather than cute, absolutely beautiful.

Right after the shock, guilt took over for even considering Luke would be chasing after such a young thing. *His daughter? Holy hell.*

"Wow, the last time I saw you, you were this big," Nelson stated, holding his hands about a foot apart.

"You remember me telling you about Nelson?" Luke asked her.

Nellie nodded. "I've heard all about you. It's good to finally put a face with a name."

And just like that, the guilt spiraled right back to shock. Luke talked about him? He would have thought, considering the way things ended, Luke would have wiped him from his mind and his name from his lips. "I hope he only told you about my positive attributes," Nelson teased lightly.

Nelson didn't miss the strange look in Luke's eyes, but he couldn't rightly say what it was because it quickly disappeared.

"Hey, you have to meet the new Mrs. Rollins," Colton exclaimed and tugged Nelson's arm. "I'll bring him right back," he told the others. Nelson was forced to follow.

Apparently Colton hadn't been all that involved in the planning of the wedding, or he would have known Nelson had already met his new bride. Colton shrugged and laughed when Nelson and Missy informed him of such. But moments later Nelson was left standing alone when the new bride and groom were called away. However, not for long.

"Your boyfriend went to get drinks."

Nelson spun around and looked up at Luke. "My what?" he asked in confusion.

"Your boyfriend, Grady. He said to tell you he was going to hit the john, then grab you two some beers."

"Oh, he's not my boyfriend. He's my assistant and much, much too young for me. Not to mention straight as an arrow."

Luke tilted his head. "Is that so?" Nelson nodded. "Well, let's keep that little tidbit between you and me, shall we?"

"Why is that?"

"Because watching my teenage daughter drool over a gay man I can handle. Over a straight man, not so much."

Nelson couldn't help but laugh. "I can see how that could cause you some distress. I'll be sure to tell Grady to be on his best behavior when Nellie's mommy and daddy are around."

"Oh, Charlotte's not here. We divorced three years ago."

"I'm sorry to hear that," Nelson said with sincerity. He'd known how important it was to Luke that Nellie grow up with both parents.

Luke shrugged. "She went off to find herself, and who would have known she was hiding in a little cabana bar in Florida with a surfer named Kip."

"That sucks."

"Nah, it's all good. I got Nellie, and she got Kip. I think I got the better end of the stick. Enough of that." Luke waved toward the bar area. "Let's grab a table, and we can catch up over a beer."

Nelson was reeling as he followed Luke toward a table. It was one thing to see Luke again, but now knowing he was no longer married, possibly available, sparked both dread and hope in Nelson. For the second time that night, he wasn't sure which outcome he wanted more.

Bullshit, you fucking masochist.

Nelson told the annoying little voice to shut the hell up and took the stool Luke indicated.

Chapter Twenty-Four

IT WAS pure hell watching Nelson interact with Grady, the familiarity, the camaraderie, the easy way they laughed together as if they had been friends for ages. Luke remembered a time when he and Nelson had such a relationship, and now he felt like the outsider sitting with Nelson and Grady. It was odd that, so many years later, the loss of his best friend was still so raw. Had they simply lost the sexual aspect of their relationship, Luke could have handled that. However, it was the closeness, the laughter, and the fact Luke could share his innermost secrets with Nelson and know they were safe that he missed the most.

Luke checked his watch again—9:37—five minutes later than the last time he checked it. Colton and Missy would be saying their farewells at ten. They had a plane to Aruba to catch at 5:00 a.m. Luke would only need to stay long enough to see them off, then would be free. Nellie was staying with his parents, so if he could get Nelson and Grady to stay until then, he was so tagging after them when they headed to the pub.

Grady tipped up his glass and downed the last of his beer. He set the empty glass on the table and turned to Nelson. "We really should get going."

"Hey, what's the hurry?" Luke asked. "I'll grab you another one." He jumped to his feet and pointed at Nelson's glass. "You need a refill too?"

Nelson glanced at Grady and shook his head. "Nothing more for me, thanks. I promised Grady drinks and a couple games of pool at the pub."

"You got room for another? I haven't played pool in ages."

"Sure, I don't mind," Grady said. "But seeing as you're part of the wedding party, shouldn't you stay here?"

Luke glanced at his watch again. "Only for another twenty minutes. I can be ready to go in twenty-five minutes tops."

Grady shrugged. "I'm cool with waiting if you are, Nelson?"

Nelson hesitated, the expression on his face unrecognizable. For a few painful ticks of the clock, Luke was sure Nelson was going to say no.

Finally after a long, drawn-out moment, Nelson shrugged one shoulder. "Hey, who am I to say no?"

It wasn't the "I'd love to spend time with Luke" he was hoping for, but he'd take it. Hell, Luke hadn't really expected it considering the way Luke ended their friendship. Nelson sitting with him in the first place without throwing a punch was a miracle. "Great, I'll grab you two a couple beers, send off my little brother to consummate his marriage, and we're out of here."

IT WAS more like forty minutes before Luke could finally free himself from the goodbyes. Christ, he never realized he had so many cousins, aunts, and uncles. Extricating himself from Mom's hug, he gave Nellie a peck on the cheek. "Be good for Grandma and Grandpa, and I'll see you at breakfast."

"You sure you don't want me tagging along? I could be Grady's partner." Nellie stuck out her bottom lip, fluttered her long lashes, and met Luke's gaze with pleading eyes.

Normally it worked on him. The little shit knew how to work him, but not tonight. No way in hell was he going to spend the evening watching his only child flirt with a man much too old for her, and in a bar no less. Besides, he was in the mood to do a little flirting of his own. Luke kissed her on top of the head. "Sorry, Princess. Not this time."

"You're the meanest daddy ever," Nellie complained, but her tone was teasing. She really was a great kid.

"I know. You can tell Grandma and Grandpa all your woes. It's their fault I turned out this mean."

"Pfft, c'mon, Nellie, have I got some stories for you," his mom declared.

Luke pointed a warning finger at his mom, who just waved him off and smiled. Luke headed to Nelson and Grady. "You two ready?"

Grady downed his beer. "I thought you'd never ask."

As it turned out, the pool tables were all in use. After dropping some coins on one, Luke, Nelson, and Grady headed toward an empty booth on the other side of the bar.

"Hey, I see someone I know. I'll catch up with you two in a bit," Grady said. He spun and hurried away before either Nelson or Luke could respond.

Luke slid into a booth. Nelson sat across from him, waved toward a waitress who nodded in acknowledgment.

"Alone at last," Luke commented.

"Yup, and if you had your hopes on playing doubles, I hate to tell you, Grady won't be back anytime soon."

"No?"

Nelson gestured toward the bar with his head. "That's Jo-Jo Banks. She's been leading Grady around by the short hairs for months."

"Poor guy."

"Ha, he deserves it. I've seen him do the same to plenty of girls."

Their small talk was cut short when the waitress came over. They each ordered a beer. She set down a bowl of peanuts before going off to get their drinks.

Luke picked up a peanut and cracked it open between his thumb and finger. "Thanks for letting me tag along. I don't know if I could handle one more dance with an old aunt or screaming two-year-old."

"No problem."

The silence stretched out between them long after the waitress set their brews on the table. Luke continued to play with the peanut shells, and Nelson picked at the label on his beer. Finally the heaviness swirling around them was more than Luke could take. "Okay, this sucks. Would you rather I leave?"

"No, it's just…."

"Just what?" Luke prodded.

"It's weird. I'm not even sure what to say or why I'm here."

"Why did you agree to come, then? To the wedding, I mean," Luke clarified.

"I almost didn't," Nelson admitted. He looked up at Luke and gave him a small smile. "Part of me felt like I'd just run into an old friend and was looking forward to catching up, and another part kept reminding me that you're a virtual stranger and I'm not sure what to say." He took a sip of his beer, and when he met Luke's gaze again, he smirked. "Then there was that other part of me that wanted to punch you in the face."

"Yeah, I can see that, and I probably deserve it too."

"Hell yeah, you do."

"I know," Luke said with a nod. "But still, when I first saw you, I was crazy excited and had this notion that we'd just pick up where we left off, and then it hit me that the left-off part wasn't a good place to start again."

"It wasn't one of our best. It took me a long time to forgive you."

Luke didn't know how to respond. Saying he was sorry seemed like a stupid thing considering how he stopped talking to Nelson without any explanation. Hell, the more he thought about it, the more of a miracle it was Nelson was sitting there drinking a beer rather than throwing that punch. Silence threatened to overcome them again. Luke needed to come up with some way to start a conversation that wasn't about their shared past, as it was still obviously as painful for Nelson as it was for Luke. This wasn't the right place for such a conversation, not when there was a good chance that conversation would end up in tears or violence or both.

Then Luke remembered something Nelson had told him years ago. "Oh. My. God. I just realized something."

"What's that," Nelson inquired.

"You finally got your dream!"

Nelson tilted his head, brows dipping down. "Excuse me?"

"Your dream. The cake. You finally got your bakery."

Nelson's face lit up. "Yeah, I opened it about eight years ago."

"That's so awesome. I remember you thought it was a silly goal."

"It was at the time. I never thought it would come true. I poured myself into my job, working as many hours as I could, worked my way up, and then after about eight years, I suffered some pretty severe burnout and needed a break. I hadn't had a vacation in years. So my boss at the time offered me the use of his rental house in Saugatuck, and the rest, they say, is history."

"And what? You find a bakery for sale while on vacation?"

"No, I found a boyfriend. The bakery came a year later."

It was ridiculous that the mention of a boyfriend would cause Luke's chest to tighten, but it did, ridiculous or not. To think another man wouldn't have touched Nelson in all these years was absurd. Especially since Luke sure hadn't been celibate. After Charlotte ran off.... Well, best not to think about that depravity right now. He shoved it aside.

"So, I take it you finally came out to your parents."

"Yeah, and you were right about them. I was an idiot to think they'd freak out. I mean, Mom said she always suspected, and Dad hoped for a while that it was just a phase I was going through, but it's a nonissue now."

"That's great," Luke said with all sincerity. He really hadn't known if Nelson's parents would take it well but figured it would be better in the end than living a lie. The thought almost made him laugh out loud, but he hid it in his beer. What a fucking hypocrite he was. He lived a lie for years within his loveless marriage. Still, he would never regret watching Nellie grow up happy and healthy every day rather than as a weekend father. "So, tell me about this bakery of yours. Was it everything you hoped it would be?"

"For the most part. I've worked extremely hard, made quite a name for myself in the biz." Luke arched a brow. "What? Does that surprise you?"

"Not in the slightest, it's just…." Luke let his eyes wander down Nelson's chest, took in his well-formed forearms and his thick hands before looking back up to meet Nelson's gaze. "I'm having a hard time picturing someone as rugged and manly looking as you making such delicate pastries and sugar flowers."

Nelson laughed. "I think the same thing every time I watch Grady do piping or make a petal." Nelson held up his hands. "These are but wee things compared to his, and he makes the master baker look like an amateur."

"I seriously doubt that."

Nelson took a sip of beer, then smiled. "Not yet, but I'm sure by the time he's my age, I'll be calling him for advice."

"I can tell you're very fond of him."

"Wouldn't be as successful without him. He's a great guy."

"Better be careful talking like that. Your boyfriend might get jealous," Luke teased.

"Doug has never felt threatened by Grady. He knows we're just friends. Plus, as you can see, Grady is quite the ladies' man."

Luke looked toward where Nelson was gesturing to see Grady standing at the bar with his face on Jo-Jo's belly, then made his way up to her mouth. "Wow, talk about exhibitionism."

"Seriously, Luke, I would have thought you would have done plenty of body shots in your day."

"Oh shit! Is that what he's doing?" Luke glanced at Grady and watched him tilt his head back with the lemon wedge between his teeth as the others around him cheered. "You forget I was married with child when I was Grady's age."

"No, I haven't forgotten."

Luke regretted his words the instant they were out, and he heard the sadness in Nelson's tone. While Nelson had claimed he understood Luke's decision and would never begrudge Luke for wanting to be there to raise his child, it was still cruel to remind Nelson he'd in the end chosen Charlotte over him.

Thanks to Luke's thoughtlessness, the tension between them returned. Nelson turned toward a pool game while drinking his beer. Luke, on the other hand, spent the time looking at Nelson. As long as he could remember, Nelson was always able to keep Luke's attention. God, he couldn't count the number of times Nelson would fill his mind when he was with Charlotte. He'd tried, tried so fucking hard to suppress his feelings for Nelson. It wasn't fair to Charlotte her husband was thinking of someone else, not only thinking about him, but also in love with that someone.

It really was no surprise when she left Luke. Leaving her daughter, yes, but not him. She deserved more than a façade of marriage. His only consolation was he'd been faithful, a good provider, and beyond that, a good father to Nellie. Sitting here with Nelson, seeing the way he could barely hold Luke's gaze, Luke knew his sacrifice had been an extremely high and painful one.

At one time there was a true bond between them. Luke could still feel the pull of the deeply woven threads. He was unsure how he was going to achieve it when Nelson could barely look at him. But come hell or high water, Luke vowed that bond would be strong once again, and nothing or no one would ever sever it.

Chapter Twenty-Five

SATISFIED GRADY would make it home safely with Jo-Jo, Nelson pushed through the exit door and breathed in the cool night air. Autumn was always his favorite time of year: football, cider, the stunning changing of colors in the trees, and sweater weather. Since opening Nel-D, he enjoyed it even more as it meant the end of the madness known as the wedding season.

"Beautiful night."

Nelson turned his head and smiled at Luke. "That it is. I love it here."

Luke smiled back. "I can see that. It looks good on you."

"What does?"

"Happiness."

Happiness? Nelson chewed on that for a moment. Was he truly happy? He knew he should be, but the more he thought about the question, the less clear the answer became. Nelson yawned. The long day, alcohol, and the ride on the emotional roller coaster was finally catching up to him. "What I am is exhausted."

"You live close?"

Nelson nodded to the right. "A couple blocks that way."

Luke slid his arm in Nelson's. "Cool, I'll walk you home, then."

"I don't—"

"I insist."

Before Nelson could protest, Luke tugged, and Nelson was forced to follow. "You really are a pushy bastard," he grumbled.

"Part of my charm," Luke responded, sounding completely unapologetic.

In his exhausted state, Nelson wasn't sure he could hold back the swell of the emotional storm that was brewing. The day had been such a whirlwind, and he needed some alone time to deal and figure out what the hell he was feeling since he wasn't sure if it was anger, desire, pain, happiness, or all of the above.

"I can see why you love it here. Such a great little town and so quiet," Luke commented. "You sure you don't want to walk along the lake?" Luke tipped his head back. "Not often you get to enjoy such a beautiful night with a full moon."

"Luke, seriously. It's been great seeing you, Colton, and the rest of your family, but I'm tired, my head and feet hurt, and I really just need some sleep. I can find my own way home from here."

"I wouldn't dream of letting such a desirable creature walk alone at this late hour."

"I'm perfectly safe. Seriously."

Luke either wasn't listening or ignoring Nelson's request. He kept walking, pulling Nelson along.

Outside the bakery, Nelson dug his heels in and jerked free from Luke. "Okay, you walked me home. Thank you, now I'll say good night."

Luke glanced up at the large sign over the bakery. "I thought you said you wanted to go home, not to work."

Nelson pulled the keys from his pocket. "They are currently one and the same."

"That's gotta suck. You never get to leave work."

"I don't mind." Nelson unlocked the door and disabled the alarm. "Besides, it's only temporary."

Without being invited, Luke followed him in. "And how does Doug feel about that? Spending his evenings watching cakes rise rather than the game."

"I thought you said you listen to me?"

"I do," Luke assured him. Then his attention turned to his surroundings. Nel-D wasn't like any bakery he'd ever seen. Sure, there were the display cases, lunch counter, and stools, but it was the funky décor and wild bright colors Luke hadn't expected.

Nelson was always a fan of muted colors, especially in his clothing. Nelson's childhood room was painted in dull browns and tans with a log-cabin feel to the décor. Nelson's apartment in Minneapolis was a mishmash of secondhand furniture, all of it without a hint of color. "Let me guess: Doug is an interior decorator."

"No, a trust-fund baby and aspiring author." Nelson pressed his lower back against the counter and grasped it with his hands.

Luke's brows shot up. "You decorated this place?"

"Yeah, I did."

"No way," Luke said, unable to keep the skepticism out of his voice.

"Why is that so hard for you to believe? I'll have you know I've gotten a lot of compliments on this place," Nelson snapped defensively.

"No, it's great." Luke turned in a slow circle, taking it all in. "It's better than great; it's fucking amazing. I just remembered you were never a fan of bright colors. I guess I expected your bakery to have the rustic and rugged feel."

"I'm not the same man you used to know," Nelson said curtly. He pursed his lips, then let out a heavy breath. "I'm sorry. I really am tired and…." Nelson looked away. "I just need some sleep."

Luke hesitated. He didn't want to leave, afraid if he did, Nelson would disappear forever. Yet he also knew he'd been pushing Nelson all night, and it was obvious Luke had pushed him to his limits. "It's me who should be apologizing. You're right. I can be a little pushy at times."

Nelson arched a brow "A little?"

"Okay, a lot," Luke conceded. He shoved his hands into his pockets so as not to give in to the urge to pull Nelson into his arms. "I'll tell you what: I'll get out of here and let you get some sleep if you'll agree to have breakfast with me."

Whether it was because Luke had worn him down or Nelson was simply too tired to fight or to get Luke to leave, Nelson agreed with a small nod.

"Awesome! Say ten?"

"I thought you said breakfast. Ten is typically my lunchtime." Nelson checked his watch and chuckled. "Damn, I didn't realize it was so late. No wonder I'm so tried. I've been up for nearly twenty-four hours. Ten works for me."

"Great. You want me to meet you here, or shall we meet at a restaurant of your choosing?"

"I have a better idea." Nelson pushed off the counter and went around to the other side of it. When he returned he stood before Luke and held out a business card. "Text me when you get up and around, and we'll figure it out then."

Luke took the card, but before Nelson could pull away, Luke took his hand. "You do realize it is fate that has brought up back together," he whispered.

Nelson held his gaze for a long moment, the look in his eyes unreadable. "I've never believed in fate," he finally said.

Luke brought Nelson's hand to his mouth and kissed his knuckles. "You will." Luke released him and walked to the door. "Sweet dreams, Nelson."

Luke stepped out into the night with a wide smile and a purpose. His footfalls were light as he walked down the deserted sidewalk, the temperature much colder than he was used to, but he wasn't bothered by it. The warmth Nelson had infused in him was enough to stave off any chill.

IT WAS years since Nelson had lain awake all night staring at the ceiling. Even through all the shit he'd been dealing with Doug this past year, sleep wasn't an issue. Luke walked into his life, and *bam*! His brain went on overload, and he couldn't figure out how to power it down. All these years later, Luke still could cause his blood to boil, his cock to harden, and his mind to shatter with a simple look.

"Why now?" he asked the dark room. "Why?"

The past year had been all about finalizing the end of one bad relationship, setting a course to a positive and happy life. Hell, being alone actually had its appeal. Nelson didn't want to think of anyone's feelings but his own. Selfish? Sure, it was, but after nine years of trying to consider Doug's feelings above his own, he was worn out. He deserved to be a little self-centered for a while. Come and go as he pleased, eat what he wanted, decorate his place the way he wanted, leave his goddamn dirty underwear on the floor and dishes in the sink if he wanted. No one to consider—no pet, not even a goddamn goldfish to care for. *It's supposed to be all about ME, ME, ME!*

Nelson gritted his teeth. "And just what in the fuck does this have to do with Luke?"

Not a goddamn thing. He was a crazy person. So why was he lying here giddy as hell that Luke was now divorced, and at the same time feeling as if the weight of the world was crushing him?

"You already answered your question. Because you're a crazy person."

Disgusted with himself, Nelson threw off the cover and rolled off the couch, his back protesting about the uncomfortable sleep spot. He was not only insane but wide-awake. He might as well find something constructive to do before he headed to the looney bin.

After a quick pee and washing his hands and face, Nelson headed to the kitchen. He fired up his oven, then proceeded to pull ingredients from the cupboard. As a boy of thirteen, he'd found comfort in cooking, mixing random things together, trying to create something new. It was the only time he could erect a dam on his sadness and hold it back, at least for a little while. Not everything turned out great, but being a young man, of course everything was sugary as hell. It was those desserts built out of sorrow that contributed to not only his dream of creating sweet, wonderful things for people but made him truly successful at it. The irony of sweets from sadness wasn't lost on him. It was his coping mechanism then and apparently still was.

For the first hour and two batches of cookies later, Nelson was still trying to keep Luke from his thoughts. They kept popping into his head, and he'd whisk, beat, or mix them away, but they always returned. He glanced at the clock. It was only a little after four. He couldn't call his mom, but he sure wished he could. That had to be what was missing. They'd talk about silly things, movies, and music, anything while they baked, and before Nelson knew it, a half hour, then an hour would fly by, and he hadn't had a second of sadness.

Funny—or perhaps not so funny—thing was, he doubted anything would help him take his mind off Luke this time. Perhaps he shouldn't even try. He was a grown man, for fuck's sake. He'd spent his entire life hiding his emotions, pushing them down deep inside and locking them away. Maybe it was time, for the first time in his life, to stop locking them away and pull them out and face them. Because seriously, how many could he shove in there before he exploded?

Nelson pulled another batch of chocolate-chip cookies from the stove, set them on the cooling rack, and turned off the oven. No baking in the world was going to help avoid the feelings that were wreaking havoc on his heart and head. He plopped down on a stool, rested his elbows on the counter, and rested his throbbing head in his hands.

In the past Luke often spoke of fate that brought him and Nelson together. Their destiny. Considering the circumstances that brought them back together once again, Nelson had to concede perhaps there was something to it. It was one thing to happen upon each other in an airport—millions of people passed through them. He could write that off as a random act. However, the chances of Nelson being hired to make Colton's wedding cake when the guy lived over a thousand miles from Nelson's shop were astronomical. He was sure winning the lottery jackpot would have better odds, so it had to be fate. Now he had to decide if he was going to thank her or hunt the bitch down and bestow a little destiny on her ass.

Chapter Twenty-Six

WHETHER LUKE had slept at all, he couldn't say. He was sure he'd spent several hours—or at least it felt like it—lying in the dark thinking about Nelson. At some point he thought he might have dozed off, but again he wasn't sure as the past, present, and fantasy all mingled together in one pleasure-filled night of dreaming. Were anyone able to see him lying there, he was sure they'd have thought him crazy as, oftentimes, his thoughts caused him to smile so wide his face nearly cracked.

Holy shit! Nelson!

As the sun rose, Luke had already showered, dressed, and was now pacing the small hotel room. Two hours before he had to meet Nelson for breakfast, and he was pretty sure he would go nuts before ten. *Wait!* Luke froze midstep. Why the hell was he waiting till ten? That was his idea. Nelson had said, *Text me when you get up and around.*

Luke rushed to the bedside table and snatched up his cell phone and the business card Nelson had given him. Christ, he was a mess if he'd forgotten their plans. Nelson had told him he was a morning person. Luke could have already been with him, dammit.

It took him a couple minutes—fat fingers and little bitty keyboards didn't work well together—but he finally typed out a semicoherent message.

I'm up and famished.

Luke considered the text for a moment. It certainly described his state both innocently and sexually. Luke was well aware he'd come on pretty strong the night before, which he could tell made Nelson a bit wary. They were virtual strangers. Luke had changed a lot in the past seventeen years, as he was sure Nelson had too. Making such a broad statement dripping with sexual innuendo probably wasn't the smartest idea. Nelson might not appreciate the humor. His old friend didn't seem to be as carefree and….

Luke deleted the text. They weren't kids anymore, nor were they friends. That was completely Luke's fault, and because of his actions all those years ago, he had no right to presume or act as if they were. It was something that needed to be reestablished. However, it wouldn't surprise Luke if Nelson didn't want that. Hell, if the situation was reversed, he didn't know if he could or would want to trust Nelson again. The idea made Luke sad beyond belief.

Luke stared at the blank screen on his phone. Part of him knew he should probably walk away again, but the grown man in him wouldn't allow it. Knowing what he knew now, he never would have done so all those years ago. Yes, he still would have married Charlotte. Watching Nellie grow, getting to put her to bed and read her a story until she fell asleep cuddled in his arms or against his side when she got bigger was something he would never wish away for anything or anyone, not even Nelson. What he would change if he could was he'd have allowed Nelson to make the decision whether he could handle their relationship being one of friendship only. Luke would forever regret not giving that to Nelson. He'd learned a lot through life experiences he couldn't have understood at twenty-three. Some mistakes he'd made he could blame on youth, but shutting Nelson out wasn't one of them. Luke now understood he'd done it not for Nelson, but for himself. Back then he couldn't handle seeing and talking to Nelson without being able to touch him, tell him how much he loved him. He ran because he was selfish and a coward. But no longer.

He typed out another message. *I'm awake and ready for breakfast. How about you?* He hit send before he could change his mind. Now that the immediate shock from seeing Nelson had worn off and Luke had a little time to think, he wasn't as optimistic as he was the night before.

He resumed his pacing, checking his phone every couple of seconds, waiting, wishing for it to chirp. A knock on his door caused him to jerk, and he stumbled over his own feet, nearly falling flat on his face. Luckily he caught himself on one of the hotel chairs at the last second. "Christ almighty," he grumbled.

Once he righted himself, he stomped over to the door and yanked it open. His ire instantly drained away when he found Nellie standing there with a bright smile on her face.

Nellie went up on tiptoes and pecked him on the cheek. "Morning, Daddy. Grandma and Grandpa already went down for breakfast. I am here to escort you and tease you about your hangover."

Luke stepped out of the way when Nellie pushed past him. "I do not have a hangover, and I'll be the one escorting you down. I'm heading out, so you'll have to have breakfast with your grandparents."

"Aww, Daddy. I don't want to have breakfast with the old folks without you. Can't I go with you?" She put her hands on her hips and pushed out her bottom lip. "Please."

"Sorry, Princess." Luke kissed her on the top of the head. "I have a date."

"With Nelson?"

"Yup."

"Is Grady going to be there?"

Luke gave her a disproving look. "No and even if he was, you're not going." Her pout got impressively bigger. "Sorry, it's not going to work on me this time. Unless you want me to go Rapunzel on you, I suggest you put all thoughts of Grady, and any other guy, right out of your pretty little head."

"But he's so dreamy," she sighed.

Luke pointed a warning finger at his daughter. He so wasn't ready for the whole dating thing, and he damn sure wasn't about to allow her to go sniffing after older men. Not on his watch. "I'm going to pretend I didn't just hear that."

Nellie's shoulders slumped. "You're so mean."

"Yes, Princess, I know. You keep reminding me." He hooked his arm in hers. "Now come with your mean old daddy so he can take you down to the other mean people in your life."

Nellie huffed, but she knew better than to push Luke too far. Most of the time she was teasing, but he wasn't so sure she was about Grady. He was a very good-looking man, and Nellie was a maturing young lady. Luke shook his head. Nope, he wasn't ready for womanhood. On the way out, he made sure he had his key and phone. He checked his cell once more—still no response—before sliding it into his pocket.

He walked Nellie down to the restaurant. She chatted on and on about what her friends back home were doing, what she was missing out on, and Luke tried to pay attention. He loved the fact Nellie shared so much with him, and normally he was very much involved in her life, but Nelson was occupying his thoughts, and he was having a difficult time listening. Thankfully Nellie didn't seem to notice his distraction, and she continued to prattle on.

He was beginning to think Nelson was ignoring Luke's text, but just as they made it to the restaurant, his phone vibrated. He pulled it out and nearly hooted out loud when he saw it was a text from Nelson.

I'll be at the bakery in five if you want to stop by for a cup of coffee.

Hell yeah, he wanted to have a cup of coffee. "Apologize to Grandma and Grandpa for me and tell them I'll be back within the hour, okay?"

"Okay, see you in an hour," Nellie responded without looking up from her phone.

"Nellie, we're at the restaurant. You might want to put that down so you don't run into anyone."

"I can multitask," she said.

Luke watched her maneuver to the table, moving her fingers rapidly over the phone as she moved. It was quite impressive she made it to the table without a single mishap. Luke had to wonder if his daughter's generation was even aware of their surroundings and how much they missed, seeing as every teen he saw had their noses in their phone rather than their eyes on the world. Luke walked away shaking his head. He wept for the future.

NELSON POWERED off his phone, slid it into his pocket, and stepped out of his office just as Doug came out of his—the one that was no longer his—his clothes wrinkled and hair mussed. It was apparent Doug had once again slept at the shop. Nelson gritted his teeth.

"Morning, Nelson," Doug said sleepily. He scratched his head and then his belly before moving away.

"What the hell are you doing here?" Nelson asked, unable to keep the irritation out of his tone. Christ, had Doug been here all night? Why hadn't he checked? *Because I shouldn't have to.*

"I slept here. What's the big deal?"

Nelson followed Doug into the main room. "The big deal is you don't own this place anymore, nor do you have any right to be here."

"Wow, aren't you just Mr. Pissy this morning?" Doug flipped on the coffee maker.

Nelson stepped in front of him. "Go home, Doug."

Doug took a step back. "I can't have a cup of coffee?"

"No. I know for a fact that you have a coffee maker at your place. You took mine," Nelson pointed out.

Ignoring Nelson's anger and his demand, Doug took a mug off the shelf. "I don't have any power at my place."

"Then maybe you should have paid your bill."

Doug rolled his eyes. "A transformer blew. They're supposed to have it fixed sometime today. I hope so, anyway." He held up the mug. "You want some."

"No. I mean yes." He snatched the mug from Doug. "Yes, I want coffee, and no, I don't want to have it with you."

Doug glared at him. "What the hell is wrong with you?"

Nelson did his best to get his anger in check, but he was seething. If this were the first time Doug showed up unannounced or the first time he acted like the bakery was still his, then perhaps Nelson could have blown it off. But it wasn't the first time, and the more Nelson thought about it, the madder he became. Doug just wasn't getting it, and it was time Nelson drew him a picture.

He held is hand out. "Key."

Doug spit and sputtered, but he reached in his pocket, pulled out the key, and dropped it in Nelson's hand. "Happy?"

"Nope, but I will be." He went to the counter, grabbed a to-go cup, and filled it. He put the lid on it and handed it to Doug. "Now make me happy and head out."

Doug hesitated with a disbelieving expression on his face. "You're serious?"

"As serious as a heart attack. We are no longer together, this is no longer your place, and you're no longer welcome unless you're coming through the front door during regular business hours. Got it?"

Nelson expected Doug to balk. He always had been a bit demanding and a whole lot conceited. He was extremely good-looking and thought that was enough to get what he wanted. Too bad the inside of the man wasn't as pretty as the exterior. However, much to Nelson's surprise, Doug headed to the front door without another word. Nelson followed him, and wouldn't he just know it, as they approached, Luke walked past the window. *Motherfucker.* Not Luke, the situation.

Doug turned the lock and yanked the door open, and of course slammed into Luke. "Hey! Watch where you're going," Doug snapped.

"Sorry, I didn't see you," Luke apologized. His face lit up when his gaze met Nelson's. "Good morning, Nelson."

Doug looked back and forth between Nelson and Luke, his face an angry shade of red. "Now I fucking get it."

"Get what?" Nelson asked with a heavy sigh.

"Why you're being such a little bitch this morning. You couldn't even wait for the ink to dry, could you, Nelson?"

Luke took a step back and held up his hands. "Oh, hey, I didn't mean to interrupt anything. I can come back later."

"No, it's fine. Doug was just leaving," Nelson assured Luke. He glared at Doug. "I will talk to you later."

"The hell you will. We're done." Doug stormed off.

No shit we're done. I've been telling you that for months! He didn't say it because he knew it was pointless. Doug would be back in a day or two, acting like nothing happened. He really didn't want Nelson. He wanted what Nelson could do for him—pay the bills while Doug spent the day researching. The thought of having to sit and listen to Doug whine again was exhausting.

Nelson swallowed down his sigh, moved out of the way, and held the door. "Come on in, Luke."

Luke came in, but he looked wary. "I'm really sorry for interrupting. I won't mind waiting if you want to go talk to him."

"Oh God no. I may end up doing something that will require bail money."

"No bail on Sunday. You'd be stuck till Monday," Luke pointed out.

"Another reason not to go after him. At least he made coffee. Want some?"

"Sure."

Nelson led Luke to the counter and pointed to a stool. "Have a seat. I'll get your coffee. What do you want in it?"

Luke took the seat Nelson instructed. "Cream and sugar, please."

Nelson watched Luke take in the place as Nelson poured them each a mug. He was coffeed out, but he was fluttering with nervous energy and needed something other than Luke to focus on.

He set the mugs down and pulled a stool over to sit across from Luke.

"Thanks." Luke took the mug, blew on the steaming brew before taking a small sip.

"Is it okay?"

"Perfect." Luke scanned the room again. "Business is a little light this morning, huh?"

"I'm closed for the next six weeks while I do a little remodeling and tweaking of the menu." Nelson cocked his head. "I thought I told you that?"

"You may have, but I admit I was having a bit of a hard time paying attention. I mean, I know I should have been concentrating on Colton. It's not every day your little brother gets married, but...." Luke smiled over the rim of his mug. "My excitement at seeing you again may have gotten the better of me. How about I take you out for brunch, and you can tell me all about your plans for this magnificent place?"

Nelson was extremely proud of his bakery, and talking about it with Luke solved one of the dilemmas Nelson had been struggling with—what to talk about with Luke that wouldn't lead to unpleasant feelings from the past creeping in. The bakery was an easy topic. Nelson could talk about it for hours. "I could eat."

"Great." Luke downed the rest of his coffee and set his mug down. "I'm not familiar with your little town, so I'll let you pick the place as long as it's in walking distance. It's absolutely gorgeous out today."

Nelson had been freaking out all night, went without sleep, and for what? To spend the morning at his favorite outside café talking about his bakery. Talking about the future was way easier than the past. He flipped the coffee pot off. "I know the perfect place."

Chapter Twenty-Seven

PINING AFTER Lucas Rollins was a position Nelson swore he'd never be in again, and yet, here he was doing exactly that. Since Luke left less than a week ago, Nelson found himself clutching his phone each night as he fell asleep on the couch and checking for missed calls each morning upon waking. The only difference this time was Luke was calling him, and each morning there was a *Good morning, Sunshine. Hope you slept well* text from Luke. Maybe this time would be different. Luke definitely seemed sincere about wanting a future with him, yet Nelson wasn't sure he could trust his judgment when it came to Luke. His love for him had blinded him and set him up for a major fall in the past. It scared him beyond all reason that he might see Luke through those rose-colored glasses because he wanted it to be true.

You wouldn't know sincerity if it came up and bit you on the ass.

"Yeah, tell me something I don't already know," he berated himself. His past proved how true that statement was. Luke. Doug. His track record with men sure wasn't something to brag about.

He pulled another tray of chocolate-chip cookies from the oven and set them on the cooling rack. It was bordering on ridiculous how many things he'd baked in the past week. It was great for keeping his hands busy, but it only resulted in a freezer full of sweets. It did nothing to help him with what was really going on in his head. He had lost interest in just about everything, including cooking. While part of him was ecstatic Luke was back in his life, another part simply couldn't let go of the memory of searing pain in his chest when Luke broke his heart in two.

He turned off the oven, pulled his apron over his head, and hung it on a hook. He checked the clock on the wall. It was few minutes after five. Luke should be there any minute. A soft knock at his front door had Nelson mumbling, "Speak of the devil."

He pushed down his indecision and headed to the door. He opened it without checking. He knew who it was.

"Hi," Luke said, sounding nervous.

Nelson frowned. What did Luke have to be nervous about? Luke was dressed in form-fitting khaki pants, an unwrinkled linen button-up shirt—which, considering the long plane ride, was pretty amazing. To look at Luke, he had every reason to be confident, even dressed the part. However, even though Nelson had never known Luke to be shy or timid, the look in his eyes as well as his posture screamed it. It ramped up Nelson's unease to a temple-throbbing level.

"Hi, c'mon in." He stepped out of the way, ushering Luke in.

Luke dropped his duffel bag before removing his shoes. "Wow, it smells amazing in here."

"Thanks, I've been baking." For days. "Can I get you something to drink?" he asked as he headed to the kitchen. He sure could use it—a big, tall, powerful drink to soothe his jittery nerves. At least Luke had focused on the smell of his new apartment and not the disarray of the unpacked boxes.

"Beer if you have it," Luke responded quietly.

He grabbed two beers, figuring he could pull out the stronger stuff later, depending on how the conversation went. He was learning bourbon could cure just about anything in large enough quantities. Stepping back into the living room, he handed Luke a beer, careful not to allow their fingers to meet, and took a seat on the couch opposite the chair Luke had taken.

Luke didn't meet his eyes as he took the beer. "Thanks."

Nelson took a long pull of his beer and picked at the label, watching the condensation roll down the bottle, anything to keep him from looking at Luke. The silence stretched out until it became too heavy. "So how was your flight?" he asked without looking up.

"It was good. I'm happy it's over. Glad to be here," Luke answered, sounding as nervous as Nelson felt.

He studied the label on his beer, wanting to say he was glad Luke was here too, but he couldn't. His throat went suddenly dry as his insecurity began to overwhelm him. Feelings from the past reared their ugly heads, and suddenly the condensation running down the sides reminded him of tears.

Nelson caught Luke out of the corner of his eye as Luke leaned forward, forearms resting on his knees, beer dangling from his fingers. He kept his head down as he spoke. "Damn, there was a time when we could talk for hours about absolutely nothing, and now…." He laughed. The sound was sad, without Luke's normal exuberance. "I know it's my fault, and I take full responsibility for the tension in the room, but dammit, it sucks. I…. Well, I guess it doesn't matter what I thought."

Fuck! This wasn't the way I wanted this to go. Nelson took another deep pull from his beer, letting it soothe the dryness in his throat before he responded. "Of course it matters what you thought, and I agree about the tension, but it's not completely your fault. I'm kind of a mess, have been since Colton's wedding."

"Which is also my fault." Luke shook his head. "Okay, so not totally since I had no clue you lived here or were making Colton's cake." Luke stood abruptly, set his beer on the side table next to the chair, and began to pace. "You know what I wish?"

Nelson jumped from the couch and rushed to stop Luke from pacing. As soon as he touched Luke's arm, the electricity he'd felt the first time they touched was still there. The sensation was a jolt that went straight to his heart. "What do you wish for?"

Luke's smile was sweet, and rather than increase the electricity, it melted Nelson's heart. "That I could go back in time and make everything right so you and I never have to experience this new weirdness, this uncertainty." Luke gestured, waving his hand between himself and Nelson. "This."

"I admit this tension sucks, but the weirdness? That's nothing new. You've always been a bit weird," Nelson commented, wanting to lighten the mood before the throbbing in his head intensified.

Luke's eyes went comically wide. "Me? Isn't that like the kettle calling the pot black?"

Nelson waved a dismissive hand. "I am completely and utterly sane and far, far from weird." Nelson's voice cracked on a snort of laughter. He was surprised he'd been able to get out that lie with a straight face. He began to chuckle. He couldn't help it. He was ridiculously happy how quickly the tension seeped from the room, and some of his unease with it.

"That would have worked better for you if you'd been able to keep a straight face when saying it," Luke responded with a sly grin.

Nelson flung himself against Luke, wrapped his arms around him, and held on as he got his laughter under control. It felt not only wonderful but right when Luke pulled him closer. "I'll work on that," Nelson said as he gave in to the sudden urge to press his lips against Luke's neck, breathing in his unique scent. He savored it, pulling it into his lungs, relearning the wondrous scent he thought he would never smell again, relishing the feel of Luke's arms wrapped around him.

He leaned back and took Luke's face in his hands, meeting him squarely in the eye. He let Luke see every emotion that was surging through him. "Tell me this is a bad idea."

"I can't do that." He took Nelson's mouth in a brutal kiss, seeking entrance with his tongue, a sigh on his lips when Nelson let him in.

Luke pushed Nelson against the wall, moving his mouth down his jaw, across his neck. "In fact, I think it's a really, really good idea."

Nelson's brain obviously short-circuited because he forgot all about the past or future, only the here and now, his need, lust, desire, and the problem of too many clothes between them. He needed skin. Nelson grabbed the hem of Luke's shirt, tugging it up and off, forcing Luke to lean back. He moved in, licking and tasting Luke's chest. He mapped each inch of skin he could reach with his hands, relearning every ridge of muscle, every valley. He soaked in the warmth of Luke, letting the heat replace the uncertainty he had been dealing with.

"I didn't think I would ever feel this again," Nelson murmured against the skin of Luke's chest, emotion welling up in him. "Missed you so much."

Luke forced him to straighten, pulled him up until their lips met. Clothes cooperated and fell to the floor. All the things Nelson wanted to say, he said with his body. He rubbed his shaft against the hard steel of Luke's arousal, their bodies saying *hello again, missed you, need you, want you*. He arched his back as Luke ground against him, their breaths coming in short pants as the frenzy of their movements intensified.

"Oh fuck, Nelson.... God, I missed you."

Nelson moaned his agreement against Luke's neck, humping against the hard belly and even harder prick. The frenzy intensified as Luke began sucking a mark on his neck, his body giving back as good as it was getting.

They cried out in unison, the other's name on their lips as they erupted against each other. They clung desperately with lips and hands as each wave of aftershock caused their bodies to convulse and jerk. They held on as they trembled against each other, hearts thundering, breath coming in harsh pants. Both were lost in the powerful moment, wrapped in each other's arms.

Luke was the first to break the quiet. "I didn't see that coming."

Nelson placed a soft kiss to Luke's lips. "That's because you were a little busy. How about we move this into the bedroom, and you can witness it this time?"

Luke gave him a smile that melted him further, and then he pulled him toward the bedroom.

LUKE PULLED Nelson tighter to him, the sweat of their bodies drying in the light breeze from the ceiling fan. Their breathing slowed back to normal as their bodies eased in the silence. He had been such a fool walking away from this man without giving Nelson the chance to have any say in the matter. He'd given up the most amazing thing that ever happened to him, the perfect friend, the perfect lover. He made himself a promise, as he listened to Nelson's even breath and felt the heat of his body against his, that he would never let him go again.

"What are you thinking about?" Nelson asked against his chest, snuggling in deeper.

"Was just making a promise to myself."

Nelson lifted his head, those sleepy eyes searching his. "Can I know your promise, or is it a secret?"

"It's a promise for you." Luke kissed the tip of his nose. "I'll never be foolish enough to walk away from you again. I want a future with you." They were good together. Better than good; they belonged together.

Luke hadn't been prepared for the distraught expression on Nelson's face, and it twisted Luke's chest painfully. God, he was an idiot. They'd just had the most mind-blowingly best sex, something Luke hadn't expected, but was elated it had happened. Why did he have to go and ruin it by getting all sentimental and start pouring his heart out? *Stupid, stupid, stupid.*

Thankfully Nelson recovered quickly, the sadness in his eyes clearing, and he changed the subject. He kissed Luke, a slight smile on his lips. "If I lie here any longer, I'm going to permanently stick to the sheets. Plus I stink."

"You don't stink." Luke drew in a deep breath through his nose. "You smell good, like hot, raw, yummy sex. In fact, you smell so good, I think we should do it again." He rolled, pinning Nelson to the bed beneath him, happy he hadn't ruined the moment.

"I'll never get it up again." Nelson laughed, squirming to get Luke off him.

The squirming was doing all kinds of delicious things to Luke's body. His cock started to fill again in anticipation. "Is that a challenge?"

"Just a fact."

Luke forced Nelson's legs closed, pinning them together with his thighs. Leaning down, he brushed his lips against the sensitive skin beneath

Nelson's ear. "That sounded a bit like a dare." He traced the shell of Nelson's ear, causing him to shudder beneath him. "Definitely a dare."

Nelson's breath caught.

Luke was more than ready for the challenge. The attraction between them was certainly still there. They had the physical part going for them, and it was good, real good. Right now he planned on claiming Nelson's body. He'd work on claiming his heart later. He moved up Nelson's body until he could feel his growing erection. "I want you to fuck me. Feel that impressive cock stretching me wide open."

Nelson whimpered, his body beginning to tremble, hips jerking.

"Want you to fuck me so hard I'll feel you for days," he whispered against Nelson's ear.

Reaching out, Nelson snatched the lube and condoms from the bedside table, throwing the lube at Luke as he began opening the foil package. "Get yourself ready, but fuck, hurry."

Luke chuckled as he slicked his fingers and lifted his weight off Nelson. "Thought you said you couldn't get it up again." His words and laughter morphed into a moan as he breached his own opening with his slick finger. God, it'd been so long since he'd had anyone inside him. His heart was slamming in his chest, his cock leaking, and his head spinning in anticipation of Nelson filling him.

Nelson watched him. His heated eyes focused on him as he fumbled with the condom and struggled to roll it on with trembling fingers, rocking his hips, making the task that much more difficult. "That naughty mouth of yours, the thought of you riding me…. Fuck, how can I not?"

"Good answer," Luke moaned as he added a second finger, then shifted over Nelson's hips. "Ready?"

"Fuck yeah." Nelson wrapped a fist around the base of his cock, lining up the head with Luke's entrance, gasping as Luke began to drop.

Luke moved down, taking Nelson inside, the bursts of pleasurable pain making his eyes roll back in his head. Nelson pulled his hand away, and Luke lowered himself slowly, feeling the burn as Nelson's cock stretched him. As his ass met Nelson's thighs, he froze, relishing his lover filling him. He'd done plenty of fucking around after his divorce, but never with anyone he cared about as much as he did Nelson. He wanted to roar with how perfect it felt, how perfectly they fit together.

He forced his eyes open to look down at Nelson. So hot. He slowly began to rock his hips, forcing a groan from both of them.

Nelson grabbed his hips, moving in sync with them, never taking his eyes from Luke. "Damn, you feel good."

Luke didn't say a word and thrust down harder, taking Nelson deeper into his body. He loved the way Nelson's eyes devoured him, how his breath hitched with each thrust, and the sexy little moans escaping his parted lips. The combination was too much, ratcheting his lust to a boiling point. He gave in to the passion, accepting Nelson's thick cock into his body over and over, the stretch and burn so sweet. One hand was braced on Nelson's chest, and with the other he pulled hard at his own cock. "Fuck…. Oh God, you feel so…." The rest of what he would have said turned into a deep growl. His entire focus was on the cock in his ass and the heat in those magnificent eyes, the perfect union of flesh as their bodies flowed together in powerful waves.

Nelson planted his feet on the bed, tightening hands on Luke's hips as he thrust harder. Nelson met every downward motion of Luke's hips with an answering powerful lunge upward. "Luke… close."

Luke grunted in response, his ability to form coherent phrases long forgotten. Their frenzied pace became animalistic and brutal. He could feel the orgasm begin to build at the base of his spine. He fought to hold on, not ready to have this phenomenal feeling end. God, how had he ever given this up? Nelson was the one person he'd ever been truly and completely in love with.

He cried out as his orgasm ripped through him with the enormity of just how strong the love was. Nelson went rigid and roared Luke's name in an echoing response. He drifted, suspended in sheer bliss as he rode out each wave of his orgasm as it crashed into him until the last shudder left his body and he collapsed onto Nelson's chest.

"Oh sweet hell," Nelson sighed.

"I take it you liked that?" he huffed into Nelson's neck.

"Enough to drag my ass up out of this bed, shower, and do it again."

Luke patted Nelson's chest, groaning as he shifted and Nelson slipped out of him. "Give me a minute." He rolled, threw one leg up over Nelson's thigh, and snuggled up against his shoulder. "I'll get my second wind in a moment."

They were going to be stuck together if they didn't get up and clean up, but, as his eyes closed, it didn't seem like it was very important. At least not as important as the way Nelson's body felt against him and the contentment it created.

Chapter Twenty-Eight

LUKE HAD arrived a week ago and Nelson knew two things for sure—one, his dick was red and raw and probably going to fall off if he didn't slow down. Second, he was totally in love with Luke. The former he could deal with; the latter wasn't as easy to handle. It wasn't as if he really had that much time to think about his feelings. Whenever he'd start, when old emotions started to bubble to the surface, Luke had an uncanny ability to sense it, and the next thing Nelson knew, he either was on his back, his knees, or pressed up against a wall with his dick down Luke's throat.

They needed to talk. Nelson was no longer a child, couldn't blame his current feelings or behavior on the immaturity of youth. He was and always had been in love with Luke—that would never change. The sex was off-the-charts scorching, but it was the tidal wave of emotions that always came up when Nelson was coming down from sexual bliss that had to be dealt with.

"I'm lonely," Luke called out from the bedroom.

Nelson wrapped his hands around his mug and took a sip of his coffee rather than answer. If he did, Luke would use his charm, and Nelson would end up in bed. They'd be fucking Luke's last day there away.

"I'm cold."

"I have hot coffee to warm you up," Nelson yelled back.

"I don't want coffee. I want you to warm me up." After a long pause, Luke obviously was changing his strategy because he added, "How about you bring me a cup of coffee?"

Nope, he wasn't going to give in this time. Nope, nope, nope. Nelson took another sip. "I also have warm cinnamon bread," he tempted.

"Ohhh, breakfast in bed."

Nelson knew what, or rather whom, would be the feast. He wasn't giving in. Instead he pushed to his feet and went to the warmer to retrieve the bread. He took it and a stick of butter to the table. Luke still hadn't joined him, so Nelson kept busy by slicing the bread, serving it onto two plates.

By the time he had the table set, including two hot cups of coffee, Luke finally came stumbling out of the bedroom. His hair was sticking up, and impressions from the sheets were etched on his face. Luke may not have been happy about getting up, but there were certain parts of him that seemed to be really excited about it. Nelson ripped his gaze away from Luke's groin.

"I can't believe you left me in there all alone," Luke grumbled.

"Poor baby, I'm sure you'll survive. Have a seat," Nelson instructed and pointed to the chair on the other side of the table. He didn't trust himself if he sat next to Luke, felt his heat, took in his scent.

Luke huffed dramatically, but he did as Nelson instructed. His pout disappeared the instant his gaze landed on the coffee, and he happily picked up his mug and took a sip. He then picked up a piece of bread and sniffed it, his smile growing. "Okay, this kind of makes up for it," he said and popped a big piece into his mouth.

"What time are you leaving?"

"I don't want to think about that right now," Luke said around another big bite.

There were plenty of things Luke didn't want to talk about. Nelson wasn't thrilled about it either, but he knew they had to. They'd been down this road before, living in the moment, allowing their dicks to guide them, and Nelson was painfully aware of how that turned out the last time. "I don't want to either," Nelson admitted. "I've enjoyed having you here, but it's kind of hard to ignore the inevitable."

"From the tone in your voice, I have a funny feeling we're not talking about my trip home."

"That's part of it," Nelson admitted.

Luke looked at Nelson with a wary expression. "And the other part."

Luke had to know there was more. They'd been fucking like bunnies, eating, and binge-watching old classic horror movies when they were too exhausted to fuck and avoiding anything serious or difficult. But some things simply couldn't be left unsaid. "Like I said, this past week has been great. After the last year, I needed some time to enjoy life, and I have, but that doesn't mean it hasn't been without stress."

"I know," Luke agreed. "You get this look on your face, and your body tenses when you start thinking about something. I know it's about us, or rather me."

"You know, this would be a lot easier if we were hooking up just to fuck and leave it at that, but you and I both know that's impossible. Too much shit has happened in the past to just fuck. Feelings, good and bad, are always there waiting to be dealt with."

"Do you mind if I put some pants on and get another cup of coffee before we go down that path?" Luke asked, sounding resigned to the fact he couldn't get Nelson in bed this time.

"Sure, you go dress, and I'll make more coffee."

Luke nodded, holding Nelson's gaze, but he didn't get up. Nelson didn't flinch, letting Luke see how serious he was about this. He refused to let Luke's charm seduce him, although it wasn't without difficulty. The years had been good to Luke, very good. He'd always been handsome, but years and wisdom made him even more so. Although the dimples still gave him a bit of a boyish look and they were the hardest to resist, somehow Nelson managed. After a few more seconds, Luke nodded again, apparently reading something in Nelson that had him up and moving.

Nelson waited until Luke turned before letting out a pent-up breath. It had taken every bit of willpower not to say "fuck it" and follow Luke and spend the rest of the day in bed with him. When he stood up and the fabric of his sweatpants brushed across his abused dick, it reminded Nelson of the soundness of his decision. He gritted his teeth. It was amazing how the soft cotton suddenly felt like coarse sandpaper. Nelson had another pot of coffee brewed and their mugs refilled by the time Luke rejoined him. Luke looked much less excited than he did earlier.

"Okay, I'm ready, but be gentle with me," Luke said. His words were teasing, but his voice was tight, giving away how nervous he was.

"I don't know how gentle I can be. If we were talking about sex, maybe." Luke shifted in his seat and arched a brow. "Okay, that may be the wrong word choice, but you know what I mean."

Luke didn't even try to hide his sigh. "Yeah, I know."

"Look, I'm not trying to force you here. If you don't want to talk, then I'll just have to deal, but honestly, do you think the fuck-buddy thing is going to work here?"

"You mean too much to me to call you that."

Nelson wasn't sure where it came from or why at that exact moment it escaped, but anger so intense came rushing to the surface that it nearly stole his breath and left him trembling. "When you say shit like that, I have a really hard time believing you."

"I can understand that."

Luke sounded so reasonable that Nelson wanted to fucking scream. It scared him a little how suddenly the anger had overwhelmed him. He tried shoving it back down so he could speak calmly and rationally, but now that the lid was off Pandora's box, it refused to be shut. "I don't think you do," Nelson insisted. "I didn't walk away from you and choose to never speak to you again. That leaves a bitter taste in a person's mouth."

"I'm not saying I understand how you felt, only that I understand why you have a hard time hearing me say certain things. I'm sure the heartbreak and pain I experienced pales in comparison to what you went through."

"That's because it was your choice, something you didn't give me!"

"I know."

For reasons Nelson couldn't comprehend, that simple statement was the proverbial match to the keg of gunpowder, and his anger exploded. He jumped to his feet. "You don't have a fucking clue, so don't even pretend to act like you do. You ripped my fucking heart out. Not only did you yank it from my chest, but you stomped all over it. I don't trust you. I'm not even sure if I like you because I don't know you! I don't even know if I want to know you. Anyone who can do what you did to someone he claimed to care about, to someone he grew up with and had at one time called a best friend, isn't someone I would choose to associate with. I don't know why you're here, what you want from me, and how dare you expect anything from me."

Well, that escalated quickly. Nelson had not planned on starting at that point, but slowly and reasonably leading up to it so they could deal with and work through the issues. But apparently his heart had other ideas, and he was unable to rein it back in. Surprisingly, he wasn't the least bit sorry Luke was looking at him as if Nelson had just punched him in the face. Another thing that surprised Nelson was Luke stayed sitting in his chair, never looked away from Nelson, and didn't interrupt. He sat there and took every hateful word Nelson threw at him instead of walking away.

Nelson didn't think he had it in him, but a part of him was rejoicing at seeing Luke in pain. He felt vindicated and horrified in equal measures. However, it didn't stop him from inflicting even more pain as he purged it from his soul and slung it at Luke with force.

"Goddammit, Luke, do you even realize how much I fucking hated you? I sat in my little apartment day after day with that fucking phone, waiting, wishing, hoping, but you never called. Each day I hated you more, and I think part of me still does. You come back in my life, force all those bad feelings out of me, force me to deal with them, and I don't know if I can forgive you for that. For any of it. I don't know what you want from me, but right now it feels like you only showed up to torment me all over again." Tears were flowing, his breathing harsh, and he was trembling so hard he was sure he was going to shake apart. Standing there screaming and ranting like a madman while Luke sat there taking it, no tears, no words, breathing.... *GODDAMN HIM!*

The edges of Nelson's vision went black and started creeping in until the nothingness took over, and he welcomed it.

LUKE JUMPED to his feet and rushed to Nelson mere seconds before his eyes rolled back in his head. Luke had his arms around Nelson, holding him tight when he collapsed. He eased them down onto the floor and carefully examined Nelson. Luke had seen the color intensify in Nelson's face, watched as his breathing and shaking increased and could tell if he didn't calm down, he was going to hyperventilate. Luke hadn't dared tell him that. Besides, he seriously doubted Nelson would have heard him. But Luke heard Nelson. Heard every word, and as painful as they were, Luke deserved them and more.

Avoiding the tough issues probably hadn't been the best idea. His intention was to reconnect on the easy part—their attraction—and holy hell, had they reconnected, time after time after time. But Nelson was a thinker, a brooder. How could Luke forget that? He should have known during the quiet times, when they were coming down from their bliss, Nelson would have been contemplating things. Looking at each event, each emotion, and each statement and turning it over and over, analyzing it. Nelson's meltdown was Luke's fault, plain and simple.

As was the reason behind it.

Luke gently brushed the hair from Nelson's damp forehead. He wasn't about to sit here and wallow in a pity party. He'd already done enough damage by not putting Nelson's feelings first.

Nelson's lids fluttered open with a dazed look in his eyes. It only lasted a second, and Nelson scrambled to get out of Luke's arms. He nearly fell back on his ass, and Luke reached out to steady him. Nelson swatted his hand away. The color in his cheeks was evidence of Nelson's embarrassment. Luke started to tell him there was nothing to be embarrassed about but snapped his mouth shut. It wouldn't help.

He pushed up off the floor and sat in the chair. "Are you okay?"

"No, I'm not okay. I'm a fucking mess," Nelson responded. He ran his fingers through his hair, then clamped his hands behind his head, glaring at Luke.

"Would you like me to give you a minute alone?"

"Yes… I mean, no, I…. Dammit, Luke, I'm not even sure what I'm feeling or what I need right now. Hell, I don't even know where all that came from. I certainly didn't plan on saying all that shit, and I damn sure didn't expect to get so worked up that I fainted like a delicate Southern belle."

Luke hung his head. "I went about this all wrong."

"What's that supposed to mean?"

"You and I have no problem with the physical attraction, and I thought if we made that the focus and had fun together like we used to, then it might be a little easier to deal with the other stuff. You know, like when we were young."

Nelson slumped in the chair next to Luke. "You didn't twist my arm. I was all on board for the fuckfest. But come on, we had to realize too much has happened between us and in the years we were apart to go back."

"Of course I realized it, but I… I'm sorry, Nelson. I was a fool to leave you, a fool to walk away and not give you a choice."

"Why?"

"Because I'm an idiot."

"No, I meant, why did you just walk away. That was the hardest part for me. No explanation, no closure, nothing."

"At the time, I honestly thought I was doing the right thing." Luke held Nelson's gaze, hoping Nelson would see the sincerity in his eyes. "I knew there was no way I could do what I thought I had to for my child. I couldn't have stayed with Charlotte or been faithful to her. I was weak. I wanted you, and I kept thinking of you going on with your life and meeting someone else. That would have crushed me." It still would. However, the more he thought about how to explain his actions, he realized there was no excuse for what he'd done.

Luke took Nelson's hand and entwined their fingers. "I was going to say, I loved you too much to imagine you with anyone else. I can't use that as an excuse for my actions. I have no excuse. I told myself I was doing it for you, to keep you from hurting, but I really did it for me. I was selfish and stupid. and I am so sorry, Nelson."

Nelson didn't say anything but, to Luke's great relief, didn't pull his hand away. After a moment, he nodded. "I'm glad you told me. I mean, it doesn't take away all the pain—there is still healing to do—but it's a start."

"So you may even forgive me one day?" Luke asked.

"Maybe."

"It's a start," Luke said, echoing Nelson's words. "And here I thought it would be better to reconnect on a primal level first."

"Figures a Brobdingnagian would want to go primal."

Luke started to laugh. He hadn't been called Brobdingnagian in forever. It made him ridiculously happy to hear the endearment pass Nelson's lips. "Oh. My. God. I remember when you used to call me that," he got out between snorts of laughter.

"It wasn't a compliment, you asshole." Nelson glared at him, but from the slight upturn of his lip, it was evident he was trying to hold back a grin.

The morning had been a rollercoaster of emotions, and Luke had no misconceptions the ride would be a smooth one. It still had a lot of ups and downs, twists and turns. However, after hitting such a low point, the fact they could cut up and laugh again was extraordinary. When Nelson lost the battle and started laughing with Luke, Luke knew they at least had a chance to move forward together.

Chapter Twenty-Nine

SITTING AMONG an avalanche of pamphlets, Luke scanned the chaos, the task of choosing one overwhelming. "You do realize if you narrowed this down to a few hundred, this would be much easier."

Nellie looked up from one of the pamphlets she'd been reading to give him one of her signature looks Luke had come to learn meant *Will you stop being so weird and annoying?*

Nellie tossed the paper aside. "This is like the biggest decision of my life. It's imperative I get it right."

"That's a bit overdramatic, don't you think?"

BAM, there was that look again. Luke pushed to his feet. He needed a drink. "You know what? I think I'll leave this to you."

"Daddy," Nellie whined. "Graduating from the right university could mean the difference between having a great career and becoming a bag lady. I so would not do well pushing around a grocery cart and begging for food."

Ah, his little Miss Drama. Luke didn't say it out loud. He'd only get another one of *those* looks. Instead he kissed her on the top of the head as he passed on his way to the liquor cabinet. His daughter was beautiful, bright, and had great common sense. He had no doubt she would succeed at anything she put her mind to. But he did have to agree with her at some level. Going into anthropology didn't seem like a glamorous career, and honestly, he had no clue as to what the job market was like for that field of work. He put a couple of ice cubes in a cocktail glass and added a good measure of bourbon. He brought it back to the table and took his seat before he said anything further.

"Do you have your favorites?"

Now that she had Luke's attention, Nellie's face lit up. "I do. The University of Chicago is well-known for its attention to classic problems in social theory along with an engagement with the latest developments in theories of history, culture, politics, economics, transnational processes, space and place, subjectivity, experience, and materiality."

Luke had no clue what language she was speaking. He knew money, making it, spending it, and saving it. Anthropology was way over his head. He hoped like hell she didn't expect him to help her with her homework. "You sound like one of these pamphlets."

"I may have memorized it." Nellie giggled.

"If you've already picked your favorite, please tell me why we are sitting here with this mess." Luke waved his hand at the papers covering the table.

"What if I don't get in? I have to have a plan B. A plan C isn't a bad idea either."

"You'll get in," Luke assured her.

"You can't know that."

Luke sat back in his chair, taking his drink with him. He took a sip and smiled. He was so amazingly proud of his daughter. She was extremely hardworking when it came to her studies, her 4.16 grade-point average a testament to just how hard she worked. She was also humble, always striving to do better. Her amazing heart brought joy to so many people. Just like her namesake, although she didn't know Nelson, but he hoped she'd get to know him in the future. Oh shit! If Nellie moved to Chicago, that would solve Luke's problem. He wanted to be near Nelson and planned to do so, but being far from Nellie didn't feel right.

"I can know that," he finally told her. "In fact, I am so sure you'll get in, I think we should go check out the housing situation over Christmas holiday."

"Really? I've never had a white Christmas."

"Sure. Why not?"

Nellie's shoulders slumped. "Oh, wait, I can't. I promised Mom I'd spend Christmas with her this year."

"Christmas isn't a day; it's a feeling. You've got two weeks off from school. We'll celebrate around your visit with your mom."

Nellie jumped up and flung herself at Luke, wrapping her arms around his neck and squeezing. "You're the best daddy ever! I have to call Chloe. She's going to be so totally jealous I'm going to Chicago."

Before Luke could respond, she was rushing out of the room. He looked down at the mess on his shirt and the half-empty glass of bourbon and shook his head. As excited as his little girl was, Luke's own might rival hers. Chicago for the holidays? His smile grew until it nearly cracked his face. It could prove to be the best Christmas he'd had in a very long time. Chicago was only a two-and-a-half-hour drive to Saugatuck.

THE DISAPPOINTMENT Nelson heard in his mom's voice filled him with guilt. She and his dad had been looking forward to him coming home for the holidays, and it sucked that he had to call them and inform them he wouldn't be making it home this year again. It had been four years since he spent Christmas with them. It was the nature of his business. He made decent money selling coffee and pastries to the locals, but the big money, the money that assured the bakery's success, came from weddings and holiday orders.

The plan had been, once Nelson finished the last order on Christmas Eve, he'd head home. Unfortunately, the contractors ran into issues with creepy crawlies that shut down the job until an exterminator came in and eliminated the bastards. Then there was damaged wood to be replaced and permits to be obtained. Delay, delay, delay. Of course they would want to resume work the day after Christmas. On the bright side, Doug had met another "aspiring" writer. The two of them were driving across the country together in search of inspiration. At least Nelson would no longer have to deal with Doug showing up unannounced and begging.

Still, the thought of what he need to do inside the shop, all he was going to miss, made Nelson's head throb. He sat back in his chair and scrubbed a hand over his face, his week-old beard tickling his palm. His office phone rang, and he grabbed a pen and pad of paper before picking up the receiver.

"Maitland Confections, how can I help you?"

There was a slight pause, then the caller sputtered a couple of times before saying, "I'm sorry, I was trying to call Nel-D's."

"You've reached them," Nelson informed her. "We've had a name change. Is there something I can help you with?"

"Yes, sir. A friend gave me your number. I'm looking to have a cake made for my daughter's birthday."

Wonderful thing, word of mouth. He went over options, set up an appointment, and was thankful for the distraction. If he had to be stuck in Saugatuck for the holidays, then at least he'd be busy. After making the arrangements, he thanked her and set the phone down on the cradle. Before he could even pull his hand back, it rang again.

"Maitland Confections, how can I help you?"

"You can tell me you're going to be home for the holidays?" Luke asked.

Nelson smiled when he recognized Luke's voice. "Nope, sorry."

"Damn, and I was planning on taking a ride up to see you."

"Seriously? Wait a minute. What do you mean, take a ride up?"

"Nellie and I will be in Chicago the day after Christmas, and I was hoping I'd get a chance to see you." The disappointment was evident in Luke's tone.

"That's great. It would be great seeing you."

"But you just said—"

"I said I wouldn't be home, but I never said I wouldn't be in Saugatuck. Renovations have hit a few stumbling blocks, so I'll be at the shop day and night, not only up till Christmas, but it looks like well after too."

"That's great! I mean, that sucks about the renos, but great news for me," Luke clarified happily.

Nelson was ridiculously happy Luke would be coming to visit. If he was stuck working, at least he'd have some company. Plus it wouldn't hurt to have some extra muscles to help with the project and cleanup. "So the day after, huh?"

"Yup."

"Alright, but you better bring your tool belt and boots."

"Mmm, you want to do a little fantasy role-playing?"

There went Luke's one-track mind. They had done a lot of talking since Luke returned to California, but even when they promised each other they were going keep their dicks in their pants, one or both of them always ended up throwing in a sexual innuendo, and bam, they were off topic.

"Yeah, that's it. I want to bang a sexy construction worker, so bring a hard hat too."

"I got something hard for you, alright."

A rap on Nelson's office door had him looking up to see Grady peek his head around the frame. Nelson put his hand over the receiver. "What's up?"

"Your two o'clock is here," Grady informed him.

"Be right there," he told him before turning his attention back to Luke. "Hold that thought. I have a client waiting."

"I'll be holding it. Rubbing it. Stroking it."

"You're done," Nelson said.

"But—"

Nelson went to his feet. He knew how this would go if he stayed on the phone a moment longer. "Gotta go."

"But—"

"Bye, Luke."

Luke huffed a heavy breath as if knowing he couldn't win this one. "Bye, Nelson."

"Call you tonight." He hung up the phone and picked up his jacket from his chair. He slipped it on and headed out the door with a huge smile on his face. He'd started out the morning in a crap mood, and with one call, his day was made, as were his holiday plans.

Luke for Christmas. Nelson's smile grew. Damn fine present.

Chapter Thirty

IT WASN'T Luke's first time in subzero temperatures, and perhaps he'd blocked it out, but he didn't remember it ever being this fucking cold. He was literally shaking like a leaf in a windstorm, and his balls were so far up into his stomach he seriously doubted he'd see them till spring.

He wrapped his arms around himself, hopping from foot to foot to keep the blood from freezing where he stood. "There is no way you can like living here in the winter."

Nelson finished unlocking the door to the bakery, then shrugged. "You get used to it."

Luke rushed past Nelson the second he had the door open. "Bullshit. Humans weren't made for these kinds of temperatures. There is no way I could get used to it."

"How soon they forget," Nelson chuckled. He pulled off his jacket and hung it on a hook, then stomped his boots on the rug to dislodge some of the snow.

"What's that supposed to mean?" Luke asked. He followed Nelson's lead, stomping off the snow on his boots, but kept his coat. He was too cold to let it go just yet.

"Remember when we were kids? We used to pray for either mass quantities of snow or temperatures of negative ten or less."

"That's because our brains weren't fully developed, so we didn't know any better. Now we do." Luke tilted his head back, then nodded to the new sign. "They did a great job on that."

"I hate it," Nelson insisted. He pulled a bottle of coffee Patron from where he'd hidden it beneath the counter and poured a good measure in two mugs rimmed with crushed peppermint.

Luke took a seat at the counter and eyed Nelson with a curious look. "Then why did you hang it up?"

"It's not the sign I hate, but the name," Nelson clarified. He took the mugs to the hot chocolate dispenser and filled them.

"I think it's a great name and a great sign. What's that you're making?"

Nelson stirred each drink, then brought them over to the counter, setting one in front of Luke. "This, my friend, is how one survives winters here."

Luke eyed it suspiciously. He'd never been a fan of fancy drinks. Beer was his go-to. Nelson taught him to enjoy good bourbon, but this? He sniffed it.

"Oh, just try it," Nelson urged.

"Well, if it helps me survive the winter, what the hell." He took a tentative sip. It was warm, chocolatey…. He took another sip, the Patron heating his throat and gut even more than the temperature of the drink.

"Well?"

"Okay, I can totally see how this could help. I'm already starting to feel warm and fuzzy."

Nelson laughed. "That's probably because you have your coat on and are about to pass out from the heat, but yeah, the drink helps."

"Oh yeah, it does," Luke agreed. He took another sip before sliding out of his coat.

"So, what are Nellie and your parents up to?"

"They are shopping, can you believe that? Nellie has spent the last week opening gifts. What possibly could she not have gotten?"

"It's a girl thing, I guess," Nelson responded with a shrug.

"I guess. What's on the agenda for today?"

"The contractors were supposed to be back today, but once again, delay. I swear to fuck, I am so sick and tired of hearing about issues that set the complete date farther and farther. Not to mention the hits my budget has taken."

Luke looked around the bakery. It looked even better than the last time he was here. Not only did the place have new name, but a new vibe. A good one. "It looks amazing. I would have thought this place was done. I don't see a single sign of construction."

"Grab your drink."

Luke picked up his drink and followed Nelson into the back room. His eyes were glued to the sway of Nelson's hips. He couldn't wait to get his hands on him. It felt like it forever since he'd had his lips on Nelson's sweet flesh. The shock of seeing the kitchen pulled Luke from his lustful thoughts. "Holy hell."

Nelson nodded. "That pretty much sums it up."

There was a small area that seemed to be usable, but the rest of the room was complete and utter chaos. The wall to the back room was nothing but studs, a large portion of the ceiling missing, exposing the rafters and wiring. "How in the fuck have you been baking back here?"

Nelson pointed to the one clean spot. "Every day we wrap my little workstation in plastic, and I do what I gotta do. Plus I've been baking at home too."

"Anything we can do to get you closer to fixing this?" Luke asked, still scanning the area in disbelief.

"Nope, unfortunately not. Something about a missing permit that shut the jobsite down," Nelson said, his tone full of sadness.

The disappointment in Nelson was palpable, and Luke would do anything to make him feel better. Unfortunately he couldn't do anything about the jobsite, but…. He stepped up close to Nelson and wrapped his free arm around Nelson's waist. "You know there is one good thing about the crew not being here today."

Nelson arched a brow. "And what would that be?"

"We have the place all to ourselves." Luke pressed a soft kiss to Nelson's lips, then spoke against them. "And I've really, really—" He kissed him again. "—really missed you."

"Is that so?" Nelson asked, pushing up even closer, rolling his hips.

"Uh-huh. What's your office look like?"

Nelson took the drink from Luke and stepped back. He set them on the table, then grabbed Luke's hand. "Let me show you."

Chapter Thirty-One

THE HEAT of desire bloomed within Nelson. He'd spent countless hours fantasizing, an untold number of nights dreaming about being in Luke's arms again. "God, Luke. I swear I will kick your fucking ass if you ever leave me again. I need you so goddamn bad."

"Never." Luke pressed his lips to Nelson's. "And I'm right here. Right where I was meant to be. Now shut up and kiss me."

With a low moan, Nelson opened his mouth and invited Luke in. Nelson could barely believe it was finally happening. They'd been skirting around it for weeks, the sexual tension growing until it threatened to explode. Yet Nelson hadn't been able to give in to the need for fear if he did, his heart would be broken. He couldn't bear it again. There was still a chance it might happen, but the thought of not giving Luke another chance was even more painful than the risk of a broken heart.

Luke shifted, spread his legs, and encouraged Nelson to move between them. "C'mon, Nelson. Want to feel you deep inside me, need to," Luke whispered against Nelson's lips.

Breaking the kiss, Nelson sat back on his calves without taking his gaze from Luke. The expression of lust on Luke's handsome face stole his breath. He reached over, snatched up his pants, and pulled a condom from the pocket and rolled it down his length, then grabbed the lube packet. He ripped it open, poured a small amount onto his fingers, and slicked his sheathed dick, moaning at the slight touch. Luke's impressive cock swayed as if in response to the needy sounds Nelson was making. Urgency rushed through Nelson, and he poured more lube into his palm, tossing the packet aside and slicking his fingers.

Luke spread his legs wider as Nelson pressed the tip of one slick finger against Luke's ass. He gasped and tensed as Nelson breached his opening. "You alright?"

"Yeah." Luke licked his lips while inhaling deeply, then blew it out. "Burns a bit."

"Good kind?" Nelson pushed deeper, slowly and gently began to slide his finger in and out until Luke's body began to relax.

"Yeah."

Nelson stilled and smiled slyly. "I don't want to hurt you."

"I know you won't. You love me too much."

"You sure about that?"

Luke nodded. "Of course, not as much as I love you, but, you know," Luke teased.

Nelson moved up to lie on the floor next to Luke, kissing him soundly and leaving Luke panting when it ended. "You sure about that?"

"Only thing I'm sure about at this particular moment is that I need to feel you inside me."

Nelson kissed him again. "Your wish is my command, and I promise I'll be gentle."

"Only until I beg for more," Luke responded with a wicked smile.

"And you will," Nelson assured him. He worked a single finger in Luke's ass, watching Luke's face as he moved it in and out, going deeper and deeper with each gentle thrust. Luke's eyes became heavy lidded, his body opening up to Nelson. Nelson added a second finger next to the first. Luke hissed, and Nelson froze. "Too much?"

"No, it's okay. Just burns."

"Bad?"

"No, in a really good way."

Nelson spent an extended amount of time opening Luke up, which gave Nelson plenty of time to explore the delicious taste of Luke's neck, shoulder, and chest. Each stroke of Nelson's finger inside Luke's ass was like one to his own cock, and far too soon, his dick was pulsing and so fucking hard he thought he'd split wide open if he didn't get some relief soon.

Nelson pressed another kiss to the sensitive place below Luke's ear. "Please tell me you're ready for my cock."

"God yes. Just go slow," Luke moaned.

"As slow as you need," Nelson promised. He kissed Luke one more time, slid his fingers from Luke's ass, and moved to kneel between Luke's spread thighs. Nelson added more lube to the condom, then guided it to Luke's hole. Pressing gently, he nudged his cockhead against Luke's entrance, teasing it with short, easy thrusts until a deep rumbling moan escaped Luke's lips.

"Fuck, Nelson. You're driving me fucking nuts." He wrapped his long legs around Nelson, trapping him, then snapped his hips. The movement forced Nelson's cockhead to breach Luke's ass. They both moaned at the invasion.

Concerned, Nelson searched Luke's eyes for any signs of distress but only found lust, inflaming Nelson. He had the sudden urge to ram his cock balls-deep into Luke's hot, tight body. The restraint it took to keep from doing that had Nelson trembling with the strain. But he wouldn't cause Luke any undue pain, no matter how badly his body demanded he thrust and rut and take.

Nelson clamped down on the urge, instead moving with short, slow thrusts until he was once again deep within his lover's unresisting body. "Oh yeah, that's it," Luke groaned and grabbed Nelson's ass, encouraging him to move.

Nelson balanced on his hands, needing to see Luke's face, to read his expression as Nelson increased the speed of his hips. Luke's body welcomed him, his ass gripping Nelson's cock like a tight glove. They found a rhythm, moving their bodies with familiarity, each stroke pushing them closer and closer to the edge. A thrill raced down Nelson's spine, and he went up on his knees, lifting Luke's hips off the floor. In this new position, Nelson was able to go deeper, each stroke hitting that sweet spot within Luke. He was close. Nelson knew it by the sounds pouring from his lover and the way his body was in constant motion.

Nelson increased his thrusts further still and wrapped his fist around Luke's cock, stroking it in time to the thrusts of Nelson's hips. "Fuck, you feel good. Not going to last much longer."

Luke opened his mouth in an apparent attempt to answer, but all that came out was a deep, throaty moan. Perhaps Luke was close, or it could have been the fact that at just that second, Nelson pulled almost all the way out and thrust back in.

"What was that?" Nelson asked and thrust again.

Luke's eyes blazed blue fire, his jaw set in a defiant expression. "Harder, then," he demanded, jerking his hips as Nelson thrust into him.

Nelson leaned down, nearly bending Luke in half until their lips were but a hairsbreadth apart. "You haven't begged yet."

"Then you weren't listening," Luke taunted. He snapped his hips again.

Luke may not have used simple words such as "please" and "more," but his begging was in every thrust, every arch of his back or moan rumbling in his chest. Well, Nelson was fucking listening now. With renewed determination, Nelson growled and pulled out till only his cockhead was breaching Luke, then rammed in again over and over, pounding into Luke again and again.

Luke draped his knees over Nelson's forearms, raising his hips to meet each of Nelson's forward thrusts, completely opening himself up so Nelson could fuck him as hard and as long as he wanted. Luke's body was muscular and strong and could take anything Nelson gave him. To be in such a position over such a powerful man only added to the eroticism. Luke was so hot, so tight, and if it felt any fucking better, Nelson feared his head would explode.

Over and over Nelson slammed into Luke, pouring every bit of need and want and love, and Luke took it, urging Nelson on, thrusting and bucking and daring Nelson wordlessly to fuck him harder, to take and give what they both so desperately needed.

A knot formed at the base of Nelson's spine, and the pressure in his balls grew. He knew he couldn't last much longer. How could he when it felt so fucking good? The tight grip of Luke's body around his cock, stroking him, demanded his release as completely as Nelson demanded his.

"Luke," he groaned. His thrusts were erratic and without finesse as his release began to race down his spine. "Going to.... Can't.... Fuck, Luke. Come with me," he pleaded with the last of his breath.

"Do it," Luke demanded.

Nelson pressed upward, arching his back, and slammed into Luke's pliable body one last time, nailing Luke's sweet spot. Nelson groaned as the orgasm overwhelmed him, building in a fury, stealing his breath, then rushed from his body like white-hot fire. As he came he heard Luke groan Nelson's name, warm wetness spreading between their bodies.

"Fuck yeah, that's it, Luke, come for me."

Nelson rode out his orgasm until every drop drained from his body. Luke's legs fell to the mattress, and Nelson collapsed on Luke's chest, spreading the wet warmth further. As Nelson struggled to catch his breath, his body melted into Luke's, complexly spent and content. Only Luke could ever make him feel this way.

Nelson closed his eyes and breathed in Luke's scent, basked in his heat. He had no idea where this new journey with Luke was going, but if he'd learned one thing from the past, it was to live in the moment because tomorrow wasn't guaranteed. What he did have was the here and now. Throughout his life, the only time he was truly happy was when he was with Luke. Sure, they'd had some bad times, really, really bad times. But that too was in the past, and Nelson either had to dwell on it or move forward. Lying next to Luke, feeling his body against his, he knew it was where he belonged. Hopefully fate would finally give up and realize she wasn't ever going to keep them apart for too long.

Epilogue

"THIS IS the last one," Luke announced, coming through the door with yet another large box.

When they'd decided to move in together, Nelson had no clue Luke would have so much stuff. They'd been unpacking the moving truck for hours. The garage as well as the living room were chock-full of boxes. Unpacking was going to be a bitch. Nelson had no idea where the hell they were going to put everything. He swiped his hand over his sweaty brow. "We're going to need a bigger house."

Luke set the box down next to the door—the last spot of floor space left—then bumped his shoulder against Nelson's. "It's not as much stuff as it looks. Half of it is Bubble Wrap and Styrofoam. Think we can make it to the kitchen? I'm dying of thirst."

"It will be tough, but I do like a challenge."

They made their way through the maze of boxes, and Nelson was right: it was a hell of a challenge. It wasn't the boxes so much that made it difficult but the fact Luke kept grabbing his ass or his belt loop and jerking him back to give him a kiss. By the time they made it to the kitchen, Nelson was laughing, and his dick was hard. A very good state to be in—happy and horny.

He got them both a glass of ice water. He handed one to Luke, then clinked his against it. "Here's to finally getting the truck unloaded."

"Here, here."

Nelson downed his water and refilled his glass. He turned and leaned against the counter. "Nellie is really okay with this?"

"Hell yeah. She loves the idea that I'll be so close to her. She's been making a lot of new friends in Chicago but likes that Dad isn't too far away."

"I meant about us."

Luke cocked his head. "I'm not following."

"I know you told me she's never had an issue with your sexuality, but it's one thing knowing your dad is bisexual, but a whole different animal when he moves in with another man."

Luke set his glass down and wrapped his arms around Nelson. "Trust me, she's okay with it. She's happy that I'm happy, but you know what?"

Nelson slid his fingers in the loops on the waistband of Luke's jeans and pulled him closer still, wiggling a bit, enjoying the feel of Luke's body against his. "What?"

Luke groaned and took Nelson's mouth in an all-consuming kiss that curled Nelson's toes and left him breathing harshly when it ended. "What were we talking about again?"

"I was asking you a question, I think," Luke chuckled.

"Was it an important one?" Nelson rutted a little. They'd been working hard all day. He'd been watching all those flexing muscles, the sweat, the bending, the tight ass on display each time Luke set a box down. They deserved a little reward for all their hard work. He rutted a little harder.

Luke grabbed Nelson's hips and stilled his movements, a serious expression on his face. "Yeah, it was. I was saying that Nellie is happy for me, but even if she was opposed to me living with you, I'd still do it. She's grown, working on her future. It's only fair that I work on mine. I've spent my life trying to make other people happy, and it's beyond time that you and I are the priority." Luke moved his right hand up and laid it against Nelson's cheek. "I have loved you my entire life, and I want to spend the rest of it showing you just how much."

Tears welled in Nelson's eyes, but he blinked them away. He'd dreamed of spending his life with Luke, and it was coming true. Did he completely trust Luke not to hurt him? Mostly. But each day his conviction and belief in Luke was getting stronger. It wouldn't be easy; nothing worth having was. But they had each other, they had today, and they loved each other. They had a shot. "I think I could handle that," Nelson finally said past the lump in his throat.

Luke smiled and leaned in like he was about to kiss Nelson, but Nelson pressed his hand against Luke's chest, stopping him. "Not so fast, Mister. Remember when I promised to kick your ass if you ever left me again?"

"Yeah."

"I meant it."

SJD PETERSON, better known as Jo, is a best-selling and award-winning author of gay romance. She lives in Michigan with her Itty Bitty Kitty and Little Man. She does her best writing when under pressure of deadlines and at 3:00 a.m. when the world is quiet. Jo loves to tell stories about real people with real flaws. The happily-ever-after isn't guaranteed unless it's earned through hard work and growth. Oh, but when it comes, the rewards are all the better!

Facebook: www.facebook.com/SJD.Peterson
Blog: sjdpeterson.blogspot.com
Twitter: @SJDPeterson
Goodreads: www.goodreads.com/author/show/4563849.S_J_D_
Peterson
Email: sjdpeterson@gmail.com

CAN DESTINY
AWAKEN A COLD,
DEAD HEART?

IUNCTIŌ CŌPULA

INNOCENCE
TO THE
MAX

SJD PETERSON

On his sixteenth birthday, Francisco "Cisco" Aguilar first sets eyes on Maximilian De Ferrari, owner of Wicked Grounds, an exclusive BDSM club. Cisco has been lost, unsure of what is missing in his life. Over a century old, Max leads a vampire clan, and Cisco is drawn to him in a way he can't explain. The moment he sees Max he knows his quest isn't about what he's been missing, but who.

Five years' wait seems more than Cisco can bear, but he perseveres and on his twenty-first birthday he walks into Wicked Ground. He's unafraid to meet the vampire he's sure is his destiny. Max has been waiting for him, too.

What Max has known all these years, and what Cisco soon discovers, is that more than fate is drawing them together. Iunctio Copula is a powerful binding link capable of restoring cold, dead hearts. With Max and Cisco bound, Cisco will be Max's greatest weakness. Unable to let Max go, Cisco is thrust into a dark world, where he's nearly powerless, left to fight for his life and his future with Max. Worse, he's at the mercy of those who will use him—and hurt him—just to get to the powerful vampire.

www.dreamspinnerpress.com

MY
HOMETOWN

SJD Peterson

Jimmy Brink and Eric Halter grew up together in a small country town. While Eric has always been content with life as a rancher, Jimmy wanted more and moved to Chicago early on to pursue a medical career.

Life has a way of coming back around. When Jimmy's parents decide to retire in Florida, Jimmy returns to his hometown to finish his residency at a local hospital. Flamboyant boyfriend Oliver in tow, Jimmy bumps into his old friend. Eric quickly takes a disliking to Oliver, though, and for good reason. Oliver proves he's not only self-centered but also a cheater.

To complicate matters, Eric finds it more and more difficult to hide his attraction to his best friend. When the opportunity arises, he needs to decide whether to risk their friendship to pursue his feelings… but maybe Jimmy will see there's more for him now than ever before in his hometown.

www.dreamspinnerpress.com

Something's Brewing at Joe's

SJD PETERSON

The promise of a dream job lures Murphy to Tampa, but he arrives to the rude awakening that the offer is on hold. Now he's got two choices: slink back to Michigan with his tail between his legs or stay and look for work. Things perk up when he goes into a coffee shop and learns the owner is looking for someone to renovate the apartment above it. He happily takes the job, only later realizing he's met Joe Sterling, Kaffeinate's proprietor, before… when they hooked up at a club Murphy's first night in Tampa.

Murphy and Joe are both proud, passionate, and outspoken. Neither is looking for a relationship, though they can't deny they go together as well as coffee and doughnuts, in spite of their tempers. But that's before Joe learns Murphy will be working for the corporation he believes is harming local businesses and the environment—and if Murphy will be supporting it, Joe wants nothing to do with him, dooming any possibility of an unexpected happy ending.

www.dreamspinnerpress.com

OVERRIDE
SJD PETERSON

An Underground Club Tale

Don't judge a book by its cover....

At over six feet, with a body honed in the gym, auto worker Donavan Gregory is used to people assuming he's a dominant top. Unfortunately, they're wrong, and Donavan's desire to explore his submissive side goes unfulfilled.

Smaller and older than Donavan, Dr. Seth Manning might not look like a typical Dominant, but when the two men meet at Pride, Donavan realizes Seth might be his perfect counterpart. The trouble is, Donavan doesn't have as much experience with the BDSM world as he'd like. What could an educated, handsome, and confident man like Seth possibly see in someone like him? Seth must convince him that despite the differences on the surface, when it comes to kinky fun and discovery, they'll fit together just fine.

www.dreamspinnerpress.com

LIMITLESS

SJD PETERSON

An Underground Club Tale

Even within the context of the Underground BDSM Club, Joshua's desires are dark and extreme. Hopelessly addicted to pain and the high it gives him, he has no limits. Joshua would quite literally rather die than use a safeword, and he accepts that might be his fate. As much as he depends on others, he has yet to find a man who can gain his trust, and he has little hope that he ever will.

For Nash, acquiring Joshua from another Dom at the club is only the first step in what will be a long and arduous road to lure the young man back from the brink of self-destruction. He must do the impossible and win Joshua's trust, and he must be the one to set limits in their exploration—something he's unaccustomed to as a Dom. But Nash knows dominance doesn't always mean pushing a submissive's boundaries. It's about establishing a bond and fulfilling another man's needs. In Joshua's case, he'll have to strike a balance between meeting the young man's expectations and drawing firm lines that will save Joshua from himself.

www.dreamspinnerpress.com